EVEN NOW

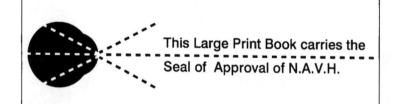

This Large Print Book carries the
Seal of Approval of N.A.V.H.

EVEN NOW

SUSAN S. KELLY

Thorndike Press • Waterville, Maine

Grateful acknowledgment is made to quote from
"Prospecting" by Catharine Savage Brosman. First published
in the Sewanee Review, vol. 101, no. 2, Spring 1993. Copyright
1993 by Catharine Savage Brosman. Reprinted with the
permission of the editor and the author.

Published in 2001 by arrangement with Warner Books, Inc.

Thorndike Press Large Print Women's Fiction Series.

The tree indicium is a trademark of Thorndike Press.

The text of this Large Print edition is unabridged.
Other aspects of the book may vary from the original edition.

Set in 16 pt. Plantin by Myrna S. Raven.

Printed in the United States on permanent paper.

Library of Congress Cataloging-in-Publication Data

Kelly, Susan S.
    Even now / Susan S. Kelly.
      p. cm.
    ISBN 0-7862-3677-9 (lg. print : hc : alk. paper)
    1. Teachers' spouses — Fiction. 2. Female friendship
— Fiction. 3. Asheville (N.C.) — Fiction. 4. Married
women — Fiction. 5. Large type books. I. Title.
PS3561.E39716 E93 2001b
  813'.54—dc21
                                            2001053018

For my mother, who let me read.

My thanks to Jamie Raab, who saw the story's core, to Rhoda Weyr for her wisdom and humor, and to the Virginia Center for the Creative Arts for the solitude of a corncrib studio.

Chapter 1

I stretched a length of tape over the lid and nudged the box toward seven other moving cartons labeled TO GO. TO STAY boxes were stacked in our bedroom. Possessions to be thrown away didn't merit marking; they were accumulating in the hall.

There's something wholly satisfactory in packing. It had been seventeen years since I'd boxed and wrapped and crated everything I owned, when Hal and I returned from our honeymoon. The bulk of my belongings then were wedding gifts gleaming with newness, each present carefully recorded by my sister, Ceel, in a white leatherette album and checked off as thank-you notes were written. Everything was "to go" then, brass candlesticks and linen napkins and floral cachepots and casserole dishes, the few silver trays and bowls and breadbaskets I hadn't swapped for Lucite versions. My mother was dismayed.

"You'll want that silver," she'd said as a pitcher joined a gravy boat to be returned.

"For what?"

"Christenings," Mother answered, and

I'd laughed. The concept was as remote as funerals. My son, Mark, was christened two years later, five more and Ellen was baptized. My father's funeral came three years after that.

No silver was going to Rural Ridge. I couldn't picture filigreed salt and pepper shakers anywhere in the single-storied stone-and-timbered house Hal and I had bought. One wing held a kitchen; the opposite arm comprised three small bedrooms. A step lower than the rest of the house, the entire midsection was a den with scarred wood floors, a rock hearth flanked by floor-to-ceiling bookshelves, and a gently vaulted ceiling of tongue-and-groove paneling. Built in the twenties as a summer home by a less advantaged relation to the Vanderbilt scions of Asheville's famed Biltmore Castle, the cottage was subsequently lost during the Depression, then defaulted, deeded, or sold to a succession of owners.

And it had been available, the scarcest and most precious of commodities in the alpine hamlet. While Rural Ridge year-rounders numbered only twelve hundred, summer residents swelled the population to five thousand.

As soon as our house in Durham sold we'd bought the cottage on sight; love at first sight on my part, from the moment I stood on the slate terrace snugged within the house's horseshoe shape. "Less space," Hal said about the square footage.

"More room," I contradicted him.

Below the terrace an inclined acre of yard sloped away. But it was what lay beyond and above, spanning the entire semicircle of horizon, that captivated me, dispatching any doubts about furnace age or roof condition or electrical inspections. In shades from denim to indigo, the ancient range of the Blue Ridge rippled in humped and overlapping folds one upon the other like carelessly unspooled bolts of fabric. Gently undulating hollows cupped sunlight with such clarity that the trees massed within them seemed perfectly separate, as if I might part them like hair, a Gulliver peering into Lilliput. Intersecting with forest and farmland were tiny houses with the diminutive perfection of model train settings. Tin roofs, clothesline poles, and heating oil drums were mica chips of glitter. The vista was vast yet comfortingly finite.

"Think of this view in the winter," I'd sighed, hugging myself with contentment.

"You mean in autumn, with the leaves," Ceel said.

"I mean in winter, with the snow."

My realist sibling had snorted. "It's North Carolina, not North Dakota."

I checked my list, surprised by the difficulty in choosing what to leave behind and what to take along. I thought it would be simple: this for the old life, this for the new one. A college roommate had always packed in leaf bags, loading her car with bulky black plastic shapes, and I'd admired the economy of her system. Or perhaps it was only laziness, carelessness.

Hal stuck his head in the kitchen door. "The crawl space and the toolshed are almost empty." He brushed cobwebs from his coarse light blond hair. "You sure you want to take all those clay pots? They'll probably bust in transit."

"I'm sure," I said, thinking of Ceel's horticultural bribe.

"Hannah, think of what you'll be able to grow!" she'd said. *"Fuchsia, asters big as plates. It's cooler here. Tulips come back a second year."*

Tulips had been blooming the afternoon she called from Rural Ridge. It was a Sunday, and I'd been outside regarding our sorry yard. Among the rampant ivy, the tulips I'd ordered especially for their rare color were just blooming. After a mild winter — no snow, not a single paltry flake — a series

10

of killing freezes in early April crippled and stunted earlier varieties, sending flower freaks hustling to linen closets for sheets to protect budding camellias.

But my tulips were a failure all round. The foliage drooped limp as noodles; the cupped petals opened bright orange instead of the expected pale pink. At the nurseryman's urging I'd purchased a drilling device to corkscrew through the drought-dense autumn dirt and had planted the bulbs too deeply. The blossoms opened a scant four inches from the ground, with stems barely long enough to pick, much less arrange in a vase.

"What are you doing?" Ceel had asked, her standard opener.

"My tulips are orange. Pumpkin orange."

"Let Ellen take them to school like you used to, you teacher-pleasing suck-up." Mother's daffodils had sprung from a bank of periwinkle outside the kitchen, and every spring I begged to pick a bouquet wrapped in a dripping handle of crumpled tinfoil for my teacher's desk.

"Easy for you to say."

Ceel laughed. She'd gotten through school on sheer personality. "The child charmed the teachers," Mother still claims. Ceel would pick Mother's flowers without her permission and smuggle them onto the bus. She rolled up jeans under her skirts to circumvent Mother's "no pants to school" rule, later stuffing her skirt into her gym bag. She'd sneaked out so often in junior high that in a last-ditch effort to keep Ceel home, Mother had taken away her shoes every night. Four years earlier the two of us had returned to Cullen for a wedding, and Ceel, who was driving, had taken an unfamiliar route into town. "What road are we on?" I asked. "I don't know this shortcut."

"You've forgotten." Ceel grinned. "While you were at home doing your first child thing, I was on the road to Chesney to buy beer."

"You'll never believe why I'm calling," she'd said over the phone that April Sunday. "The Academy has an opening for an upper-school social studies teacher." Ceel's husband, Ben, was head of a kindergarten-through-eighth-grade Episcopal day school in Asheville.

"You're going back to teaching?" I asked. Ceel had taught fourth grade for six years, before trying to have her own child became more important than teaching someone else's.

"Not me. *Hal.*"

"Hal?" I parroted.

"Isn't he sitting there with his business sold, waiting for something to grab him? He's talked about teaching for years, the way other people talk about opening a bar, or going around the world on a sailboat. This is his chance."

"Hal doesn't have any teaching background or certificate."

"We're talking about a private elementary school here, Hannah. You could move this summer after Ellen and Mark are out of school," Ceel went on. "It's just for a year, while Ben looks for a permanent replacement. Hal can get his ya-yas out teaching — before he finds out what academia is *really* about. You could live up the mountain in Rural Ridge, far from the madding crowd. I've even found you a house."

I smiled, tempted. "With room for a garden?"

"Shade and sun. Plus there's a university in Asheville, and you know what Mother's always said" — Ceel's voice had risen in mimicry — " 'There's always something going on in a college town, speakers and seminars and whatnot.' Now don't tell Hal I called. Let Ben offer the position first. Act surprised."

I stood up as Mark walked in wearing a thick braided silver choker of mine. "Look what I found. Ugh," he grunted, straining his neck muscles against the metal twists. "See how thick my neck is?"

"Put that back."

"I'm bored."

"Obviously." *Were we ever bored in Cullen?* I thought, walking outside. I wedged my toe beneath a tree root that had surfaced through the dropped soil line. As a child, my closest friend and I constructed entire villages within knotty tree roots in which to steer our Matchbox cars, earnestly debating who would drive the milk truck or the police cruiser, who would deliver firewood with the pickup truck. While Ellen, who apparently inherited Ceel's hostessing genes, used the weedy produce of our yard — crumpled violet blooms and wild strawberries — to accessorize her dolls' tea parties, I'd never seen either of my children spend an entire afternoon contentedly entertaining themselves outdoors. They were too busy with lessons and sports and organizations. Overinvolved, overentertained, with karate, cotillion, guitar.

But that was all going to change now. "Haven't you and Hal discussed moving?" Ceel had asked.

We had. Idly, ideally, hypothetically. Even before Hal sold his grocery cart manufac-

turing business, whenever our Durham life-
style seemed stressful and scheduled and
superficial. A small textile town like dozens
throughout the South, Cullen had had no
social echelons, no pecking order. No
country club or swim teams, no team sports
at all but for boys' Little League. Summer
evenings, while twilight deepened and small
children scrabbled in the red dust, I'd watch
Geoff from the rickety bleacher with the
O'Connors. Everything in Cullen was
public: pool and school and single tennis
court.

Rural Ridge offered more than a career
change. More than adventure, yet less. The
move seemed a beacon to me, an opportunity to restore and reclaim what once had
been. Some simplicity and sweetness I'd
lost, left behind, or cast off in the intervening years no different in some ways from
clothing my leaf-bag roommate had left
with a shrug in dorm room dresser drawers.

I wasn't so naive as to believe our moving
could duplicate or re-create for Ellen and
Mark the benevolence of my small-town
childhood, but debate had evolved into
longing, and with the decision made,
longing had become excited anticipation.

"There's nothing in the house to eat,"
Mark complained from the door, and I au-

tomatically waved my hand at him in a family code. A directed complaint required some corresponding gratitude, no matter how trivial; a parental system of checks and balances that amused my friends.

"But," Mark conceded, "you took me to the mall to get a CD."

The CD was the one item on his recent birthday list that had failed to materialize in the stack of wrapped gifts. My list-making gene had been inherited by Mark and Ellen, who routinely typed out their birthday and Christmas requests, lists I sentimentally saved along with drawings and report cards. For this birthday, his fifteenth, Mark's list had been a comical compendium. A new putter and as many used golf balls as twenty-five dollars would buy at Play It Again, the used-sporting-goods store. A five-foot down body pillow: cuddling company, no doubt, to melon-breasted models in the Victoria's Secret catalog I'd found poorly hidden beneath a beanbag chair. At the other end of the teenage spectrum, Mark asked for a computer game called Blood Bath. A gooseneck lamp he could clip to the headboard for homework. A waffle maker, of all things, because a friend had one, a friend with a mother apparently more inclined to special Saturday breakfasts than

I. At least the list was, in a favorite phrase of my mother's, "well rounded," covering sports, sex, cooking, technology, education. And of course the battery-operated fart machine with remote control, guaranteed to embarrass anyone within twelve feet. There was the child I knew and loved, the one who hadn't yet outgrown the useless but intriguing items that resist categorization — faucets that run into a never-full beer stein, lava lamps, fake arms to dangle from car trunks.

"Heat up some of that turkey tetrazzini Martha Dawson brought over," I suggested.

"I want something *new*."

"There's bologna."

"But no white bread."

"Fry it."

"Huh?"

"How has a child of mine lived so long without eating fried bologna? Denied a delicacy all these years." I peeled red strips from three slices, slapped them in a cast-iron frying pan, and turned on the stove eye. The fleshy pink circles ballooned obscenely, sizzled and blackened at the edges.

"Good," Mark mumbled between bites. "How'd you know about that?"

"Mark," I said with mock weariness, "I know everything." Mark rolled his eyes at my ritual response, coined by my father some Sunday night as he walked through the den, where I sat rapt before *Lassie*.

"Watch," he'd said, "Lassie's going to pull that badger away from the trap."

"But how did you know?" I pestered, awed, after the plot had transpired exactly as he'd predicted.

"I know everything," Daddy had said, laughing. Though dead for seven years, small things — a phrase, a song title — could resurrect him and pierce me with fresh loss.

"Friend showed me," I amended my answer, thinking of fried-bologna Saturday lunches at the O'Connors', forked straight from pan to mouth and washed down with Tab colas in pebbled bottles. "Next time," I told Mark, "eat it right from the frying pan. Tastes even better."

His eyes widened. This from a mother who required glasses for orange juice.

I glanced out the kitchen window. Styrofoam packing peanuts from a neighbor's overturned trash can littered the yard. "I'll pay you a penny apiece to pick those up," I proposed, pointing. "Same offer Mother made me and my friend after storms, for fallen sticks."

"*Please,*" Mark said. "Times have changed."

I thought of our moneymaking childhood industries: sticks and lemonade stands, a handwritten neighborhood newspaper. "We bought an Illya Kuryakin briefcase with our earnings. *The Man from U.N.C.L.E.*"

"Who's Illya Kuryakin?"

"Never mind. Have you finished packing your room? All those — *things* — on your bureau, and your bookshelf, and your desk, and —"

"Mom. It's my stuff." *Muh stuff*, I heard, a gruffness to my son's voice that wasn't merely pride in ownership, but maturity.

I let it go, content that Mark had been willing to undergo a seismic change in school and friends. An August move had advantages. Summer vacation had grown stale for both children, yet school, with its social and academic whirl, was still distant enough to forestall separation pangs. Mark would be a high school freshman, and while Hal and I had discussed boarding school with him, the move had postponed any decision. Mark's only real regret about leaving Durham was not being able to complete his driver's ed course.

"You've been great about all this, Mark. Seriously. I really admire your attitude."

The compliment flustered him, but only momentarily. "As a reward can I get a car when I turn sixteen?"

"Don't push it, pal."

"Would you settle for not having to write thank-you notes for my birthday presents?"

"No bargains." I dried my hands. "My father made a deal with me. He said if I didn't drink or smoke before I was twenty-one, he'd buy me a car. How's that for a bargain?"

"Did you get it?"

"Hardly. I need to finish packing."

"Would you settle for takeout dinner tonight?" he said, wandering from the room.

I knelt before the bookcases. At least these were easily packed items, easily chosen or disposed. There were few volumes I couldn't live without, and some that were downright embarrassing. To go were the books I hadn't read but meant to. To throw away were the encyclopedias, made obsolete by on-line information and out-of-date before I'd even been born. They'd originally belonged to my mother, and though as a schoolgirl I shunned the volumes, with their black embossed covers and flimsy yellow pages, Mother maintained that as long as Abraham Lincoln stayed dead, the set was perfectly fine. I'd longed for a set like the O'Connors', luscious red-and-blue *Encyclopedia Britannica* with glazed pages and colored illustrations bought from a door-to-door salesman. Out too went dog-eared copies of *Sweet Savage Love* and *The Flame and the Flower*. A coffee table book on interior decorating. Nor would I need Spock's *Baby and Child Care* any longer, I thought with a twinge for myself and for Ceel.

Pushed behind the taller books, the way my children used to destroy the neat shelving during library visits, was a small paperback that stopped me. Titled *Letters to Karen*, the cover pictured a young woman whose face was hidden by falling, golden-lit hair, madonnalike. The book had been a premarital counseling gift from my minister. I fanned the stiff pages bound within an uncracked spine, wondering if Hal too had failed to read his corresponding volume, *Letters to Phillip*, and what had become of it. "You hang on to things too long," Ceel has told me, and true to form, I boxed it with gardening volumes, ones in which I could finally consult the cool-weather chapters.

Ellen came in as I was leafing through a yearbook, and I beckoned to her. "Come over here. I need a you fix," I said, family shorthand for a hug. She leaned over my shoulder, arms around my neck, enclosing me in her sweet scent of shampoo and skin.

"Who's that?" she asked, pointing.

I laughed. "Me."

"You look awful."

I couldn't argue. My ninth-grade smile was obliterated by braces, the most obvious feature in a face half-hidden by chin-length hair. "My best friend told me a thousand times that parting my hair in the middle looked terrible, but I didn't listen to her."

"What are those stripes on the sides?" Ellen asked.

"I slept in bobby pins so my hair would curl, and all I got was those dents."

My daughter's fingers traveled down the page. "But someone scratched out your name and put Angela."

"My friend did that, too. She was making fun of me."

"Weren't you mad at her?"

"Oh no. When we were little girls playing pretend-like, I always wanted to be called Angela instead of Hannah. She could do a perfect English accent, like Mary Poppins. Ahn-je-luh," I imitated.

Ellen giggled appreciatively. "I like your name."

I turned to kiss the smooth cheek warm against my own. "Thank God for small favors."

"Let me see her picture."

"Who?"

"The friend." I obediently flipped to the Os. "Her hair looks good," Ellen said.

"Yes." I sighed. "It always did."

"I would've hidden if I were you," Ellen said with nine-year-old confidence and four-year-old tactlessness.

I laughed. "In a way I did. I went to a different school the next year." Seeing an opportunity, I seized it. "Like you are. Where your daddy will be a *teacher.*"

"Was she your best friend?" Ellen persisted.

"Yes, she was."

"Did you cut yourselves and press your fingers together? Were you best friends like that?"

"Oh no. We didn't have to prove anything. We just . . . knew. Like you and Lila."

Ellen's brow creased. "Lila says she'll write to me, but she said that when she went to camp and never did."

"Don't hold that against her. It doesn't mean you aren't still friends. Sometimes people mean to do things and don't."

"What happened to her?"

I stood up, surprised by Ellen's interest. I forgot that about children, their intrigue with facts beyond their own timelines. It's both fascinating and impossible to picture parents in any guise other than their grown-up roles. Hard to imagine that those giants of logic and imperturbability once wept over skinned knees and hurt feelings, schemed or cheated or climbed trees. Children long for access to those people they can't personally know. "She always liked her name just fine. Isn't that weird? Very weird," I said. There, that was a fact.

But not enough fact for Ellen. "What happened to her?"

I scrunched up my eyes and forehead, pulling down the skin to make a gruesome face. "We both grew up and got all old and wrinkled."

Ellen rolled her eyes. "*Mommy.* So?"

"So she moved. Like us." I grabbed her bare foot. "So, so, suck your toe, all the way to Mexico." She giggled again, and I held up a sleek, also unread version of *The Velveteen Rabbit.* "Are you ever going to read this? Your godmother gave it to you."

"Oh, Mom," she said, breezing from the room, "I'm too *old* for that."

I added the Wyndham Hall yearbooks to the To Go box. Embossed on their covers was the school motto my classmates and I ridiculed in sonorous, melodramatic tones: *What we keep we lose, and only what we give remains our own.* Surrounded by years of accumulation, of possessions segregated into containers, it seemed that despite its intent, the motto fell short. What about those things we never intended to lose, yet never intended to keep, those things that by our not deciding remain part of us through simple default?

It was near dusk before I finished. Hal found me outside, trowel in hand and knees buried in ivy.

"So it's come to this," he said, and pressed a cold beer against my temple. "Burying a time capsule."

I smiled at his reference to a family joke. I'd been married and a mother before I finally relinquished a timeline I'd made for a seventh-grade history project, and only then because Mother herself was moving, six months after Daddy died.

"That was very important to me," I said huffily, and tugged his pants leg. I'd liked the precision and detail required in creating the assignment, liked the pungent chemical scent of Magic Marker, the bold black hash marks of history angling off the line of decades and centuries. Certain, definite, unalterable events both in history and immediate deed since a trembling stroke, an accidental omission of a single event on the unscrolling paper, and the entire project would be ruined. "You ought to assign a timeline to *your* seventh-graders." I wedged all ten fingers into the earth and carefully pulled out a crumbling chunk.

"What are you doing?" Hal said. "Taking dirt to Rural Ridge?"

I picked root threads from the moist handful. "This is a valuable plant."

"Oh, I see. Because it's invisible."

"It's arum. Just because it's vanished doesn't mean it doesn't exist. Arum dies back every year this time." I eased the invisible plant into a plastic sandwich bag for transporting to Rural Ridge. "You can't buy arum. Someone has to give it to you. This came from our house in Cullen."

The sky was deep violet. I sat on the top step, patted Hal to sit beside me, and took a long swallow of beer. Dark tufts of grass poked through cracks in the entrance sidewalk at my feet. *"How nice,"* Mother had said when she first saw our house, *"a brick sidewalk when so many homes just have concrete slabs."* Bricked entrances were an amenity I hadn't known to appreciate. Hollow-core doors I knew. Our Cullen house had hollow-core doors, and Mother had often commented enviously on the solid wood doors at the O'Connors' older house across the street. I sat forward and wrenched free a clump of the wayward grass.

"All done?" Hal said.

"Just about."

"Good," he said. "Wouldn't want you to go to bed without closure."

Hal teased me about my need for closure, a term that, like the brick sidewalk, I'd never known existed before it was pointed out to me. It was true, though; I couldn't help it. I liked things tidied and completed. Open-ended decisions and circumstances left me floundering.

"Just think," I said softly. "This time tomorrow we'll be watching the sun set over the mountains."

From beyond the treetops, beyond our neighborhood, floated the familiar summer sounds of organ chords and muffled loud-speaker voice from the baseball stadium downtown. In two weeks the sound would change tempo and direction as a high school band began its nightly marching and practicing on the athletic fields in preparation for football season.

"You never hear children playing after-supper games anymore," I said.

"After-supper games?"

"Red Light, Giant Steps, Mother May I." A game called merely School, in which a small pebble was passed, or pretended to be, from one pair of prayer-clasped hands to another. Evening noises in Cullen weren't insect zappers and baseball announcers, but the calls of children and bobwhites. As he challenged me to make my bed tight enough to bounce a dime, my father would sit on the stoop and challenge me to count the bobwhite calls. "Listen," he'd whisper with cocked head, "they say their name," then whistle his own identical three-note plaint: *bob bob white.*

"Sad?" Hal asked, clasping my knee. "Melancholy baby?"

The chill stripe of his wedding band warmed against my skin. "You know, this spring was the first spring in five years that cardinals didn't build a nest in the smilax."

He gasped. "My God. Shunned by the birds. Good thing we're leaving."

"It's not that simple, Hal." But I smiled with him; after seventeen years of dailiness you know what can't be explained, know that the insufficiencies of love can't be punished. I leaned my head to his shoulder. If I was sad, it wasn't about leaving. "Moving gets a bad rap in movies and stories. Packing is always associated with some kind of sadness. Change, flight, departure, death. This is different. This is hopeful. I feel as though I'm returning, not leaving. Going back to something I've always known."

"How philosophical of you."

I looked to see whether Hal was mocking me and decided it didn't matter. "Maybe a little sad," I admitted. "Sad to leave the driveway where I spent so many hours watching Mark and Ellen drive their Big Wheels."

"I don't think it's the driveway or the Big Wheels you're missing," Hal said, touching his bottle to mine. After a moment he added, "It isn't permanent, Hannah."

I didn't answer him. There is something attractive and irresistible in a limited arrangement, a plan with predetermined closure. Perfect job, perfect house, perfect small town. A perfectly clear path toward rediscovering lost simplicity, or whatever it was I'd lost. The move to Rural Ridge seemed ordained, fated. It had been a Sunday when Ceel called, and the eve of our leaving was a Sunday again. A godsend all around. And thus does He arrange to give us what we want.

From Hannah's quote book:
. . . the past came back to her in one of those rushing waves of emotion by which people of sensibility are visited at odd hours.

— Henry James

Chapter 2

"Hope the good stuff isn't gone," Ceel said as we climbed from her car. "I have six vases to fill and need a dozen tomatoes." She and Ben were hostessing a casual get-together for Hal and me that night.

"A foot-long sub is Mark's idea of perfect party food."

"It ain't only for you, honey," Ceel drawled. "Don't be offended by the double billing, but I'm entertaining our new interim minister and his wife, too. Wait till you see St. Martin's–in-the-Mountains tomorrow," she said. "Even the name is wonderful, isn't it? Looks just like a storybook church."

"Careful," I said. "You're turning into Mother. 'Mark my words.' "

"Mark my words," Mother had predicted during every family road trip, "the sweetest-looking church in any town always turns out to be the Episcopal church." And though I'd sat picking at the backseat upholstery, perversely hoping the church would be something awful and prove my mother finally wrong — contemporary hacienda or a low-slung, pink-bricked monstrosity — it was invariably charming, nestled beneath swaying pines or sweetly white and ivy covered behind wrought-iron gates.

Inside the cavernous shed of the farmer's market, giant fans spun lazily from a ceiling still draped with crimped Independence Day bunting. Makeshift wooden counters were heaped with shucked corn, yellow squash, and tomatoes in varying stages of ripening. Fingers of carrots, dusty beets, and string beans competed for space with shelled peas — dun crowders, speckled pintos, pale limas — bagged in clear plastic. I touched leafy vegetables meant for day-long simmering with the fatty scraps of country ham one vendor hawked. Aproned women in a far corner sold crocheted toilet paper hats and calico lid toppers.

Ceel headed for the flower aisle while I browsed, buying new potatoes no bigger than grapes, Big Boys and German Johnsons, baby cukes for sandwiches and salads.

Ceel appeared beside me, her face half-hidden by sunflowers and zinnias, loose-strife and bachelor buttons. "What army are you feeding?" she asked at the sight of my bulging bags.

My sister had no conception of feeding a family. "I got carried away with the atmosphere," I said; Ceel's childlessness resurrected itself when I least suspected it. "Look." I displayed my prize find: two quarts of wild blackberries, dark nubbed jewels mounded in paper cartons, a roadside treasure not available in any Durham grocery store. "Still warm from the sun. What a treat. Another plus to add to my list of reasons for moving. There's enough here for two cobblers. Remember picking blackberries?"

"Huh," Ceel said. "I remember the chiggers."

"Maybe I should get some more," I debated. "To make jam."

Ceel rolled her eyes, sneezed into the weedy musk of a Queen Anne's lace. "Let's go. Five more minutes and you'll be buying a sunbonnet and butter churn."

An architect's sleight of hand, Ceel and Ben's house seemed nothing but roof and windows, a lit lantern in the dusk. Their home was as sleek as ours was rustic, and I admired its minimal spareness, consisting of only three rooms: kitchen, living area, and bedroom. Distinctively contemporary, the house boasted a two-storied ceiling checkerboarded with skylights. Honey-stained wood floors were enclosed by sliding glass doors giving on to a wrap-around porch.

"Hello, boss," Hal said, shaking his brother-in-law's hand.

"I locked up the Academy to make sure Hal made it tonight," Ben said to me. "Classes haven't begun, but the professor here is already working overtime. Come on in. Ceel's making sure the lemon slices are precisely a quarter inch thick."

We followed Ben through the open room to a planked table Ceel had covered with bright bandannas to serve as a bar. Frosted green and amber longneck beer bottles poked from an ice-filled wheelbarrow.

"Martini on the rocks, please," I said to the young man behind the table.

"That's a tall order for a moonlighting teacher's aide," he said with a rueful expression. "I'll need some instructions."

"Watch this highly technical process," I said, and dribbled vermouth over an ice-packed glass, then quickly upended it over my palm. The clear liquid dripped through my fingers to a dish towel. "Now, gin and three olives, minimum. Perfect every time." He bowed with mock respect and laughed as I added, "Call if you need my sophisticated skills."

I stood at a window and watched Ceel light citronella torches on the deck. Ceel and Ben had chosen a snug forested hollow over a prized mountaintop lot, and sunset's colors had nearly faded here. The dying day remained only in the smeary pink undersides of high cloud wisps rippled like tidal sand.

"You're Hannah Marsh, aren't you? Welcome to town," a cheery voice said. "You'll just *love* it here in Rural Ridge, love it. Bill and I only wish we'd come to our senses and left Atlanta earlier." I turned to a petite woman wearing gold jewelry at wrists and neck and earlobes. "Doesy Howard," she said, "your neighbor behind the overgrown hemlocks."

"Doesy?"

"Short for Doris. Our daughter Wendy is just ahead of your son in school. Mark, right? Wendy can tell him everything there is to know about the Blue Ridge Rangers!"

"I'm sure he'd appreciate it," I said, smiling at Doesy's effusion and wondering if

Wendy Howard was equally enthusiastic. "He's unhappily baby-sitting for our daughter, Ellen, tonight."

"You should have called Wendy! Most weekends you wouldn't *ever* catch her home, but she's grounded for two weeks for cutting her piano lessons. Wendy resists all my efforts to make her well rounded — don't you agree piano is a good life skill? Told Mrs. Biddix she had an orthodontist appointment. Unfortunately Wendy forgot that she's no longer wearing braces." Doesy shook her head happily. "The little liar! A social creature if ever there was one. Always has something going on. Of course, it's all my fault. I couldn't wait for her to be a teen-ager so I could live it all over again. *Frances!*" she trilled to a woman wearing drawstring pants and a needleworked tank. "Come meet Ceel's big sister, Hannah."

Frances Mason greeted me and regarded Doesy skeptically. "You're resplendently overdressed. What kind of soiree did you think you were attending?"

Doesy was unfazed. "I'm trying to im-press our new rector. The parish offices are dire, haven't been touched since the fifties." In a stage whisper to me she added, "Frances is our village agitator."

Frances tipped her bottle of beer and took

several long swallows. "Loosely related to the community curmudgeon."

I laughed. "Who do you agitate and curmudgeon?"

"Anyone who'll let me."

"Oh, hush," Doesy said, wagging a finger. "Frances gives me a terrible time. And I'm Picky-Picky's *best* customer. Anything new in stock?" she demanded. "You know I get *first* choice." Doesy gave me an earnest look. "I'm an interior designer. Give me a holler if you need help with your house. I know a place where you can get *darling* kudzu-vine furniture." I thought of the decorating books I'd consigned to the Dumpster.

"Jesus, Doesy," Frances said. "You're the kind of female who gives the South a bad name."

Doesy stuck out her tongue. "Look after Hannah," she directed Frances. "I'm going to mingle."

"Mingle, mingle," Frances called after her.

"*The Mary Tyler Moore Show*," I said.

She was clearly surprised. "Showing your age. And your good memory."

"I'm afraid so. Doesn't she mind the way you tease her?"

Frances gave an economic shake of her head. "Nah. We know each other so well that we don't have to fake anything."

"What's 'Picky-Picky'?"

"My store. I run a sucker joint."

"Velvet Elvises?"

"Other end of the scale. *Up*scale. Cutesy cocktail napkins, placemats made of leaves, yard art, hideously overpriced hand-smocked nightgowns. You know, useless essentials."

I did know. I'd been introduced to useless essentials — monogrammed jewelry pouches, quilted checkbook covers, piped and plaid garment bags, satin-padded coat hangers — at boarding school. Before Wyndham Hall I'd never seen a fingernail buffer, much less a matching manicure set. "Can you make a decent living on summer tourists alone?"

"Suckers know no season, fortunately. And fortunately I'm not in it to make a living. You've heard of 'marrying well'? I divorced well. You married?"

"Yes, he's . . ." I glanced around. "Somewhere."

Frances Mason drained her bottle. "Excuse me while I get another."

Left alone, I wandered outside and gazed appreciatively at the fringe of forest, black feathers against the navy sky of evening. Dangling from hooks above me, moss baskets dripped pink blossoms of fuchsia. I closed my eyes and tilted my face to the delicate cascading blooms.

"Sorry," a man said, sliding open the screen door. "I didn't realize this hiding place was taken."

Feeling foolish, I swiveled. "I wasn't hiding, I was —"

"Oh, go ahead, admit it." He smiled from a face still ruddy with summer's sun, made darker still by the faded aqua-striped shirt and the dim gold of torchlight. Smiled as if he'd caught me. His eyes were dark, the pinpoints of reflected torchlight seeming to emphasize his accusation. "Just listening to the quiet, then," he said.

"You must be Rod McKuen." He was wearing white tennis shoes, old-fashioned thick-soled canvas versions not meant for any activity but comfort. "Except you're too young to know Rod McKuen." The sneakers inexplicably charmed me. "I like your shoes."

"I keep them in the closet right beside my Wallabes. Proof enough that I'm old enough to know Rod McKuen?"

I laughed. "I *was* hiding." It was enjoyable to flirt with this man, whoever he was; to indulge in harmless play with its harmless message: *This is fun. Your turn.*

"And I'm Peter Whicker," he said, extending one hand to me and raking hair from his forehead — a funny backward sweep of his knuckles — with the other. A pale slice of untanned skin flashed before the hair fell disobediently forward again.

"Hannah Marsh." His hand closed around mine. He must be another teacher at the Academy . . . English, I decided. The eighth-grade girls probably wrote about him — transparently disguised — in their short stories and creative writing journals. I would have.

His dark eyes narrowed into a squint, thinking. "I forgot my cheat sheet, with everyone's name and two-word description. You're the sister who assists with the children's choir, right?"

"What?"

"No," Ceel said, stepping through the open door with a platter of crudités, "that's me. So you've met . . ." She hesitated. "Nowadays you all have different titles. Are you 'Father Whicker'?"

I was confused. " 'Father'?"

"Didn't he tell you?" Ceel asked. "This is our other guest of honor, St. Martin's new rector."

"Oh, I . . ."

Peter Whicker drew a thumb across his

upper lip. "I saw that."

"Saw what?"

"You rearranged your attitude. Changed your entire manner — and opinion — of me. Didn't you? Don't lie." He knit his brow, frowning sternly. "Thou shalt not, et cetera. See? See how terrifying I am, quoting commandments?"

I laughed. "No, no, it's just that I was expecting —" *Someone not so nice looking. So relaxed and regular, unstern and unsomber.*

"Wait, let me run through my file of stereotypes." Again, the backward-knuckled gesture through his hair. "Fat. Bald. Friar Tuck."

I opened my mouth to say, *Exactly. Precisely. You read my mind,* and said only, "Something like that."

His grin was wry. "Fat and bald all in good time, probably."

"It's that you aren't . . ."

He touched his bare throat. "Wearing a collar."

Right again. "Is that allowed?"

"Allowed?" He laughed.

Ceel sighed noisily, reprovingly. "Jeez, Hannah. No thought unexpressed." She slipped between us, heading for the door. "I'm leaving before she says something worse. You two come get a plate soon."

Hal's silhouette was momentarily framed in a large window before he strode out to join us. "*Interim* rector," Peter corrected my introduction. "Here to wean the congregation from old alliances, and sentiments and" — his expression was mischievous — "grudges, maybe."

"To ready the flock," I offered.

"Exactly. One of those good Episcopal edicts. What brought the two of you to Rural Ridge?" Peter asked.

I hesitated, reticent. Peter Whicker's earlier assessment was correct. Knowing what I now knew — that he was a priest — inhibited me. I couldn't imagine admitting, *To look for something perfect and good and uncomplicated.* "To garden," I finally blurted. "And because of the mountains."

Hal looked at me piercingly, evidently annoyed by my insufficient answer. "I sold a business recently, and when Ben called offering a temporary teaching position, I jumped. We, I mean." He touched my shoulder, adding, "Hannah and I thought our lives might be simpler here." I sipped my drink to cover embarrassment at his forthrightness and immediately choked on the alcohol's fiery bite.

"Are you okay?" Peter asked. I nodded, coughing. "And is it simpler?" he asked Hal.

"Too early to tell."

"We're in the same temporary category, then. Leaving is part of my job description, too, no matter how much I fall in love with the people, or the parish, or" — he gestured toward the enveloping blackness — "even the mountains. And I have, just like Hannah."

The admission felt not factual, but personal, lovely. In the small silence Peter tapped my glass with his. "Can I get you another drink?"

"I'll get it," Hal said. "Need anything from the bar, Peter?"

"Thanks, no."

As Hal wove through the guests indoors, I laced my fingers, lacking the social prop of a glass. "My mother always says if you put three Episcopalians in a room together, they invariably start talking about the Church, uppercase."

"*My* mother always says never to discuss dogs, children, or religion with other people. Maybe they're related."

"I guess it's a tough topic to avoid when one of the three is a priest."

"Were you avoiding it?" Peter said. "Or does the topic just make you choke, like gin?" The corners of his eyes crinkled with amusement.

I relaxed again. "No, actually it's *you*. Proximity to priests makes me uncomfortable. I'm afraid you can read my mind, divine my thoughts and faults. When I was young I was sure Father Edwards knew I was holding my Advent calendar to the light to see what picture was behind the closed flaps."

He snapped his fingers. "I knew I'd forgotten something tonight. I meant to bring my mind-reading X-ray glasses."

"You had some, too?" I said, delighted. "My best friend and I saved our allowance for weeks to order some from the —"

"Back page of a comic book."

"Yes," I said softly, "exactly." I stepped backward, away from him. Proximity to this priest was making me decidedly uncomfortable.

"So you and Hal are members of St. Martin's?"

"Will be, I guess."

" 'Will'?" He was curious, not chastising.

"Maybe one of these Sundays. I've been . . . unpacking."

Peter lifted his chin. "Careful. I'm reading your mind."

I smiled. "Isn't it written somewhere that Episcopalians don't go to church in the summer? I grew up thinking it was the only perk we had."

"But Ceel comes, and she grew up in the same house as you, no?"

I reached and sliced my finger through the flickering flame of a torch. "Touché. Okay, read my mind. Can you see I was hoping I'd move and find a little parish here still doing things the old way? There's an irony for you, rebelling on behalf of the old. I miss the litanies and liturgy, I miss it all. The pageantry and drama, and the . . . privacy."

I waited, but he only said, "I'm listening."

"Remember when the only issues Episcopalians got heated about were getting married and buried in ten minutes and growing English box in the churchyard?" Now he laughed, and I did, too. "But you know what I mean. I even miss the old words, the pretty pronunciations."

"Sustaineth and maintaineth?"

"Yes. And apocrypha and apotheosis and pro-, pro—"

"Propitiation."

"Yes, propitiation, and —"

"What does it mean?"

"I — Okay, uncle. I have no idea."

He waited, dark eyes merry, glass to lips. "Go ahead. Dig yourself in a little deeper."

"It's just that . . ." I struggled, inhibitions abandoned. "You could lose yourself in those phrases."

"You go to church to lose yourself?"

"Maybe." Realizing how the answer sounded, I looked at him guiltily. "Another mindless blurt. I'm sorry."

He touched my shoulder. "It takes more than that to hurt my feelings."

"I think I went to a huge university so I could be a Social Security number. Don't you ever want to do that, lose yourself?"

"Often."

"Doesn't seem you picked the right job."

"You'd be surprised."

I was surprised. At his candor. It was appealing in someone you'd expect to have all the answers. "I guess I just don't like change."

"You won't like me, then." The soft tone of his response, the almost melancholy admission, was nearly obscured by the twangy forest chorus of crickets and frogs.

"Why?" I asked. Stubble shadowed his jaw. Tennis shoes, and he hadn't shaved. Not like Hal, in his loafers and beardless cheeks. Not that I didn't like my husband's loafers or his razored skin. But. Had I been in Durham, had Peter Whicker been a friend, I'd have stroked his face, teased, "Ouch," no differently and with no more significance than murmuring, "Feels good," after touching a man's arm and discovering

45

the unexpected softness of a cashmere blazer. But Peter Whicker wasn't an old friend and not likely to become one. He was a priest.

"Know why it takes four Episcopalians to change a light bulb?" he asked.

"Is this a test?"

"It's a joke."

It was my turn to wait. "Because," he said, "one person changes the bulb, and three say they liked it better the old way."

I bit my lip to keep from laughing. "How nice that I'm in the majority."

He smiled broadly. "Come to church tomorrow and give me moral support. It's my first sermon at St. Martin's."

I stood on tiptoe, craning over his shoulder to peer indoors. "*Where* is Hal with that drink?"

"Say you will," he pestered with all the insistence of an adolescent. "I'll wear my sandals and rope belt. But you have to call me Peter. No Friar, and no Father. My wife thinks 'Father' is — let me get this right — an offensive term of the patriarchy."

Wife. Why wouldn't there be a wife? Because he wasn't wearing a wedding ring. Once I'd told Hal that I automatically checked for wedding bands. In elevators, restaurants, on anyone I looked twice at.

"Why?" Hal had asked in a tone that was partly curious, partly annoyed.

"No reason. It's just something women do habitually. Like men checking out breasts. Admit it. After the face, your eyes drop right to the boobs." Hal shook his head, refusing to agree.

I'd asked Ceel. "Of course I look for a ring," she'd said. "Always. It's an age thing. After you stop looking at butts."

I realized that Peter Whicker and I hadn't talked about our spouses. Nor had we swapped information about where we were from or where we went to school or whom we knew in common. He hadn't asked me what I *did*. Typical social fact-finding had never materialized in our conversation. We hadn't needed it, and I hadn't missed it.

I pointed to the window, looking among the guests for the woman who might qualify. "Which one is she?"

"Running late." Peter pulled a thick old-fashioned pocket watch from his pocket. "Still getting her office organized."

"What does she do?"

"Keeps the world safe for capitalism. Investments."

"A stockbroker? I have a little inherited stock. Maybe I should call her."

"Actually, she's been hired to run the

western N.C. office of Burke and McConnell."

"Sounds like a big job."

"She's more than up to it." Peter Whicker's face had become a mask backlit by the house's interior, where people mingled and moved, laughed and chatted, in a pretty party tableau. Ceel, ever attentive to food and drink and conversation, touched an arm here, inclined her head to listen there. With darkness had come chill, autumn's forecast, and I shivered.

"You're cold. Let's go inside." A car door slammed faintly from the other side of the house. "Maybe that's her now," Peter said, steering me through the open glass doors. "There she is." Across the room of milling guests a tall woman stood out, self-assuredly greeting Frances Mason. "Come meet her."

My mouth went dry. Thick, blunt-cut hair brushed the woman's shoulders, a straight inky curtain framing high brow and pointed chin. "Daintry? You're married to Daintry O'Connor?"

"Yes," Peter said with puzzled surprise. "Do you know her?"

From Hannah's quote book:
(I love you as) . . . I love my vanished youth — which is as much as a human heart can hold.

— Zelda Fitzgerald

Chapter 3

Know her? Know Daintry?

BFF we scratched with an opened paper clip on any available surface: her bunk bed headboard, the ledge in her telephone booth, the armrest of a terrace chair. **BFF** we inked on canvas-bound three-ring note-books and the smooth rubbery soles of sneakers. Best Friends Forever.

"Striking," Mother once described Daintry, and she was yet. Not classically beautiful, Daintry O'Connor was nonethe-less arresting, even commanding, in appear-ance. I stared at the woman she'd become, watched as she placed her purse on the fire-place mantel. The early and ungainly ado-lescent height had become stateliness, the skin was a smooth pale porcelain, the black hair fell Asian straight and gleaming. Hair I'd once watched her chop off with a single ruthless scissor slice.

She seemed to shimmer, standing there, to radiate the wavering glow of mirage. Though perhaps it was only the gauzy haze of memory that cloaked her in the dazzle she'd radiated for so long to me.

Since I was six years old, I might have said to Peter Whicker, and reeled backward, propelled by memory.

The hot June morning the O'Connors moved to Cullen I was just out of first grade. My mother burned the breakfast toast in her absorption with the activities across the street, a Tiffany lamp prompting the first in a series of derogatory groans. "My God, mock French provincial furniture," she observed of a gold-trimmed dresser and bureau. "An entire *suite*."

It took less than an hour for me to discover Daintry O'Connor. It would take seven years for Daintry to evolve into mentor and guide — always more and less than friend.

I was never to examine that gilded suite in the years to come. But Daintry's marvelous beds I knew well: the double-decker thrill of bunks. While I was required to straighten my bed, Daintry's went unmade for days, and the drooping sheets and blankets created a secretive cave for the two of us, a private burrow. I campaigned for the top bunk when I spent the night with her, enthralled with its height and claustrophobic closeness to the ceiling. Mornings, Daintry kicked the mattress slats to jolt me awake, and, sated with Saturday cartoon idiocy, we contentedly slurped cereal and plaited each other's hair until noon. Our lives became similarly braided. Same age and street and grade and gender, Daintry O'Connor and I were destined to be friends.

She hadn't seen me. I swiftly crossed the room to her. "Daintry." I put down my drink and reached for her across nearly twenty years of separation. "Daintry." How long since I had seen her, even uttered her name aloud?

Yet she made no move to touch me, didn't so much as extend an arm in a semblance of embrace. A slight smile crossed her lips, and I recalled how Mother hadn't rushed across the street to welcome the O'Connors to Cullen three decades earlier.

"Hannah," she said. Even the timbre of her voice — husky, rich — had hardly altered. "What a coincidence."

Instantly I forgave her the stunted casual greeting. Not for Daintry the effusive hellos of Southern women. And she knew I'd be here, must have known who was giving the party. How many other Ceel-short-for-

Cecelias could there be?

"What a shock," I said. "Sometimes in airports or restaurants I'm overcome with absolute certainty that I'll run into a person I know from some other phase of my life — a girl from camp, a sorority sister or Wyndham classmate. But never anyone from Cullen. Never you."

"And here I am."

Daintry's stance, her attitude — all polished poise and cool graciousness — was bewildering, but I plunged on. "I'm trying to remember the last time we saw each other. Though I heard you'd gone to graduate school. And now you're married to a minister. Our minister, Peter, whatever," I stammered, feebled by this sudden, slippery collision of past and present. Hers, mine, ours.

"You know Peter?"

"Just introduced . . ."

Daintry gave me a long, assessing gaze. "Two birds with one stone. Peter and I met in divinity school."

How many more surprises? "You were studying for the priesthood, too?"

"No, I was only there to learn."

I fought down the impression of belittlement implicit in her response, as though I ought to have known better; known that she'd choose hard work merely for the pleasure of *learning*. "Kind of a crooked path, isn't it?" I said. "Theology to stockbroking? God and mammon?"

Something softened in her expression, and I still recognized it: amusement. I remembered the pleasure of making Daintry laugh, coaxing and cajoling her from the occasional black mood she was prey to, long hours of a sourceless, stubborn gloom. "You have to decide whether Daintry's friendship is worth it," Mother would tell me as I moped and waited. I'd worked so hard for the privilege of her company.

"Well put." She laughed. "Strange bedfellows."

I wasn't sure I wanted to know what she was talking about. Despite those times I had wanted to know, shamelessly asking even though — unenlightened and inexperienced — I'd had no sexual tales of my own to swap. *"Okay, I'll tell you what it's like. I almost choked on his tongue."*

"He put his tongue in you?"

"So far in I could feel his taste buds. Then" — her eyes flickered toward mine, as if gauging my reaction — *"he felt me off."*

"You let him?" I breathed.

"Hannah, grow up. It feels sooo good. Better than his tongue." She giggled, snapping the ten-

53

sion. *"But you can't ask me anything else because I won't tell you. Not after second base."*

"I just had no idea . . ." I tried again, childishly tongue-tied.

Small diamond studs glittered at her ears. "No idea of what?"

It had not faded, that old power. "Anything. Everything," I said lamely. *Where would I have been without you? You who convinced me that I needed a shirt with a poor-boy collar. You who persuaded me to replace bulletin board pictures of Julie Andrews with teenage idols. You who corrected me in the song lyrics of "Don't Sleep in the Subway" before I made a sing-along fool of myself before other, less kind peers. Unprotected from the land mines of nonconforming, where would I have been without you during that dangerous age? You were savvier and smarter and better in every way.*

"You've hardly changed, Hannah. You look just the same."

"I hope not," I said. "But thanks. You either. All those afternoons baking our faces didn't affect your skin." She smiled then, a gift, and I knew she was recalling the homemade reflectors of tinfoil-wrapped shirt cardboards we held under our chins in our determination to be what the fashion magazines termed "tawny."

"Your freckles have disappeared," she said, and brushed two fingers over my cheek. The touch was intimate, surprising. Grown women don't touch. They hug and they tap and they even shove each other with teasing, but they don't *touch*.

"Finally. You were lucky that way." *Always lucky.* "After all these years," I said softly, risking sentiment. "I can't believe it." She stood there, the very embodiment of my childhood. Returned to me was this cherished friend with whom I'd fashioned bracelets from the colorful ganglia of wires beneath the dashboard of her father's broken-down sedan perched on blocks in the driveway, to my mother's continued dismay. This friend with whom I'd conducted solemn funerals for overfed goldfish and cat-mangled birds we coffined in shoeboxes. With Daintry I'd concocted a Raggedy Ann salad from a peach-half face, shredded cheddar hair, a pimiento mouth, and raisin eyes. A lettuce leaf was her dress, and though we wouldn't think of tasting our creation, we'd won first prize at a school fair. Here was Daintry, from whom — long before needing the information — I'd learned about sex while her brother Sean beat on the locked bedroom door. This was Daintry, with whom I'd pooled savings to buy a

Barbie wedding dress and four years later a shared set of electric rollers from, of all places, the Western Auto.

Here was Daintry, developed at thirteen when it would be another two years before I could covertly check to make sure my small swells were still there. I'd liked the feel of the thick elastic band hugging my chest, the reflexive shoulder ripple of adjusting, the unfamiliar binding tightness both a comfort and a torture. In the wake of her early spurt of hormones Daintry had dragged me to try on bras in what passed for Cullen's department store.

"Watch," she'd said, and bent over, naked to the waist. Her breasts bobbed downward, and she fitted them into the bra cups with her hands. "Always lean over for the best fit," she said behind the ebony drape of her hair. I laughed so hard that I fell to the dressing room rug, where scattered straight pins pricked my rear. "It's true," she'd asserted calmly. "I read it in one of Heather's magazines."

For she was lucky even with birth order, blessed with an older sister, Heather, a font of romance and grooming advice I had access to only through Daintry. Or on the occasional weekend when my mother shelved her poorly veiled scorn for the O'Connors and hired Heather to baby-sit. Wise, glamorous Heather, with her "fall," a hank of fake hair. "That James West," she'd say with sly admiration, lounging with feline grace on our den floor as Ceel and I watched *The Wild Wild West.* "Those tight pants," she'd say, twirling her fingers through a bowl of popcorn between legs shaved smooth as plastic. Like snapshots, the scenes replayed themselves with eerie, eidetic detail.

"Your new position sounds like a lot of responsibility."

"Who told you that? Peter?" The query carried sarcasm. She glanced at her husband, talking to Hal and Ben.

"Hal has no idea what I do all day, either," I said, the automatic ally. Easily, helplessly spiraling back to an earlier role.

But Daintry only smoothed the lapels of her suit, and I felt stumpy and matronly suddenly, diminished by that implacable composure. "I'm not worried," she returned.

"No, of course not," I said, and meant it. Leadership roles were nothing new to Daintry. She'd been demonstrating that talent since I'd left Cullen for Wyndham Hall and Daintry had stayed behind to conquer Cullen Central High. She'd become a member or officer of a dozen organizations — Debating Club, Hop Committee, Keydettes, Yearbook, Glee Club. She was elected class president three successive years and awarded Girl Scouts' highest honors.

"The title is both privilege and albatross," she was saying. "All the credit or all the blame." But I couldn't picture Daintry failing at anything. Never had I known her to doubt herself.

"How are your parents?" I asked.

"They're living in a double-wide outside Nashville."

"Oh," I floundered.

Daintry grinned. "Gotcha last."

"Stop that," I said. *Don't.* Don't let this become one of those artificial reunions where acquaintances declare, *I never get to see you anymore,* and mean, *We have nothing to talk about anymore.* "Didn't those O'Connors live across the street from you?" a Wyndham Hall friend had drilled me at a reunion function. "Tell me what they were like. Whatever those parents did for those kids, I want to do for mine. I've heard Heather's NPR essays, met Geoff once at a medical awards dinner. And didn't the youngest — Sean? — make a perfect sixteen hundred on his college boards?"

58

I assumed the classmate was joking. "Well. They weren't allowed desserts, so they came to our house for sweets."

My classmate stared, nonplussed by my glib response. "The O'Connors were *born* perfect," I'd finally told her, and that, she'd accepted.

"Does your mother . . . still have the organ?" I asked Daintry now.

"What next?" my mother had mused to no one that moving day as she'd watched a wicker chair with peacock-fanned headpiece hauled indoors, a bristling hedgehog foot wiper placed on the front step. What next was Kathleen O'Connor's organ, a massive electronic instrument installed boldly in the foyer. I loved the organ's double rows of ivory keys, the flanking knobs that added rhumba or bongo rhythms, instantly changing the music's tone to mournful or mysterious. I loved the complicated symmetry of the foot pedals, the sheet music carelessly scattered about the organ's slickly varnished veneer: "Born Free," "Danny Boy," "My Funny Valentine." I loved Daintry, and I loved the O'Connors, and thus I loved whatever was theirs.

Kathleen O'Connor taught piano and directed the seventh- and eighth-grade chorus at Cullen Elementary, and I was anxious to age, to fall under her tutelage and dress for performances in a navy skirt and stockings. To wear loafers rather than my black-and-white saddle shoes Daintry referred to as "fairy stompers." Even now I recalled the pleasure, the glad warmth, that suffused me during an afternoon of errands when a clerk had touched my head and asked Mrs. O'Connor, "Is this one of yours, too?"

"No," Daintry's mother had said with a smile. "But she might as well be."

"She still has the organ." Daintry ran manicured nails around the rim of her glass. "Do you still have your quote book?"

"I . . ." The unexpected question silenced me. I did, though I hadn't thought of it in years. An aunt had given me the blank-paged book when I left for Wyndham, and throughout high school and college I'd faithfully penned treasured snippets of popular songs or movie dialogue into it, French phrases, lines lifted from novels or poems or speeches.

"I still remember some of those quotes," Daintry said.

My neck warmed. "Sentimental stuff."

Daintry's smile was wry. "I was sorry to hear of your father's death," she said, and I was glad for the tough curtness of the word,

60

no euphemism of "passing away." "So sudden." Her eyes met mine again, and I glimpsed something truthful there. "I remember . . . ," she began.

I remembered, too. Daddy had "traveled," his year in the women's apparel business dictated by and divided into five seasons rather than four: spring, summer, fall, winter, resort. Mondays through Thursdays he walked Manhattan's crowded streets, but often on Sundays he took the two of us to the deserted asphalt of the Winn-Dixie parking lot to roller-skate. He sat on the curb smoking until Daintry and I complained of pinched toes and feet itching from friction.

"He brought us those wonderful surprise balls," she said, an almost wistful tone, and in it I heard the girls we were. Big as grapefruits, the surprise balls with clown or princess or pirate faces seemed too pretty to unwrap. But we did, slowly unwinding yard upon yard of tightly bound crepe-paper strips, savoring the process far more than the worthless trinkets hidden at the center.

"Your father had the rings," I said, motivated by some pathological need to mete fairness, equality in advantages. The rings were cheap, glittering bits of tinted glass nested in foam rubber slots, "good behavior" bribes at his two-room pediatrics office decorated with a flop-footed Goofy mural Kathleen O'Connor herself had painted. Daintry and I had selected a new ring every week, the length of time it took for the previous one to bend, break, or turn our knuckles green. "They were wonderful, too."

But Daintry was still thinking of my father. "And he brought you that paper dress. It was . . . a cat."

"Yes." A shift of thick newsprint whose countless dots viewed from the proper distance formed a cat's face. "It didn't fit me, so I let you have it."

"One time your father told me I could do anything I wanted if I put my mind to it," Daintry said. She smiled. "He ate that candy medicine all the time — what was it? Something minty."

"Tums. Now Mother's hooked, for the calcium. She badgers me about taking them."

My quotidian observation had brought her back. "Is your mother still so much in your life?"

"She's just trying to —"

"It must have been very difficult to lose him," Daintry interrupted, "as close as you all were. Are," she concluded crisply. I sensed reproof in her self-correction, but she merely gazed placidly about her. "I like the openness of Ceel's house. The rectory is so 'quaint' — all nooks and cubbyholes and crawl spaces. Makes me feel like a giant in a dollhouse. At least some former priest had the sense to renovate the upstairs bath. Though I've never understood what people see in clear shower stalls."

"Maybe that's the point?" Daintry laughed, and I was absurdly pleased. "Ceel loves the rectory. She looked into our buying it."

Daintry wagged her finger. "But unavailable to laymen. Lay*people*. It's too much like our house in Cullen, which has sold again, I hear. Something like the fifth set of owners since we left."

I was surprised and saddened. With the O'Connors' arrival I'd finally been allowed entry to the eccentricities of recently deceased Mrs. Payne's house and came to know it as well as I knew my own. Daintry and I pressed our faces to the wavy leaded glass of the front door. We regarded the telephone closet off the kitchen as our personal indoor phone booth. Even Mother was envious when I reported that the house boasted an attic flight of permanent steps rather than flimsy fold-downs like ours. I ate

untold numbers of grilled-cheese sandwiches in the O'Connor kitchen, its wallpaper patterned with canisters and soup
cans whose not-meant-to-be-legible labels
Daintry and I spent hours deciphering.

"And the rest of your family?" I said.
*"Why don't we ever do something with the
O'Connors as a family? Cook out together, or go
swimming together, or something?"*

*"Because we're only neighbors, not social
friends."*

"They're all fine, of course," Daintry said,
shaking the black hair she shared with all
her siblings, an uncanny resemblance noticed by all of Cullen. "I'm adopted," she'd
asserted to me that first summer together.
"We all are" — claiming the fact with such
superiority that I'd scurried for my baby
album, checking the language on the copy of
the birth certificate pasted to its pages in
hopes of possible fraud. But I wasn't
adopted by anyone, except Daintry.

"They're living all over," she said. "Habits
die hard."

For they'd come to Cullen from Ireland,
the most recent setting of Jack O'Connor's
career, and thus the pretty litany of those
Irish names: Heather, Geoffrey, Daintry,
Sean. A pediatrician who shunned the security of group practice for charity cases, their

father had spent ten years treating the poor in far-flung locales but had decided his family needed a home base and consistent schooling. Before Ireland they'd lived in Mexico, and when her children misbehaved Kathleen O'Connor scolded them in Spanish, sparing them the humiliation of a public upbraiding. Whatever their country of origin, I thought even their names were beautiful, musical as Kathleen herself. Geoffrey with a G, Sean with no h, the Heather on the Hill. And of course Daintry, a name I'd never heard at all.

Mrs. O'Connor's tales of foreign hardships and oddities entranced me. She shook her head as she recalled the unrecognizable cuts of beef and lamb dangling from butchers' hooks in Mexican *mercados,* the gamey taste of meats lacking American-mandated preservatives. She described Irish weather, the rain so constant that a stroller fitted with a zippered bonnet of clear plastic was required to take her children to the village for daily shopping. In Ireland the O'Connor children weren't *bad;* they were *bold.*

"What did you *do* all the time?" I pestered, fascinated by their self-imposed exile. They stayed in bed beside their mother until noon, playing with toy soldiers and puzzles amid the messy sheets and blankets, present-day Robert Louis Stevensons. As a result of that forced confinement the O'Connor offspring were industrious, self-entertaining children, never at a loss for something to do. For me, everything about the O'Connors was fabulous, fabled. Even their history.

But their history had taken an ugly turn, because Jack O'Connor's business had not only been the business of pediatrics. When panicked young girls in Cullen and its environs came to him with their pregnancies, he delivered the unplanned and unwanted babies. And then delivered them a second time — to childless couples around the state. Birth mothers and adoptive mothers were equally grateful for his go-between humanitarianism, which, like his medical practice, was charitable. But illegal: His Good Samaritan efforts were outside formal adoption agencies or statutes of law. Years later some citizen's long-held suspicion became conviction, and the authorities were notified. It was no accident after all that the O'Connor children looked alike. Jack O'Connor had personally known their mothers.

Though his medical license hadn't been revoked, though he was never arrested, accused, or tried, he was sentenced all the same. His reputation in Cullen was too marred by the scandal for him to continue practicing there. I was already a mother by the time the O'Connors moved to Tennessee.

Snared in memory, I hardly noticed that Hal had materialized at my elbow. "You must be Daintry Whicker."

"I use my maiden name, O'Connor. Even though Peter thinks it scandalizes the parishioners."

"Doesn't it get confusing with children?" Hal asked.

"Not in our case," Daintry said. "We don't have any."

No children, I thought. And realized, *We never got around to that topic, either, Peter and I.*

"That's certainly understandable," Hal continued. "As busy as you both must be. Not to mention moving from parish to parish."

"No, no," Daintry said. "We opted not. I had enough domestic chaos the first twenty years of my life." A disorganization and communal chaos I myself had craved. Often left to fend for themselves, the O'Connor children existed on frozen pizza, ants on a log, fluffernutter sandwiches, or whatever they came across in the cabinets. Dishes went unwashed, food was taken to bedrooms, and if Heather or Daintry decided to change the furniture position in their rooms, no one objected. With no adult present, arguments were decided by strength or cunning. The last Popsicle or the stereo volume, the best chair before the television — and even the particular television show — depended upon the first sibling to claim it and keep it. When Daintry was assigned the task of bathing Sean, she was merciless with her taunts, calling him spaghetti dick, making fun of his tightie-whities. The ruthlessness thrilled me. My household, with its dull requirement of taking turns, was prim and rigid and straitlaced by comparison.

Doesy Howard approached us. "Isn't it a wonder what Ceel's done with these sunflowers? They're so perfectly arranged! Where *is* Ceel? I've been looking for her all night."

Daintry glanced away from me, as though she might oblige Doesy's intrusion by locating Ceel. I didn't look, didn't help, didn't want Ceel to be found. Couldn't bear for my sister, yearning desperately for a child, to hear Daintry's easy explanation, the cruel, casual rhyme: *"We opted not."*

Doesy tapped Daintry's arm. "You must

be Daintry Whicker. I'm Doesy Howard."

"O'Connor," Daintry corrected again, bemused but never wavering.

"Welcome to you, too. Are you as talented as these two sisters? I swear, they can do anything. Ceel's the hostess with the mostest, and I hear Hannah's a dirt wizard. Can I bring over my ailing orchid, Hannah?"

But I scarcely acknowledged Doesy, because I'd suddenly remembered the last time I'd seen Daintry. A spring afternoon late in my junior year, when I'd left sorority sisters basking on the sundeck and gone to the little-used stacks in the graduate library. Smitten with Hal, in the throes of dreamy romance, I was combing through Tennyson's *Idylls of the King* to find Arthur's instructions to his knights on the topic of love, a particular portion I remembered from Wyndham Hall and wanted to enter in my quote book.

A phantom, she appeared from around a bookshelf. I was flat on my stomach in the carpeted hush, the open book before me. "Hello, Hannah."

She was wearing a bandanna. Not around her neck in the current style, but tied tightly to her head, covering her hair. I hadn't seen her in months, and only then when I glimpsed her walking somewhere across campus. We weren't . . . *together* anymore.

"What are you doing?" she asked with typical boldness. Boldness I had reason to both admire and fear, and I swiftly shut the volume on the passage it had taken an hour of tedious searching to locate.

I'd showed Daintry my quote book when we roomed together our freshman year. When we were still friends. Or at least when we were still close, trading notes at the end of the day, not only from classes, but from whom we'd seen, what boys we'd talked with.

I lied instinctively. "Working on a paper."

"Mmm."

"C'mon, O'Connor," a male voice said. He'd loomed up behind her, bearded and blue jeaned, hooking his fingers through the belt loops of her jeans. I was jealous of that obvious possessiveness, a possessiveness that Hal, for all our parking lot passion, never demonstrated.

"This is my preppie friend," Daintry said. "Here in the library just like in the movie. Of course, *Love Story* never came to Cullen. Too intellectual."

"Cullen?" he said. "Or *Love Story*?" The two laughed with private glee. Laughed the way Daintry and I once had, excluding everyone else. As though he didn't need to

70

know me, she didn't call me by name, never introduced him. His name was Ford, I remembered from the masthead of the campus paper. Ford-something. An out-of-stater, a Yankee.

" 'Oh wonderful, wonderful and most wonderful wonderful, and yet again wonderful,' " her voice called as they walked away. "Shakespeare, right?"

Chilled, I hadn't answered, heard only their low laughter rows away, the sound of books tumbling to the floor, then a pregnant silence. Had Daintry stumbled, toppling books with her elbow? Or had she been pushed against the shelves in a spontaneous passionate embrace? That. That was the last time I'd seen Daintry O'Connor.

"So you're a gardener," she said to me, ignoring Doesy. "Like your mother."

"I'm jealous! I feel left out," Doesy squealed. "You two already know each other!"

I waited for Daintry to answer, certain of her response. Once upon a time we knew exactly what the other would say, spoke in unison more often than not. *Jinx you owe me a Pepsi onetwothreefourfivesixseven.* I'd let Daintry find the words, define and encompass for Doesy our strong, long ties.

71

"Hannah and I were just neighbors for a while," she said, gazing over my new neighbor's head, and mine. "Like the two of you."

From Hannah's quote book:
Moments big as years . . .
— John Keats

Chapter 4

"What are you doing?"

My sleep-fuzzed brain was slow to respond to Ceel. "Being woken up by you," I said into the phone.

"Jeez. Of all the gin joints in all the world."

Breakfast aromas wafted into the room. Then I remembered. The party. Daintry.

"What are the odds," I agreed, stretching. "I move to Rural Ridge for the way things used to be, and she appears. Answered prayers."

"Yeah, and there's some quote about grief and answered prayers," Ceel said. "I hardly had a chance to speak to her. What's she like now?"

"She's . . ." I curled my toes. "Did you know you were double-billing me with Daintry?"

"No, but that's nothing new, is it?"

I hesitated, caught by a question that, however playful and casual, held a darker, more tangled truth in its answer. Something smelled scorched.

"Coming to church? It's Peter Whicker's first service."

His face — open, teasing — replaced Daintry's, a face I'd known much longer. *"Come support me,"* he'd said. "I know."

"You do?"

I sniffed again. Burned batter, from Mark's waffle iron. The first one off the griddle is never right.

Ceel hadn't exaggerated. St. Martin's–in–the-Mountains was lovely, picturesque. Tiny and stone walled, the church was sequestered from the curving road amid tall oaks and poplars. The arched entrance was a single planked door whose handle was a thick iron bracelet.

"A rich family who summered in Rural Ridge built it as their personal chapel," Ceel whispered as we took a pew. "All the stained-glass windows are given in memory of some Chisolm or another." Scanning the congregation for Daintry, I scarcely heard her.

The church's interior was dim, lit only by sconces on the rough rock walls. The wooden pew was glossy, and I was touched to see squashed velvet cushions, kneelers of another era, tucked beneath them, though as a child I'd hated those square lumps. My Methodist peers didn't kneel, and I longed to be one of them, to attend their youth fellowship meetings and retreats to Lake Junaluska, wherever that was. Sundays after spending the night with a Methodist friend, I admired the orderliness of their communion, the miniature cups of grape juice and cubes of white bread passed like cocktails and canapés. First Methodist had been so *white*, pristine and uncluttered. I'd even envied their sincere and clean-lined rectory, home of my eighth-grade boyfriend, Alan Geer.

St. Francis, my family's church, was located on Cullen's outskirts and populated with strange characters who genuflected or crossed themselves at mysterious intervals in the service, elderly women wearing lace doilies on their heads. In contrast with First Methodist's clipped square of churchyard and wide, marble Main Street steps, the grounds of St. Francis seemed neglected and spooky, dotted with irregular stepping-stones, a cracked concrete birdbath, and a forlorn-faced knee-high statue of the church's namesake saint. As an Episcopalian, I was a denominational oddball in Cullen.

Until Daintry moved to town, saving me in a way religion hadn't. The O'Connors attended St. Francis by default. Since no Catholic church existed in Cullen, the few Catholics made do with St. Francis, where incense was burned on high holy days.

"High church in Cullen, of all places," Mother said. "Catholics need those smells, bells, and yells." All I'd known of Catholics was that they were responsible for fish sticks in the school cafeteria every Friday.

Craning my neck, I looked again. Hal frowned at me, so I faced the altar, where Peter Whicker was beginning his promised sermon. His message was connected to the Gospel, not the path he'd taken to find himself at St. Martin's. I'd hoped for something personal, including Daintry. Thinking of her boldness in not attending her husband's service made me smile. Where I'd feel obligated, Daintry was evidently fearless. That, I could tell Ceel, hadn't changed.

Beside me in the pew, Ellen placed her open palm in my lap and smiled inquiringly, wordlessly asking me to trace her fingers with my own to pass the time. The high point in the Sunday service for Ellen was the offertory — action at last! audience participation! — when she could clasp her fingers around the chill golden heft of the platter filled with bills and coins. With predictable sibling torture, Mark tried to deny his sister's pleasure by reaching over her head for it. She fished the bulletin from the hymnal rack to play hangman.

I sympathized with their fidgeting. As a church-captive child I'd tapped fingers against the pew to count, calculating the ages of dead patrons who'd donated the stained-glass windows. I looked at St. Martin's Chisolm windows. Muted reds and blues of light leaked through the stained glass and rainbowed my hands. Grown now, I wasn't bored, but neither was I attentive. Church, if not religion, had begun to nag me with its expectations.

Yet even as I fought its invisible imprisonment, I was prisoner to the familiar. I ached for changelessness, missed the old responses and prayers replaced with contemporary, "accessible" language. I was missing not faith, not belief in God, but simply what had once been. *Propitiation,* Peter Whicker had challenged me last night. He understood.

We rose for the beginning of Communion. After years of the new prayer book I still had to consult it for the creed, the Prayers of the People, unable to recite from memory.

"I've killed off too many brain cells," I'd sighed to Mark. "Or maybe they just died. Use it or lose it." Prepped for confirmation, he'd challenged his new knowledge against mine, winning handily. In Mark's confirmation classes he visited different denominations and watched *A Man for All Seasons*. Mine had been tedious after-school sessions culminating in the bishop mashing my head into my neck, and receiving a charm that read *I am an Episcopalian*. But at least Daintry had been with me, stopping on our way to confirmation classes at Rexall Drugs to share a warmed oatmeal cookie gooed with icing.

Peter Whicker was deep into the Eucharist. His every gesture seemed wholly personal, replete with reverence as, palms opened toward the communion offerings, he touched his thumb to lips and shoulders and finally to heart. I watched. It's hard to think of priests as only men: sons, fathers, husbands. "Thus we proclaim the mystery of faith," he said, and, closing his eyes, extended his arms again. As he raised the wine and bread he shuddered slightly, and as though I'd stumbled and intruded upon a private rapture, I quickly looked down again, joining the rest of the congregation's bowed heads. That was what I wanted: what Peter had.

So that I almost missed her, the last to come. And not parading, no, just that leisurely gait I knew immediately, even from behind. Were her pace faster, Daintry's arms would swing side to side past her stomach rather than front to back as mine did, a difference we'd noticed in our shadows one summer evening.

Her black jersey skirt was ankle length, noiseless and fluid as she made her way down the aisle. She wore a hip-length sweater, hiding, I knew, her short waist, a torso trait she'd despaired of and despised. Daintry knew, too, that I'd have traded my evenly proportioned but short-legged stature for those long legs of hers. Several heads turned or bent to remark to a partner, and I sensed the parishioners' curiosity about this person, the rector's wife.

Coolness drifted from the rock walls, blending with the mountain scents of wood rot and stray skunk and bitter galax. She walked down the aisle oblivious of me, just as she had before.

Religious fervor had arrived in Cullen three weeks before I would enter Wyndham Hall as a high school sophomore. Not the revival energy that annually overtook our Bible Belt community, tented camp meetings advertised on rainbow-hued cardboard placards in the barbershop window no different from those for stock car races or country bands. It arrived in the form of Up with People, a roving troupe of young evangelists whose target audience was teenagers. Their medium was an evening show of patriotic and religious anthems, a clapping, foot-stomping musical presentation held in Cullen High's auditorium.

I knew the auditorium well, had sat there for lectures, band recitals, Tuesday assemblies when a minister from a local church would visit to preach. Except our church, of course, mine and Daintry's. We laughed, a united front pretending not to care. Still, we felt hopeful every Tuesday morning on the bus and disappointed when an unfamiliar face invariably appeared at the podium.

The huge high windows were open, and in the low-lit room Daintry and I and six other girls sat where we pleased instead of alphabetically by class. People jostled and talked as we waited to be entertained, flipping the wooden seats up and down in excited anticipation. Parents had dropped us off, so we were in charge of ourselves; it was night; it wasn't school; it was mysterious. The atmosphere in the auditorium was charged with a carnival air.

I remember it well, that peppy professional presentation, orchestrated and choreographed with quick-step dancing to rapid tempos and the harmonizing voices of clean-cut performers. A spectacle of pure, rousing fun. But not like I remember what happened afterward. At the conclusion a sweet-voiced soprano sang "America the Beautiful" and we waited for the houselights to brighten and signal for applause.

Instead, the born-again choir started swaying hypnotically as they began an unfamiliar song, slow and throbbing. At the microphone, the leader implored each person present to come forward and pledge their commitment to Jesus. Members of the chorus stepped down from the risers and wept as they spoke of their transformation, their sins, their beliefs. The lights indeed came on, and there was no hiding.

Daintry elbowed me. "There goes Laura Hodge," she whispered. "God! Did you see Jimmy Stoneman *trip* when he went up the stairs?"

"Listen to Becky Yelton," I murmured in return, giggling as a girl from Latin class tearfully whispered something into the leader's ear and he translated for the benefit of us sinners still in our seats. We knew this act. Wasn't it *stupid?* Could you be*lieve* it?

81

But our snickering was silenced as one by one, a slow trickle from the audience became a steady stream. Classmates made their way to the lighted stage and sobbed a personal testament into the microphone. "Jesus loves you!" the leader crooned, moaned, beckoned, pleading for another sinner to join the newly saved. The aisles teemed, and what had seemed comical became menacing. A hairball of anxiety knotted in my stomach as, trancelike, surrounding friends left their seats for something that might have been magnetic, that might have been mesmerizing, but wasn't God.

I was grateful for Daintry, experiencing the same unease as I. But watching the stage, Daintry had grown quiet. And then, incredibly, she stood. Her seat clattered up.

"Daintry," I said, tugging at her skirt. We'd made them together, of blue jeans ripped open at the crotch and resewn as minis. She ignored me, strode purposefully toward the crowded stage where people clapped as though the last drowning holdout had been pulled from the waters. Rooted, alone, brutally visible, I watched Daintry far away and above me, her arms flung around and shoulder to shoulder with fellow penitents. She didn't gesture *Come*.

She smiled, and she sang, and she left me.

Two hours later the Up with People bus left Cullen and its converts, spirit-bound for the next town and the next auditorium. Daintry and I managed to avoid each other for three long weeks, until I left Cullen, too; the first time in my life I felt the pull of the new.

What peace I'd taken from the service and from Peter Whicker's visible faith was shattered when Doesy Howard found me outside. "I want you to meet my daughter. Wendy!" she called, gesturing. "Looks like she and Mark have already found each other!"

A pretty, long-haired teenager wearing a flimsy spaghetti-strapped dress slouched over with the studied nonchalance available only to those who are wholly aware of their attraction. Wendy greeted me minimally, Mark trailing her like the sweetish cologne the girl exuded. If the collection plate had been the high point of Ellen's Sunday morning, finding Wendy Howard was obviously Mark's.

"And you'll be going to Blue Ridge High, too, honey?" Doesy asked. Mark nodded. I made a mental note to tease him later as my father had done to me: *Catching flies? Close your mouth.*

"Didn't you just *adore* high school?" Doesy asked me. "Wendy got a new car for her sixteenth birthday and would *love* to give Mark a ride to school every day! Although now that Wendy has her license, we hardly see a hair of her, do we, darling." Doesy clutched my sleeve. "Wendy's so popular!"

I thought of Daintry's mother. "Aren't they wonderful?" she agreed if someone complimented her children. Kathleen O'Connor must have seemed an oddity and aberration to my mother and her self-deprecating friends, Southern women quick to deflect a compliment. *Oh, it's nothing.*

"I'm so glad your family will be coming to St. Martin's," Doesy was saying. "We switched from West Methodist because we knew everyone there. It's just wonderful the way you Episcopalians do things. Sunday school only lasts thirty minutes and the rest is all socializing. Got to run. Coming to Sunday school?"

It was hard to know which astounding sentence or question to respond to first. "I . . ." I looked for help in the form of Hal, but he'd taken Ellen to find her classroom. Mark, for a change, had been only too happy to go to Sunday school as long as Wendy Howard was going, too. People were dispersing to cars and classes and parish house coffee. Then I saw her, walking toward the far side of the church.

I nearly trotted, determined to move beyond the remnant discomfort of our stilted greeting the previous night. Hoping I'd imagined it. "Daintry," I said, not wanting to overwhelm her with gushed enthusiasm as Doesy had me.

She turned, eyes hidden behind dark glasses. "Hannah."

"Where were you?"

"Pardon?" Incredulity tinged the question, as though I'd presumed a claim upon her. Once, though, I did. We both did, demanding, "Where *were* you?" of one another after an absence of only hours. "I was sitting in the organ loft, upstairs out of sight," she said. "The perfect Episcopal position: in the back, and above the hoi polloi." I laughed at the deadpan tone, the ironic truth of it. "Not going to Sunday school?" she asked.

"I'm not a big Sunday school person."

"No, we never were, were we?"

I was happy, warmed. "I can still plink out 'Fairest Lord Jesus' on the piano." To escape church we volunteered to keep the children's nursery at St. Francis and lead their abbreviated chapel.

"No," Daintry corrected me, "it was 'All

Things Bright and Beautiful.' "

"I doubt my children even know those hymns."

"I saw them from the loft. Two?"

"Mark's fifteen and Ellen is nine. She's fretting over school starting tomorrow, and I don't blame her. I wouldn't go back to those days for anything. All that . . . savagery. Wondering if you were going to be the last pick for dodgeball. Getting paired with someone who hated you — and vice versa — for a project."

Daintry's gaze was even. "But you escaped, though, didn't you? To Wyndham Hall."

" 'Escaped'? I'm not sure that's the right verb." Still, I self-consciously tucked hair behind an ear, knowing and remembering how ready I'd been to leave. Ready to distance myself from high school intrigues I couldn't follow, a far cry from elementary grades, where hard work and good marks and obedience mattered. In high school, looks and perkiness and popularity mattered. Other friends had made memorizing the names of upperclassmen at Cullen High — and even the cars they drove — their reason for living.

But not Daintry. Not sensible Daintry. The summer before I was slated to go, while peers passed hot nights perched and flirting on car hoods at the Putt-Putt, Daintry and I were side by side before my bathroom mirror. We were practicing smiling without showing our gums. Or rehearsing for my upcoming adventure, pretending to be roommates brushing our teeth in the communal bathroom, speaking from a wholly imaginary script.

"Can I borrow your notes for history?"

"Sure! That Mrs. Thompson has it out for me, I swear!"

"Want to go to breakfast together tomorrow morning?"

"Yeah, let's not forget to set the alarm."

"What about Ceel?" Daintry asked. "Where are her kids? Too young to come to church?"

"She and Ben don't have children. Yet."

"Are they trying?" Daintry said.

How like her it was, that unabashed bluntness. Except that *trying* no longer applied to Ceel, who'd undergone fertility treatments with little regard for distance or expense. She and Ben had attempted every means of conception, whether herbal, homeopathic, or sheer old wives' tale. Financially depleted and physically exhausted, they were pursuing adoption now, subject to fat application packets, exorbitant and ever-rising fees, the maze of dead-end avenues, and the waiting. "I don't know," I said.

Daintry knew I was lying. She looked toward the empty church lawn. "I didn't talk to Ceel long enough last night to catch her up on Geoff. She'd probably like to know what he's up to."

She probably would. Leftover love for Geoff O'Connor prevented Ceel from resenting him. I pictured his handsome teasing face, long legs banging the kitchen cabinets as he sang Simon and Garfunkel's "Cecilia" to my sister. Ceel had had no same-age O'Connor sibling to latch on to and became an ignored or scorned tagalong to Daintry and me. When the O'Connors adopted Sean, she was already six. But eventually Ceel too had fallen under an O'Connor's sway — later, when age made no difference.

Canny, candid, quick with pitch and smile, and eight years older than Ceel, Geoff was a pharmaceutical salesman using his parents' house as home base for road trips across the Southeast. From his first swift but serious appraisal of Ceel in a long white dress during her graduation festivities, this next-door scamp grown lovely, ready, ripe, Geoff had wooed and pursued Ceel throughout her four years at Sewanee. Smitten with his salesman's charm, complimented by his affection, she'd been easy prey, giving her heart and body completely to Geoff O'Connor and what she'd believed was his love.

"How is Geoff?" I asked only from politeness. I didn't care how Geoff O'Connor was. Hadn't cared since that terrible Christmas of Ceel's senior year. Just after Thanksgiving Geoff ended their relationship for someone else, a name Ceel had never even heard. During exams she'd become ill with infection and fever — and heartbreak — and had to be flown home.

Daintry shrugged. "His Catholicism seems to have reasserted itself. He's got five kids."

A fact I wouldn't report to Ceel. "God's paying me back for being such a wild child," she'd joked of her infertility. "The great checks-and-balances system in the sky."

I didn't laugh. "Don't be absurd."

"How do you know? Does God talk to you? Damn, I thought he liked me better."

"It doesn't work that way, Ceel," I'd said softly. "I just know." But I didn't know whether what my sister would always fear and wonder was true: if her determination not to conceive then had left her with an inability to conceive ever. Because over that Christmas vacation Mother had nursed

Ceel's wounded psyche and a gynecologist had dug out her embedded IUD.

I wanted to hear no more of Daintry's brother, think no more of the multiple heartaches he'd caused my sister. "Doesn't St. Martin's remind you of St. Francis?"

Daintry's mouth twitched in a slight smile of agreement beneath the black lenses. "But no playground or swing set."

I'd forgotten. Like the bulky hassocks, the St. Francis swing set was old-fashioned as well, a twelve-foot steel structure uncomplicated with the ladders and winding slides and chin-up bars of contemporary playground equipment. The swing seats were wide straps scavenged from a local textile mill, conveyor belt lengths that snugged the behind. I could picture us easily, pumping and pumping and climbing, the gradual rise and falling away, the thrilling momentary conviction that you might circle the top of the set itself, then leaning our heads far back and down to drag our hair in the dust. Stomachs to seat, we twisted the parallel chains so tightly that we were flung spiraling as they unwound.

"Haven't seen one of those old sets since," I said.

She lifted the sunglasses. "Have you had an orgasm since?"

"What?"

Daintry's laughter sang out in the church-yard. "Scooting up the poles, trying to reach the top. Unless there's something you haven't told me. I used to know your sex life pretty well. C'mon, Hannah," she said, "you remember."

I looked into those pretty eyes — gray, impaling, and, even lacking the shades, fathomless — and did remember.

" 'Course, once I figured it out, I was humping hard as you." A breeze flattened her skirt against her thighs, leaving her crotch in clear veed relief. She pulled it away, rolling her eyes the same way she had when our health teacher pronounced "hormones" as "harmones." "The only thing that feels that good nowadays is" — Daintry tapped her chin thoughtfully — "gouging your ear with a Q-Tip." She put her finger in her ear, rotated it, and moaned.

I laughed. There was no one like her. "God, it's good to see you."

"What, got nobody to talk nasty with?"

"And all morning I was congratulating myself on *my* good memory."

"Really." She lifted her chin. "What were you remembering?"

If she could tease me, surely I could reciprocate. "Up with People. How you . . ."

When I look back, comb through the

countless little ways it began disintegrating, that summer after our high school freshman year glows as our last happy span of time together. Because we were still young, I believe. Still willing to suspend belief about the future, about the way things would be, would become, once I left.

"How I what?"

"Went," I said softly, "left me."

Daintry's fingers tightened around the purse strap on her shoulder. I'd ruined something, immediately rued my frankness and wanted the brief shared hilarity back, even if it had been at my expense. Like the double billing, it wouldn't be the first time. "I should have known then," I said lightly, "that you'd go off and marry yourself a minister. You started hanging out with religious types early."

A horn honked from the parking lot, and Mark beckoned from the car window.

"What, no van?" Daintry said.

"No van," I said evenly. "Let's get together."

"Yeah, yeah, yeah."

I knew the refrain, a song from *The Parent Trap*. But there was nothing nostalgic, no elbow-poked reminder in the answer, and I strained to decipher the subtext. *Don't, Daintry, don't,* I wanted to say, *it's me.*

"Where were you during Sunday school?" Hal said at home as he stood at the kitchen counter, forking pickles from a jar.

I stared out the window over the sink, where a wooden bird feeder squirrels had gnawed nearly to splinters hung motionless from a branch. "Talking to Daintry."

"So you knew her growing up?" he asked.

"Yes."

"Well?"

Well? "At their Sunday lunches, Dr. O'Connor would go around the table and make each child summarize a portion of the sermon. His eyebrows grew in a straight line across his forehead."

Hal's own eyebrows, fair and chamois colored in the noon sun invading the window, lifted at my non sequitur. He clattered the fork in the sink. "Small world."

Yes. And here we were, reunited in another village so small that it barely graced a map. Yet Daintry was distant, different. I wrenched free from a swamp of emotions too varied and complex for categorization — gladness, embarrassment, sentiment, anxiety.

"You two can pick up where you left off," Hal added blithely, unaware that was precisely the problem. What hindered our new relationship was the loose ends and rough edges of our old one.

From Hannah's quote book:
. . . but she — after the nature of women and cats, which will not come when they are called and which come when they are not called —

— Carmen, Merimee

Chapter 5

I breathed through my mouth to avoid the smell of canned ravioli rising from the lurid orange sauce bubbling and burping in the saucepan. "Are you sure you want this stuff for lunch?"

"*Everyone* at AA brings ravioli in a thermos," Ellen declared.

I'd hoped for another year or two of uncomplicated innocence for my daughter. "But do you *like* it?" I persisted, knowing even as I asked that I'd wanted to be like everyone else, too. Or at least like Daintry O'Connor.

An image of Daintry preparing for her own day rose before me. Across the village, dressing before a mirror, perhaps, as we once stood before my full-length mirror. Daintry hadn't had such a luxury, and she'd taught me to dance the dirty dog before it:

"Don't buck your knees like you're about to fall," she'd said. "And point your thumbs."

Now she would be buttoning her chic and understated outfit, pulling on stockings. Or *hose,* as Kathleen O'Connor called them, a term I'd never heard.

Hal straightened a batch of papers, stuffed them into his briefcase, and sighed.

"What's the matter?" I asked. "Flunking someone already?"

"If only that were it. I'm meeting with a mad mommy today whose seventh-grader was issued a white card for leaning back in his chair."

Two white cards in one month resulted in suspension hall. "That seems a little extreme."

"Not when falling backward might take a computer down with him. It would be funny if it weren't so irritating."

Ellen interrupted. "Don't forget to get my stencils, Mom."

"Since when am I 'Mom' and not 'Mommy'?"

But in answer Ellen gave me only a secretive smile. Spooning the gummy pasta into a thermos, I remembered crouching beside Mother in her garden and announcing that I was too old to call her "Mommy." To shield myself from her stricken expression I'd pressed my face into the soft ruffled whiteness of cottage pinks, drinking in their sweet scent.

I'd never succeeded in finding the identical pinks for my own garden, to duplicate that perfume. Pinks were "dianthus" now, flash-and-show hybrid varieties: multipetaled, brightly colored, and odorless. As if in some horticultural conspiracy, the spare simplicity of the old strains had been bred out.

Hal put his coffee mug on the counter. "What's on your list today?" His A.M. query was regular as the sun.

"Just errands," I said. "The usual."

Balancing newspapers in one hand, I struggled to open the heavy steel door of the recycle bin with the other. Twice it slammed shut, practically taking off my fingers.

"Here, let me help."

An arm grazed the back of my head, and I ducked beneath it. He'd surprised me. The lot of the community recycling center had been empty when I parked. As he lifted the lid and dumped in my load, I stepped aside and watched Peter Whicker. He was a physical opposite of Hal, with the kind of sturdy, wholly male physique that intimidated me in college. Peter was dark where my husband was fair. Stocky and broad where Hal was lean and rangy.

"That it?" He'd caught me staring. My head reached Hal's chin, Peter's shoulder.

I nodded. "My good citizen deed for the day."

"What's next on your list?"

I started at the question, an echo of Hal's. "Why?"

"Forgive my nosiness. I was driving by and saw you. Thought I'd catch you in Sunday school yesterday, but you obviously didn't attend my Inquirer's class. I got tangled up with Frances Mason instead. She had the bound-tos to harass me with unanswerable questions."

" 'The bound-tos' must be related to 'the re-and-res.' "

"Which are . . . ?"

"If my father said too much or drank too much or did anything too much, the next day he suffered from the re-and-res: regrets and remorses."

"So what class did you attend?" He laughed. "How's that for on the spot?"

I hesitated, but Peter's frankness was contagious. "The abstainer's class. If you'll *teach* me something, I'll come. But classes where you break into small groups and *discuss* . . ."

Peter folded his bare arms across the charcoal expanse of his buttonless shirtfront. "Then I don't suppose you're waiting for me to make a call on you." At my alarmed expression he added, "Don't worry. I'm not the pastoral-care type. I'm the rabble-rousing type."

There was that unexpected irreverence again. "What were you trying to 'catch' me for?"

"Your horticultural reputation precedes you. I was hoping you'd come look at the columbarium. Or the weed pit that passes for it."

"Me? Now?"

"Just a look. Please?"

I debated, stalled. "Hal did ask me to pick up a lectionary study guide at the church."

"Put them in the narthex myself," Peter said. "Let's go."

He was reaching for the car door before I'd turned off the engine. "I can't remember the last time someone held a door open for me."

"Mean mother," he said. "Meaner nuns. My good Catholic upbringing."

"Catholic? But —"

"I don't *look* Catholic, do I?" he said, deadpan. I laughed, and he shrugged.

"Jumped the fence."

"What happened?"

"What makes you think something happened?"

The answer was abrupt, and I regretted the question. "I'm sorry. Forgive my nosiness."

Recognizing his own earlier apology, he shook his head. "No, I'm sorry for snapping. Too many rules. I was just a classic bad boy."

I could see it in him still. In his bearing, loose limbed with pent energy. In the quick eyes and stubborn sideways flop of hair. An appealing shagginess. "The choirboy with the whoopee cushion?"

"No, acolyte." He grinned, restored.

On either side of the church's arched stone entrance, sugar maples were crimson tipped with fall's first touch. The sky was pure blue, the hue of spring forget-me-nots. I appreciated the pretty solitude of the scene, the weekday vacancy. "When I was a child my mother claimed that every Episcopal church was left unlocked so anyone anytime anywhere could go inside," I said. "It's a Wednesday. Is St. Martin's unlocked?"

"Care to test it?"

"If it's not true, I don't want to know anymore. It was the *idea* that I loved."

The parish house door opened and a frizzy-headed older woman walked briskly toward us. "The messages are piling up, Mr. Whicker."

" 'Peter,' Maude. I keep telling you, call me Peter."

"Yes, well, you need to get to them." She peered at me suspiciously.

"Soon, soon. Hannah, this is Maude Burleigh, the church secretary and my jailor. Hannah's going to overhaul the columbarium garden." I opened my mouth to protest.

The woman frowned. "I'd talk to the vestry before proceeding with that idea."

Peter ignored her. "Have the new visitor cards come back from the printer yet? And the sexton needs to install hooks for them on the pew backs."

Maude Burleigh dramatically shifted her belt upward on her thick torso. "I'm not at all sure our parishioners will approve of the yellow ribbons that you want pinned to the visitor cards. Much less their dangling from the pew backs when they're trying to kneel."

"But Maude, our parishioners are already members now, aren't they?" Peter said, undeterred. "They don't need to like the ribbons. They just need to be welcoming. You know my job description. Comfort the afflicted and afflict the comfortable."

Unconvinced, Maude frowned again and crossed her arms over her wide bosom.

"And what about that new font for the newsletter and bulletin?" Peter continued. "Something clean and contemporary instead of that English Gothic." He stepped on my toe. "Mrs. Marsh here told me it looks just like the title for that *Dark Shadows* soap opera. Did you ever watch *Dark Shadows*, Maude?" I looked at my foot to keep from laughing.

The woman only pulled at the collar of her dress and turned to go. "It's going to be expensive to change. Don't forget about the messages," she added over her shoulder.

"No, ma'am," Peter called uselessly as the parish house door slammed. "I'm following instructions. Daintry thinks my first job in a new parish is to charm the underpants off the OG."

" 'OG'?"

"Old Guard. Humor the natives."

Suddenly I knew Daintry had devised the cheat sheet Peter had referred to at Ceel's party. I wondered what two-word description she'd used for me. Best friend? Old friend? "Daintry always was . . . instructional."

"Do it this way, Hannah. You turn a cart-wheel like this. You're not doing it right."

"Of course it hurts. It always hurts to change the part in your hair."

"You should eat more Jell-O. It makes your fingernails stronger."

"Maude doesn't seem like much of an ally. Can't a new rector hire whoever he wants?"

"*Interim* rector, and I *am* hiring who I want — you."

Beyond the crumbling blacktop of the rear parking lot, the grounds sloped steeply downhill to a primitive split-rail fence separating church property from the Rural Ridge Cemetery. As if protective and proprietary, a thick hardwood forest spangled red and gold surrounded the graveyard. Gentle inclines and barely leveled terraces of the dilapidated graveyard proper fell away to a valley boundaried only by the notched and curving shoulders of the Blue Ridge. Square specks of barns and houses pegged corners of pastures and Christmas tree farms. An isolated pocket even for Rural Ridge, the cemetery had an ancient air, still and undisturbed. I leaned my elbows on the fence. "I had no idea this was back here. So peaceful."

A dry gust ripped leaves from the trees,

and acorns rained down, rattling with percussive snaps on railings and headstones. The graveyard's maintenance was minimal, only enough to check wilderness from reclaiming it. Leggy shrubs crowned hummocks and plumed jutting boulders; thick tufts of scraggly weeds and grasses overran burial plots, if they could even be termed such. For there seemed no formal delineation of plots, no planned design. An obelisk kept counterpointed company with a humble rounded headstone; listing, lichened monuments shouldered glossy modern markers. Rock outcroppings formed natural stopping places together with rough levels carved in earlier decades on the steep hillside to accommodate visitors. Above and beyond, the distant mountains floated powdery blue, merging with the sky.

"I love cemeteries," I said. "So tranquil and contented."

"Came here myself last week to write my sermon. What did you think of it?"

"I . . ."

"Caught you again," he said, and cleared his throat loudly. I remembered that from Ceel's party, a throaty cough that said *I know what you're thinking* and *I'm right, admit it* and *We agree* all at once. "Even

103

without my X-ray glasses. Half the men are thinking about their golf game, afraid I'll go over the eleven-minute limit."

The sleek tabby that had followed us arched sinuously against my bare leg, and I stepped away. "She came with the rectory," Peter said. "A church cat instead of church mice."

"Where's the rectory?"

"Just a good pitch from the church." He pointed up the hill to a white clapboard barely visible behind full-grown magnolias. I wondered if either of the two windows I glimpsed were Daintry's. Daintry and Peter's. I straightened, as though my father's knuckles had prodded me in the spine. "Hold your shoulders up," he'd say.

Peter nudged the animal with his toe. "Scat, Cheshire. Can't you tell when someone doesn't like you?"

"Is it that obvious?"

"Bird lover?"

"Yes," I said, thinking of the cardinals in my Durham smilax, the disintegrating feeder outside our kitchen window now. "But ..."

"But what?"

"There's something sly about cats. They're stealthy and secretive. They ..." I tried, "*Withhold* things." Peter laughed.

"You know what I mean," I insisted. "No matter their gender, cats seem female. Females . . . turn on each other. They're predatory."

"I should probably have her neutered, but she doesn't really seem mine."

"There you are, that's another thing. No ownership. No loyalty. It's like . . ." I gave up. "If you don't know what I mean, I can't explain it." *"If you don't understand why Thursday's the best day of the week, I can't explain it,"* she'd said in sixth grade. And later: *"You can't define 'sexy.' You know it when you see it."*

"But I do understand," he said. "The way they play with things, torture their victims for fun."

Years before he was to torture Ceel with more lasting effects, Geoff O'Connor had invented spit tortures. Occasionally he deigned to play Monster with us on summer evenings. Insane with suspense, Daintry and I invariably ventured from our hiding places and were trapped as easily as the wild mustangs in my *Misty of Chincoteague* books. A mute spectator, I watched Daintry pinned to the ground by her older brother, his head a foot above hers. He worked his lips to form a bubble of saliva. The bubble became a bead, and the bead grew into a dangling glutinous worm that Geoff sucked quickly back inside his mouth at the crisis moment when Daintry shrieked and writhed, and I was certain the glob would splat on her face. The spit torture became one in our repertoire of playful cruelties that escalated from roughhousing on the grass, immune to my mother's warnings: "Don't blame me if you get itchy!" But with its opposing elements of pleasure and fear, it wasn't so different after all from Daintry's appeal to me.

A rumble and blossom of dust signaled a truck's passage along the unpaved service road no wider than a cart path that wound through the graveyard. I squinted at a barely visible, curiously shaped statue and swung my legs over the fence. September sunshine was hot on my back as I made my way down the hill toward the headstone, Peter just behind me.

Except that it wasn't a headstone, but a concrete rocking horse no higher than my knees. Astride it sat an angel, a plump cherub whose stocky thighs were clamped round the pony's girth. But the child's moss-mottled fingers held no reins; they were forever clasped in prayer. Or entreaty.

Nearly hidden by brambles, a porous stone was embedded in the earth just beneath the little statue. I lifted the thorny branches gingerly and read the plain and plaintive dates etched there. "Isobel. A little girl. Only seven. She'd be . . . eighty." I blinked back sudden tears in my eyes. "Every now and then you're reminded of how much you take your children for granted." Stalling to collect myself, I touched the grainy chubby cheek of the angel child and stood.

Peter, though, had seen. "Need my hand-kerchief?"

A handkerchief. My father had always carried two items in his pocket, a Chap Stick and a handkerchief. *Snot rag,* Daintry had called it. *Gross.* I shook my head. "Little hay fever."

He held out the limp white flag. "Hannah —"

"It's okay, really. For a minute there my heart was punctured."

"Translate?" he said, and I loved that single-word question, implying it was all he needed to say.

"Once after soccer practice, Mark's chest hurt from all the running and he told me his heart felt *punctured.* He was about Isobel's age."

Peter's hand closed over my forearm. "Everyone does it. We're all guilty."

"Does what? Of what?"

"Taking people for granted, like you said."

So he'd listened, not turned away in embarrassment from my emotional moment. *Of course he did,* I told myself, *he's a* minister.

Now he tugged gently on my sleeve. "This way, in the woods."

Within the forest ten minutes later, Peter halted, pointed. A plot of ground barely fifteen feet in diameter was outlined with cinder blocks. Some persevering soul had planted fall pansies in the hollows of the rough bricks, and the purple-petaled faces bloomed valiantly.

"This is the columbarium?"

"So-called," Peter said. "Not terribly hallowed, is it?"

It wasn't. It was perfectly square, perfectly plain, perfectly terrible. Invasive wild strawberry vines competed with airier but no less determined honeysuckle tendrils for dominance of a tree stump in one quadrant. The spreading, palm-shaped leaves of violets matted and overlapped another corner, and above a thatch of grass gone wild, dandelions sprouted. Peter leaned to pick one of the tempting downy spheres.

"Careful," I said. "That's poison ivy beside your foot."

He pointed to a two-foot-high tree. "At least there's a magnolia."

"See how spindly the trunk is? Just a volunteer seedling. It'll probably never bloom, and we don't want a magnolia. It drops leaves, and the shade kills anything under it eventually. The three smaller trees are keepers, dogwoods." I stepped within the enclosure and knelt to read the few markers. They, at least, were lovely: small, simple plaques of black marble inscribed with no more than dates and names. "Only four?"

"Can you blame anyone? Ninety-nine percent of the world can't bear the idea of cremation, and this place would hardly change anyone's mind."

I brushed away nut hulls and stroked the marble's cool surface, thinking of the mahogany box that had held Daddy's studs and cuff links, now holding his ashes. It had rained for five full days before Mother and Ceel and I accompanied the minister to the Cullen cemetery for a private interment beneath still gloomy skies. Coffee-colored runoff had pooled in our footsteps on the marshy earth, and the hem of the rector's vestment quickly grew sodden and discolored with wet. Through the fog of my grief I'd sadly marveled at how little of the red Carolina clay required unearthing to accommodate a container smaller than a shoebox.

"Hannah?"

I looked over my shoulder into his sun-speckled face. "My father was a one percent."

"Was he?" He squatted beside me. "Will you help me, then?"

"You're very persuasive."

"Persuasion was my best subject at seminary." His eyes fixed on mine. "Shake their hand hard and look them in the eye," I was constantly advised by my father. Common advice, yet I've found that truly *looking someone in the eye* — not briefly, fleetingly, but direct and unglazed — is one of the most difficult physical things for people to do. Did he learn that at seminary, too?

I stood, moving away. "What was Daintry's best subject?"

He lifted his shoulders. "Daintry made straight As in everything."

Of course she did. *"I'm gonna flunk our English test for sure,"* she'd say as we waited for the school bus. *"I didn't study a bit."*

"Me either," I'd say, an immediate partner in disingenuousness. Because we both had studied and we both were lying.

"Daintry gets a dollar for every A," I'd report to Mother, hoping for equal treatment.

"It's poor practice to pay for grades," she'd answer, unmoved.

I roused myself from childhood's far corners. "I ought to go," I told Peter, and together we climbed the hill. Again he opened the car door for me.

"What's a fair wage for your services?"

"I'm not a landscape designer. You can't do that."

"Hannah," he said with easy reproval as I ducked inside. "The choir's paid."

Another surprise. "Are they?"

"I wish I didn't have to be the one to tell you that the church is as much about illusion as anything else."

I knew about illusion. Daintry had taught me that, too.

We spent our summer afternoons at the town pool, the public swimming pool down the steep, rooty incline from the Kiwanis cabin. Playing Keep Away, Marco Polo, or Sharks and Minnows — the O'Connor version, with different, tougher rules. The pool lay behind a chain-link fence and beneath top-heavy pines that cast the deep end in chilly, shifting shadows. The painted-plaster, false-blue depths scared me, and I avoided them as instinctively as I avoided the dank basement bathroom of the cabin, where teenagers sought the airless gray isolation to grind against one another.

"Go for it," she'd prodded me. Something shiny and silvery and round — a button? a dropped locket? a quarter or half-dollar? —

111

was lying on the bottom. "Go on."

"I can't hold my breath that long."

"Yes, you can. Then we'll be able to get a Coke and nabs."

I looked again. It had to be money: The circular shape never moved but wavered back and forth invitingly, shrinking and enlarging with the constant motion of the water.

"You," I said, and toed the wet concrete lip that read **12 FEET**.

"Don't be a baby," Daintry said. We were eleven. "Besides, I brought the money for a snack yesterday."

Frightened but commanded, I summoned courage, stamina, and the lungful of air needed for a plunge past thrashing bodies, past the lifeguard's unalert eyes, to the overchlorinated, high-pitched pressure of the silent, sunless bottom.

"Go on," she said, and I dove, arrow straight, for the cold, ear-pounding deep.

Kicking, blinking, I raked my hand over and over on the scratchy surface of the pool floor, groping at the spot where the treasure had to be. Had to be, I'd seen it, Daintry had seen it. But nothing was there. No medallion, no locket, no coin. Until, lungs and ears and eyes afire, I kicked frantically back to the surface toward the slimy runoff gutter littered with pine needles and paper scraps. "Daintry," I gasped, prepared for commiseration.

For we'd been tricked, fooled by nothing more than the peeling blue paint of the swimming pool floor; deluded by a circular patch of ordinary gray concrete laid bare by negligent maintenance.

Or only I'd been tricked. Because Daintry hadn't waited to congratulate or commiserate, to pull me out or buy a treat or play a game. Far up the hill I saw the flag of the towel around her waist disappear into the squalid wet-walled cave of the changing rooms. She'd sent me down deep and left me.

Peter Whicker's arms stretched on either side of the car door as if safely enclosing me within the opening. Outlined by the sun, his silhouette was like that of Sunday's Eucharist, when I'd glimpsed that brief bodily shudder. I remembered something I'd meant to tell him, to test him, to see his response. " 'To make favorably inclined,' " I quoted from the heavy *Webster's* Hal and I used to arbitrate our casual challenge of definitions. Routinely stumped by the words in my husband's unparagraphed, undialogued tomes of history and philosophy, I never guessed correctly. " 'To appease,' " I went on, " 'conciliate.' "

Peter looked at me a long moment, amusement and admiration playing across his features. "Say it," he said. "Say you will."

"All right, I will. I'll do it."

He smiled broadly, knocked on the windshield, and began walking toward the parish hall. I watched his dark figure — trousers and shirt and head — in the rearview mirror. Suddenly he whipped round, never breaking his stride in a backward walk. "Propitiation!" he called, laughing.

Peter Whicker had remembered something from the party, too.

" 'Solipsism,' " Hal said from behind the newspaper.

"A figure of speech? Sounds like 'soliloquy,' " I guessed. "Maybe something related to a Freudian slip?"

"Impossible — doesn't fit in this sentence." He riffled through the dictionary and read aloud. " 'The theory that only the self exists.' "

"Foiled again," I said, looking over the school list of teacher workdays and holidays that had come home in Ellen's bookbag. I opened my calendar and began marking the dates. "Easter's early this year, mid-March."

Hal turned on a floor lamp. "And six

months away. I can't believe you're entering those dates already. Is there a single spontaneous bone in your body?"

I thought of the magazine quizzes — *Teen, Young Miss, Seventeen* — Daintry and I had taken, reading aloud the coy questions and advice. *Keep him guessing! Mysteriousness is interesting! Don't be predictable! I spontaneously took a job today,* I could have said. I curled my hair forward over my forehead, creating a ragged fringe. "Maybe I'll cut bangs. How's that for spontaneous?"

"Unh-hunh. You self-destruct every time you go into a beauty parlor."

I flicked a finger against the newsprint hiding his face. "How was the mad mommy?"

"Placated."

"Is that it? No tantrums, no threats to withdraw her child, no bargains for behavior?"

Hal was silent. Finally from behind the paper he said, "I can't discuss it with you. It's confidential."

"What?" The answer was stunning. "Confidential to me? Your wife?"

Wordlessly he folded the section, rose, and stretched. "So how was your day? What did you do?"

I thought of my day, the church and the

columbarium. Of Peter with his handkerchief and tennis shoes and mean mother
manners. The way he'd looked at me, listened to me, surprised me. "I didn't do anything today," I said to Hal, and slit open the
electric bill. "Nothing at all."

From Hannah's quote book:
*It's a shock . . . growing old — suddenly
finding yourself on unremembered corners
surrounded by a flood of forgotten associa-
tion.*

— Zelda Fitzgerald

Chapter 6

The flat-roofed roadside emporium looked
afloat on a bubbling orange sea, the parking
lot teeming with pumpkins. In a gaudy Halloween hallucination, late afternoon sun
glinted off the slick rinds.

Searching for the big, bigger, biggest,
Ellen scrambled nimbly among the pumpkins. But I headed to the rear in search of a
different kind of treasure and discovered it
behind decorative tepees of dried
cornstalks: a jumble of potted plants left to
their own survival on brick-and-board
shelves. The plastic pots were crowded one
against the other, the soil within them
crumbly, the perennials uprooted from
some backyard garden grown leggy and
brown edged. I touched a black-eyed Susan
bloom dried crisp as paper.

Yet everything I wanted was here in the

unsold, unseasonal inventory priced for quick riddance. Lacking that early, enticing florist-perfect glory, the drooping, stalky, bloomless flowers were forgotten, abandoned. I saw their invisible promise, though, knew that with pruning and a winter's dormancy the faded specimens of coreopsis, echinacea, and platycodon would be hardier, tougher, come spring rains and summer sun. The promise of the future is the only reason to garden.

A bright burst of pinks and yellows wedged beside a flat of monkey grass caught my eye. Someone had crammed a Mason jar with the last of summer's snapdragons.

"Ellen," I called. "Over here." I pulled a stem from the jar and plucked off a single blossom. "Look." With thumb and forefinger I gently pressed the end of the delicate flower. The odd-shaped bloom obligingly yawned open and shut, exposing a furry tongue of pistils. "Grr," I growled. "See? It's a dragon's jaw. Snapdragon."

"Let me try," Ellen said.

"Careful. It's fragile."

"If you do it too much, it'll break," someone finished my warning. I turned, took in the red sweater draped across her shoulders, the starch-creased shirt. Black hair escaped a toothed clip, spilling over in soft spikes. "Know what I'm talking about?"

I knew instantly what Daintry referred to: Mrs. Payne's gliding electric chair rising along the stair banister in the O'Connors' house. With children's innocent disregard for mortality, we'd dubbed it "the Heart Attack Ride." The family had inherited the wondrous machine, and we'd ridden it up and down for hours at a time. Or until Kathleen O'Connor shooed us away with the warning Daintry had just delivered.

"Peter asked me to buy a pumpkin for the church entrance." She looked around at a row of painted plywood cutouts meant to be stuck in hay bales: witches on broomsticks, snaggle-toothed pumpkins. "But I don't know. This stuff is *awfully* enticing." She drilled an index finger in her cheek. "But what'll I do next August, when there are no wooden Easter eggs or wooden hearts or wooden Uncle Sams or wooden turkeys?"

I laughed. "Still cutting to the chase, I see."

Daintry looked down. "You're . . ."

"Ellen," I supplied. "This is Ms. O'Connor. She's married to Pe— Mr. Whicker, from church."

"Call me Daintry," she said, and smiled. Though I called Kathleen O'Connor by her first name, my mother had never granted the same privilege to Daintry.

Ellen's eyes brightened. "The one who said I can take communion."

Peter had announced the previous Sunday that a child of any age, whether or not confirmed, could receive communion. A parent might even dip the bread into the chalice wine and guide it into a toothless infant's mouth.

"Ellen brought her wafer back to the pew," I said. "It finally disintegrated. How can a ten-year-old comprehend communion?"

"The Eucharist is essentially a mystery to everyone." Daintry looked at me with a mild, frank expression. "Unless you can explain it."

I picked up the box of my pathetic plants. "I don't think I'll argue with a master's in theology."

And then she rescued me, as she'd done in countless situations decades earlier, asking Ellen, "What are you going to be for Halloween?"

"A rock star," Ellen answered from the side of a caramel apple.

"Has your mother ever told you that the two of us dressed up in identical costumes every year? Twin hoboes, twin Gypsies." Daintry turned to me. "I think our least successful costume was the mummies. I came undone because you didn't roll the toilet paper tight enough."

"It wasn't my fault. You had to go to the bathroom."

"With the toilet paper!" Ellen giggled.

"Convenient revisionist history," Daintry said. "Remember when we went as the Kennedys? We had a fight about who got to be Jackie."

"You won," I said with mock glumness.

"Moot point," Daintry returned. "JFK was assassinated the next week."

Kennedy's assassination had as much significance for Ellen as Illya Kuryakin had had for Mark. She was recalling a more recent reference. "Can you talk like Mary Poppins?"

A smile spread across Daintry's face. "Is that what your mother told you?" she returned in a lilting English accent. Ellen nodded, delighted. "What else did she tell you?" Daintry asked. As though I were invisible.

"That you were her best friend."

"Did she?"

"Yep." Ellen dragged her sleeve across her taffy-gummed mouth. "Are you now?"

"Ellen —"

"Grown-ups don't have best friends,"

Daintry interrupted me. "Their husbands are their best friends."

Ellen looked dubious. She'd eaten breakfast that morning in uncustomary silence, her face closed with the worry spawned by subtle parental warring, a tense morning exchange.

About Daintry.

"You should call her," Hal had said, "get together for lunch or something."

"She works."

"Seems you'd want to see her after spending half your life as friends," he persisted.

Half a life? What constitutes half a life? "We were apart after ninth grade."

"For three years. Didn't she go to Carolina with you?"

"She didn't go with me. We went together. So did twenty thousand other students, including you. Daintry and I aren't . . . not friends, but we're not . . ." I'd hesitated, unable to categorize, to portray for Hal the uneasy ambivalent limbo of our recent relationship, if it was even that.

"What's the problem, then? What happened between you two? A man, I bet. Isn't that the classic wedge that splits apart women friends?"

"Give me a break. Leave it to men to think

122

they're the reason for everything."

"Whoa. Back off."

"Are y'all having a fight?" Ellen asked.

"Oh, El," Hal said, immediately congenial. "If Mommy and I ever fight, heaven will open and the angels will cry. Time for school."

Now Ellen said, "I like your hair. Mommy — Mom, I mean — won't let me grow my hair long."

"Neither would her mother," Daintry answered, but she was looking at me. "Right?"

Not that the ruling had stopped me from trying to imitate Daintry's smooth braids. My short stumps were brushy, more pigtail than plait. "Until Wyndham Hall," Daintry said.

"What's that?" Ellen asked.

"Your mother hasn't told you about where she went to school?" Daintry bent to Ellen's height and said earnestly, "There were hair dryers on the bathroom walls, like in hotels."

"There were not!" I denied, and changed the subject. "We're on a double mission, for flowers and birthday favors. Those seed bells are nice, El, for the birds." Ellen curled her lip with distaste.

"Is it your birthday?" Daintry asked.

"Right after Halloween. See, here's my

list." She held up the piece of paper, numbered like Mark's, with fervently desired items in an elaborate, curlicued font.

" 'Hang-head baby,' " Daintry read aloud. "What's that?"

I loved Ellen's term, the apt description. "A life-size doll, limp like a real newborn." No sleek, plastic-limbed Barbie, no stiff, unyielding body of a bright and fake-eyed pseudoinfant.

"I've changed my mind," Ellen said. "I'm too old for hang-head babies." I was stricken, and not only because I'd already purchased the doll.

"Turn around, turn around . . ." Daintry hummed for my benefit, the refrain to an ancient Kodak ad. Not even old enough to know the meaning of poignancy, we'd nevertheless adored the mournful lyrics and melody and choreographed a halting ballet we danced whenever the advertisement aired. One of the many performances we staged solely for ourselves.

"Mom, come pay."

As we walked toward the store's entrance, Daintry said, "When I think of birthdays, I always remember yours."

"Why? Yours were the best." Because of their stint in Mexico, O'Connor birthdays were celebrated with piñatas, and I'd been among the blindfolded, bat-wielding partic-ipants scrambling for candy when the papier-mâché burro or sombrero burst.

"No," Daintry said. "No, I mean your six-teenth."

"Oh." I made a deliberate effort not to slow my stride. "That surprise party. I hated it."

"Because you don't like surprises?"

"Because . . ."

Because it was hard. Under the guise of a dentist appointment in Charlotte, Mother had secretly picked up four classmates from Wyndham Hall, springing them on me for an afternoon of sunbathing and gabbing and spending the night. Daintry was there, too, of course. So hard, watching my old life mesh uneasily with my new. And painful. Painful trying to include and translate for Daintry the subjects and incidents and names and situations she had no knowledge of or link to. The wretchedness of that after-noon reached across the years to engulf me.

"I still remember their names," Daintry said. "Meg and Amelia and Charlotte and . . . Sissy?"

"Yes."

"They were . . ."

I knew what they were. Giggly and twittery with girly excitement and gossip and information: where they'd been, whom they'd seen, what they'd bought, who was in love with whom. "We hadn't seen each other in a while," I offered. But I knew what Daintry meant.

"*I* hadn't seen you for the whole school year," Daintry said.

And I saw it all, too, standing there among baskets of apples and onions, autumn's bounty. Saw the six of us that hot afternoon sprawled in the backyard where Daintry and I had spent our childhoods. Saw Meg's legs slowly scissoring above her monogrammed towel while Daintry tried to draw up her long legs that hung off her own shabby towel. Cheap and short and thin enough to have fit, years earlier, in a box of detergent. I'd envied that free gift once, envied that Kathleen O'Connor purchased such commercial wonders: flexible straws and jelly jars you could keep as drinking glasses, while the products at my house were so dull, so ordinary. Not advertised.

I heard the peals of laughter as a bottle of Sun-In was passed around — Daintry silently demurring with a shake of her ebony head — and a crumpled tube of bronzing gel, Ban de Soleil, where baby oil had always sufficed for Daintry and me. I heard the fizz of popped sodas and saw the bright tin rings slid down fingers against gold signet rings. Saw Daintry's wide-eyed amazement as Charlotte sat up to do breast exercises, then dropped her bikini top.

"What do you think?" Charlotte had said, grinning, "Can you tell a difference or should I order Mark Eden?"

"One of them had a . . . weight belt," Daintry said, wonder tingeing her voice the way it hadn't twenty years ago. Twenty years ago she'd hardly spoken at all.

"Sissy," I said, remembering the sandbag contraption secured around her waist with Velcro. "Sissy was always dieting."

Tourists milled about us in the narrow aisle, but I was sitting cross-legged under a cloudless sky again, grass warm and prickly against my thighs as I watched my Wyndham Hall friends squint at their split ends, bite them away with perfect teeth, chattering all the while. They wore bright purple-and-gold embroidered dresses as cover-ups, with tiny round mirrors stitched into the fabric, hippie garb. But Daintry wore a shirt of her father's, the same shirt she'd shown me two years earlier before we packed for a classmate's sleep-over, advising me not to bring my nightgown, that everyone wore their father's shirt to sleep in now, just *everyone*. I'd wondered, watching her, sensing her acute discomfort, whether she still had the fake alpaca V-neck cardigan we'd searched for so diligently every week in Cullen's lone clothing store the previous summer. *Everyone* at Cullen Central wore fake alpaca V-neck cardigans.

Oh, those girls, with their big-city up-bringing, their wealthy fathers. "Your mother stopped the car in the driveway of this ungodly awful house to play a joke on us," Amelia said. "She announced, 'We're here!' and waited to see what we'd do. You should have *seen* this place!"

Over the ring of the cash register I heard it all. "What do you *do* around here? There's not even a mall! Do they roll up the side-walks at night? Let's go to the *Putt-Putt!* No wonder you went away to school!"

I saw the whole painful scene. Painful then, painful now. Heard the peals of laughter and teasing and ribbed disbelief. Oh, those girls. They weren't especially pretty. They weren't especially thin. They were soft with the obligatory dormitory pounds of consoling late night sweets and care package binges. But as they carried the extra weight they also carried assurance. They were fat with their supremacy, careless with their confidence. They knew who they were. Gifted, privileged, secure, and oblivious of their cruelty. To Daintry and her feelings as she looked for four-leaf clovers.

I had hated it. I was miserable for Daintry, because I'd encountered it myself. For though I might have escaped the social intricacies and unwritten requirements of Cullen Central, the first few months at Wyndham Hall were an equally frightening initiation. While prepared for the academics, I was unprepared for the minute scrutiny bred in girls who live every moment together. Girls who are judging one another, assessing and comparing their possessions and personalities and talents. Who got more phone calls from boys, more letters in their mailbox, who had more shoes, for God's sake. Who was cuter, skinnier, funnier, richer, smarter. Ratings never spoken aloud, but ceaselessly, silently tallied. And through that initiation, I'd ceaselessly, silently longed for Daintry, my cuter, skinnier, funnier, smarter, small-town friend.

I imagined how it must have felt to be Daintry that afternoon: outnumbered by these girls as sleek and groomed and petted as cats. And outranked. She must surely have assumed I'd aligned myself with them, shifted away from her. Believed that she was no longer the one I would turn to, listen to, imitate.

"Daintry," I said. "They didn't mean it. They . . ." What could I tell her with some belated apology, some tardy explanation? That there is nothing like boarding school to make you tough. You adapt and survive or are flattened and die. They didn't mean it. It was just the way it was.

"Mean what?" Daintry said, picked up a jar of honey and turned it upside down. The viscous golden nectar inched down the glass.

Daintry was invited to spend the night, too. But instead she went home, to pack for a three-week youth leadership conference in Raleigh. ("*Youth* conference?" Meg had laughed as Daintry made her way back across the street. "What's *that?*") I never invited classmates to visit Cullen again. What had Daintry done? She went to her conference. She accomplished and organized and achieved. She became student body president. She had an affair with the driver's ed teacher.

A tendril slipped from the barrette's grip to her shoulder. "You had a crush on somebody from a boy's school," Daintry said. She tucked the strand into the swept-up coil, and I looked at her hands, the manicured nails, and didn't remember the way we wrote messages on our palms in junior high,

130

self-important reminders to ourselves; did not remember inking smeary puppet lips and eyes on closed fists in elementary school; remembered instead her hands picking, plucking through the grass that sixteenth birthday afternoon. "Those girls were all singing 'Son of a Preacher Man.' Teasing you."

I remembered. Tim Todd, whom I'd met at a mixer and was exchanging letters with. Timothy Emerson Todd. "Because his father was a minister," I said.

"Just like Alan Geer's father." Alan, the Methodist rector's son who'd finally noticed me at the end of our freshman year at Cullen High after I'd mooned over him from a distance. "I brokered Alan for you," Daintry said.

She had — managed to persuade Alan of my charms or convince him that my being interested in him was reason enough for reciprocation. Alan and I had gone out a few times that summer — "gotten together" — at some meeting place or another, before I left for Wyndham. "Wonder what happened to him."

"You mean *after* you told him how stupid his letters were?"

Surprised and guilty, I looked at her. At Wyndham I'd read Alan's sweetly gushing

131

epistles aloud to my big-city roommates from Atlanta and Tampa. "Hometown honey," they'd chorused until eventually I'd adopted their derision and become determined to shed Alan. A scorn that must have been evident in my replies. His final letter to me was neatly scissored into strips except for a small corner where Alan had written that I'd "torn his letters to shreds." Remnant remorse made me squirm. "How did you know that?"

"He showed me. He showed everyone."

I swallowed, stunned.

"Alan fixes VCRs now. Has a beer belly and wears a gold chain."

"Oh . . ."

Daintry's responding laugh was crueler in its way than Meg's or Sissy's or Amelia's. "How would I know what happened to him, Hannah?" she said, condemning my ludicrous suggestion that she might. The sympathy that the recollection of that summer scene had elicited dissolved under her adversarial certainty.

"It's funny how you never . . ." I hesitated.

"What?"

"Never think about someone specifically, and yet they're alive somewhere. They've gone on living in Denver or Boston or Pittsburgh. They've gotten out of bed every day

132

just like you have, and eaten breakfast and watched television, and filled their car with gas and . . . people you once knew go on *living.*"

"They tend to do that, yes," Daintry said, rebuffing any tenderness in my sudden realization. Yet I was glad for the return of that authoritarian air. A similar assurance, in fact, to Meg's and Sissy's and Charlotte's. "No," Daintry went on, casually running her fingers through a bushel basket of peanuts. "I'll tell you what's funny: What's funny is that you've always been attracted to PKs."

"PKs?"

"Preacher's kids. Eighth grade, tenth grade." Heat rose in my face. I turned to the bins of spring bulbs. "So you're — what, designing? implementing? — the new columbarium. Peter said you'd volunteered to take it on."

Volunteered? Had he told her this intentional lie? Or was it a misinterpretation on Daintry's part, an obvious assumption? Had he told her that he came to visit as I cleared weeds, dug up the spindly magnolia? He surely hadn't told her of teasing me that I looked like Mary Lennox from *The Secret Garden*, scratching in the dirt. Or that we discovered that we'd memorized the same poems in elementary school. Because if finding a common bond in something as small and specific as a passage from a book or a poem is surprising and thrilling, it's also dangerous. Dangerous because of the thought that immediately follows: *If we have this in common, there's surely more.*

I wandered lonely as a cloud. Like everything else, Daintry and I had memorized together, coaching each other through "Daffodils," "Trees," "The First Snowfall." What Peter and I also had in common was Daintry.

I began putting knobby bulbs into bags. "Maybe your church cat will keep the moles from eating these."

"Slutty animal," Daintry said.

"What?"

"I think she's pregnant."

"Don't tell Ellen. A kitten would get the top slot on her birthday list." I turned back to the bulbs, selecting the hardest, the roundest, the healthiest.

"Mom." Ellen displayed an ivory kernel for my inspection. "I lost a tooth in the taffy. It was ready to fall out, see? It's barely bleedy."

I turned the tooth, no bigger than a pearl, between my fingers. "Oh, El, another one gone." I peered into her open mouth. How could that tiny hole leave such a crater in my heart?

Daintry paid for her pumpkin and looked over Ellen's list again. "Now is there anything here that I can give you? Too bad it's not April. I have a meeting in New York then. Would you like to go to New York, Ellen? See the Statue of Liberty and the Empire State Building?"

"*New York,*" Ellen breathed.

"We could combine it with Take Our Daughters to Work Day."

"April's months away . . . ," I began.

"How about a kitten?" Daintry said. "Our cat's going to have kittens."

"Oh, boy," Ellen said. "Can I, Mom? Can we?"

"I'll think about it. Let's go. We need to stop by the drugstore and get some things for Daddy. Plus he'll be home soon and I haven't started supper."

Daintry laughed. "You're so *married,* Hannah."

"Tell Ms. O'Connor good-bye, El."

"It's *Daintry,* Mom. Didn't you hear her?"

Of course I'd heard her. It was always Daintry.

Long after her bedtime Ellen padded into the kitchen where I was folding laundry.

"It's thundering," she said.

"I know." Low grumbles were echoing over the mountains and valleys. "Probably because it was so warm this afternoon."

"But it's not *supposed* to be warm anymore. It's Halloween in three days."

"I know." I tossed a sock ball at her. "I know *everything*."

"Mom," she asked hesitantly, "will you not fold my underpants on the counter?"

I stopped midroll. "Why, babe?"

"Because . . ." She shrugged helplessly. But I knew why. Ellen still wore baggy, bloomer-type panties decorated with eyelet. The undies were comfortable, but not stylish. Not acceptable. Not like everyone else's, and she didn't want them in plain view. "I'd be happy to buy you some bikinis."

"No, I like mine, they feel good, I just . . ."

"Don't want anybody to see them," I finished, and she nodded gratefully. "No prob, sweetie." I tucked the panties under a bulky stack of jeans. Who would guide — or force — Ellen into clothing conformity? Because it had been Daintry, naturally, who'd dragged me into skinny-ribbed turtleneck sweaters and bell-bottomed pants, saying, "What you want is that long, lean, hungry look." Daintry who'd ordered me to throw away the book satchel and carry textbooks by hand, hardbacks against hipbones.

Ellen lingered, picking at the peeling Aladdin appliqué on a nightgown grown too short. "Can I have a you fix?" she asked timidly.

I crooked my finger. "I'll do you one better. How about a back tickle?"

Ellen flopped stomach down on her bed, pulling the gown to her shoulders. I pressed palms to warm flesh, pliable and soft as dough. "Mmm," she hummed softly.

"Know what? If it thunders like this — when it's not summer — it's supposed to snow in two weeks."

She arched to look at me, and I watched hope and skepticism clash. "That's one of those old wife things."

I silently marveled at the soft flawlessness of her skin. One penurious Christmas I'd presented Hal with a stapled booklet of back-scratch coupons, and I wondered now what had become of that homemade gift. Whether Hal had lost them, or never cashed them, or I'd reneged on redemption. Or had each one begun with playful rubbing and ended with passionate loving? "But I'm an old wife," I said.

"Moooom. But you should wear lipstick, like her."

"Okay," I resolved. I knew who *her* was. "You help me remember."

Ellen's hands slid beneath the pillow. "The tooth fairy hasn't come."

"She stays up late. Besides, you have to be asleep." Daintry had demolished those fantasy gift givers for me — tooth fairy and Santa Claus and Easter bunny — only months after her move across the street. *"It's all 'tend-like. Ask your mother."* I was dazzled, not deflated, by her wisdom, and everything else about her, and had no intention of asking my mother for corroboration. If Daintry said so, it was surely true. "Relax," I said to Ellen, and she obediently turned over.

"Mark is so lucky, having Wendy right here," Ellen said, her voice muffled by the pillow. Luck was one word for it, I thought, picturing Mark at the Howards' now. "We're studying together," he'd said. In her room, on her bed, thigh to thigh and shoulder to shoulder. No one *only studied*, not unless you were locked away at a single-sex boarding school. I instinctively recoiled from Wendy's frequent, clipped, "Mark there?" over the telephone.

"You just don't like Wendy's style," Hal had joked.

What I disliked was Mark's infatuation

with her. "He's not old enough to be involved," I'd worried aloud.

Hal had laughed. "No, *you're* not old enough for him to be involved."

"I wish I had a friend who lived across the street," Ellen said, "like you did."

"Last month you wished you had a twin. Remember how we decided that sometimes it would be good and sometimes it would be bad? Fun, then not fun." I spread my fingers over Ellen's scalp, the firm sphere of skull beneath the fine hair. "A friend across the street is the same way."

Her head raised beneath my hand. "Did you hear that creak?"

"It's just the house settling. The wood contracts at night." My fingers drifted to her neck, the sweet vulnerability of its downy groove. Oh, Ellen. By the time we're old enough to understand what makes the noise, we're old enough not to be afraid. By the time we have answers to our questions, it's too late to change the outcome. My daughter's back relaxed, and I kissed the cornsilk hair. When the phone rang in the kitchen, she was asleep.

"What are you doing?"

Ceel, with her usual opener. I stooped, squinted. "Cleaning out the refrigerator."

"How disgustingly domestic."

139

"I saw Daintry today."

"So?"

"I don't know. She used to make me jump, now she makes me jumpy. I devolve around her."

"Why should she unnerve you? It's not like me with Geoff. I was *in love* with him."

"But —" But I'd loved Daintry, too.

"Listen, I'm forcing paper whites for Christmas presents this year, so I have to start early. Can you dig up some sheet moss for me while you're scrounging around in the woods, doing whatever it is you do at the columbarium?"

I thought of Peter, who'd brought me a muffin late that morning. "Left over from the Episcopal Churchwomen meeting," he said. "What's new since yesterday?"

"Are you there?" Ceel went on. "The moss has to be in place before the bulbs start growing."

I cradled the phone in my neck, took out a can of thawed orange juice, and slowly peeled the sealing strip. "Ceel . . . do you remember that dish towel in the O'Connors' kitchen? It always hung on the oven handle."

"*What* dish towel?"

In the refrigerator's crowded rear, I saw them. I moved the bottles and jars and tinfoiled dishes and tugged gingerly, afraid the cardboard baskets, no longer green but purply and damp, might collapse. "It said 'Be kind to married women, the wife you slave may be your own.' "

For a long moment I heard only my sister's faint exhale. "Hannah," she said finally, her voice low with amazement, "how can you remember things like that?"

"How can you not?" I answered, and cupped the mottled containers in my hands. The shiny jewels of blackberries had grown gray and fuzzed and pulped, rotten with neglect.

From Hannah's quote book:
When a woman is speaking to you, listen to what she says with her eyes.
— Victor Hugo

Chapter 7

Some summer past, Ceel and I sat on a sofa beneath a flaking mounted sailfish in a rented beach cottage. Our husbands and my children had long since gone to bed, and we were watching David Letterman. "Stop drooling, Dave," Ceel said. His guest was Madonna, and he was quizzing her about past lovers.

"What about Warren Beatty, your *Dick Tracy* costar?"

She looked from beneath thickly mascaraed lashes. "What about him?"

"I hear he's sexually insatiable," Letterman said, leering. "And . . . ?"

Madonna fingered the fringe of her skirt, purred knowingly: "He's *satiable.*"

As the audience howled, Ceel asked me, "If you were going to have a torrid affair with a movie star, who would you pick?"

"I used to say Jack Nicholson."

"Why?"

"Because he was masculine and incorrigible and looked, well, insatiable."

"Why 'used to say'? Because he's old now?"

"Because *I'm* old now. That was a good girl's predictable fantasy of a one-night bad-boy stand."

Ceel picked at the paint-clogged wicker. "But when you're beyond the knight-in-shining-armor stage, beyond the bad-boy-one-night-stand phase, what would attract you now? What's sexy?"

"Those are two different things. What attracts and what's sexy. Apples and oranges. I'd have to think."

She called a week later. "Callused hands."

"What?"

"That's what attracts my friend Janie. I asked her."

So I'd begun asking, too. When I thought of it, when I ran into someone. A casual poll of women of a certain age, my own. The range and variety of answers were surprising. But most surprising was their immediacy. No one hesitated, paused to ponder; to a one, the women were ready with their unabashed responses.

"Someone who doesn't change the subject," Emily said. "Who doesn't ask if I've had the oil changed while we're having dinner out."

"Naughtiness," Hillary said. "Sassy is sexy."

"A man who's at his professional peak," Martha said. "Can't help it: Power attracts me."

"Fixes smoke detectors. Hangs pictures," said my divorced friend Susan.

"A touch," Kathy said. "Not a grope. Just . . . a touch on the wrist, or the waist."

"Survey says?" Ceel would say when she called.

I read my friend Kathryn's postcard to her. " 'I am attracted to gentleness above almost all other things.' "

"How eloquent," Ceel said.

"How's this for eloquent?" I quoted my cynical friend Donna. "Too many women have traded one pile-of-shit relationship for another pile that turns out to be doody in a new form."

Here's what no one said: Muscles. Money. Looks.

"Brains," Ann said. "Plus a good dancer who can make hollandaise and recites poetry."

"Someone who makes me laugh," Julie said.

"You know it when you see it, even if you can't describe it," Ceel said. "Like looking for a pair of new shoes."

"Wonder how Mother would answer," I said.

"You know what she'd say: 'Timing is everything.' "

All those different answers, like fingerprints, no two alike. Later it occurred to me that I'd never cast my own vote. I hadn't canvassed myself.

While the columbarium's design took shape in both my imagination and on paper, I tackled the physical preparation, clearing away a jungle of undergrowth, weeds, brambles, stumps, even the blameless pansies. The warm dry autumn weather was an Indian summer boon for the tourist leaf season and a blessing for the columbarium's creation as well. Or re-creation. I'd come to view the project that way: not as a task, but as a re-creation, a private Eden.

"I called three times this morning," Ceel said. "Where *are* you every day? You're never home."

"At the columbarium. Working."

"Yawn," she said.

But it wasn't work, it was pleasure. Because most days, he came, too.

"Hannah."

I hadn't heard him approach over the

scratch of my raking and the hammering up the hill. He'd read the surprise in my eyes.

"They're reroofing the parish house, and the racket's making me insane. Not one of *my* changes."

Peter Whicker had wasted no time in enacting — or forcing, depending on the point of view — changes at St. Martin's. The bulletin and newsletter font, the beribboned visitor cards, doodling crayons made available for bored children during the service. Wicker baskets had replaced the heavy brass collection plates, sold in turn to an Asheville antique store with the proceeds earmarked for outreach. Moreover, the contents of those collection baskets were being routed to a poor mission church rather than used to purchase periodicals for a diocesan rest home as they had been for decades. Every night now the parish hall was made available to community groups, ranging from Alcoholics Anonymous to Single Parents to Parents with Homosexual Children.

"I've watched those roofers for two days now, and have decided they've got the ideal career," Peter said. "A biscuit in the truck with your buddies at six in the morning. On the roof at first light. That wonderful" — he grappled for the word — "*release* of ripping off shingles one after the other and pitching them down with total abandon. Hammer like hell for three hours, and by four the day's done, the team's earned three thousand dollars, and you go home, drink beer, and watch TV." He snapped his fingers. "And you don't work when it rains."

I laughed. He circled a finger within the white collar at his throat. "This thing can get pretty binding. Literally and figuratively."

"I like it," I said without thinking. He made me do that, unafraid to be frank. Or let me.

The dark eyes widened with gratitude, or surprise. "You do?"

What could I tell him? That the snowy circlet and fresh haircut and lack of a coat over that plain shirt made him look boyish, youthful as a twenty-year-old. "Mark wanted to wear a tie when he was only six, but I made him wait. He has all his life to dress like a man."

Peter pointed to the leaf pile. A squirrel brazenly nosed the fringes where the heavier acorns, resisting capture between the rake tines, accumulated. "Won't you just have to do that again tomorrow? A new batch of leaves overnight?"

"You don't feel that way on Sundays, do you? There they go, sinners again tomorrow."

He laughed. "I refuse to answer that on the grounds that it may incriminate me."

I leaned my chin on the tip of the rake handle.

"What?"

"You're the most unminister minister I've ever known."

"How many have you known?" Then the teasing tone vanished, and his expression sobered. "We're only ordinary people." I felt both chastised and confessed to. He shoved his hands into pockets of slaty twill pants, knuckles moving against the fabric, then pulled out his pocket watch as he had that night at Ceel's. "Duty calls." But, turning to leave, he pivoted slowly. "Can I come again, to visit? To escape?"

He was asking permission. *"Don't you ever want to be anonymous?"* I'd asked him at Ceel's party. *"Often,"* he'd answered. I nodded, shook my head, nodded again. Yes, no, please, come. And proximity must have been part of it, that Peter became the person I saw most often.

He did come. At no particular time, for no particular reason. Sometimes he helped, more often he watched. And always we talked, of everything and nothing. "Talk to me," he said, chin between his palms.

I knew the distress symptom. "What is it?"

"Phone's ringing off the hook. My abolishing the parish dinner, and announcement — or pronouncement, rather — that the vestry vote will be taken during a Sunday service instead is creating a new and different furor." He sat on a stump, hands dangling over his knees. "So talk to me. In person. Tell me something trivial."

So I did: what I was reading, what I was cooking for dinner, of friends I'd left in Durham, my father's army stories of Okinawa. I taught him a little of gardening, how pansies need to be picked, how plantings should be done in threes, how a rusty nail made hydrangeas bloom blue, how tuberoses would winter over only if they were dug up in fall and saved.

He picked up a spiral notebook lying on the ground. "This your journal?"

"Nothing so fascinating," I said, liking that he didn't move to open it. "A list of plants for the columbarium. Quince, spirea, dwarf euonymus, daphne, if I can find a protected place. And those are just the shrubs. Perennials on this page, daylilies and columbine and coral bells and Lenten rose and . . ." I trailed off and looked at him apologetically. "Sorry. Completely carried away."

"Carried away gets things accomplished."

Though the day was still, a sudden shower of leaves fluttered down as thickly as snow. Not dried and brittle, but perfect yellow ovals still pliable with the velvety texture of living. They caught in our hair and shoulders, softened stones and tools and earth with autumn camouflage. "Carried away is another word for passionate," he said.

Perhaps that was it. Peter took me seriously.

Couldn't a string of impossibly perfect fall days, blue skied and golden hued, lie behind an attraction? Crystalline mornings when every filament of a spiderweb glistened, dogwood berries shone plump and red, light filtered through branches in distinct rays like a child's drawing of sunbeams. Warm noons and breezy afternoons and solitude interrupted only by dropping nuts and rustling leaves and the chink of a shovel, scratch of a rake.

Hands on hips, I critically surveyed my work. The precise and hideous cinder-block outline was now painfully visible, the flat marble plaques shiny perfections within rich black soil, a by-product of time and nature that couldn't be purchased at any price anywhere.

"Busy?"

"Just about to start digging up these lovely cinder blocks. How about you?"

"Busy making enemies. The narthex has sign-up boards for covenant groups and prayer groups, tutoring at schools, a walk for the hungry, and female ushers. And I've sent out a notice for parishioners to bring powdered milk on Sundays — there's an ugly rubber barrel smack in the middle of the narthex, too, for collecting the boxes. That enough?"

Was he looking for solace or reassurance? Didn't matter; I gave it. "They're small atrocities."

"Depends on who's judging."

"Ceel —"

"Yes?" His eyes asked for affirmation.

"Ceel always says to ask yourself, How sorry will I be? How sorry will I be if — oh, I don't know. The question applies to every ridiculous situation. How sorry will I be if I leave the car unlocked and someone steals the book I left on the front seat? How sorry will I be if I postpone buying milk until tomorrow? How sorry will I be if I wash this sweater when the tag says DRY CLEAN ONLY and it's ruined? How sorry will I be if I tell this person something they might not want to hear?" I lifted my shoulders at his laughter. "You asked."

"Now that I know Ceel's, what's your philosophy of living?"

"Oh, don't. You're as bad as Ellen. She was doing an assignment for school and wanted to know if I could give only one piece of advice to a child, what would it be? Whatever I said wouldn't be right. Wouldn't be enough, couldn't possibly be the best or wisest or kindest advice." I drew a stick across the marble surface of a plaque. "Besides," I said, "I don't even break the unwritten rules."

"Tell me one."

"Don't bring a baby into a movie theater. Don't have more than one transaction at the bank drive-through. Don't take up two parking places."

Peter gazed out at the panoramic mountainscape where vivid blocks of red and gold cozied with green corridors of conifers. When he spoke again, his voice was filled with doubt. "Do you think I'm making terrible changes?"

I looked at him but saw only the dark bowed head, as though the need to know shamed him.

"Do you?" he said, raising his head.

He was entrusting me with his misgivings. Asking for encouragement is a gift. "No," I said. "Not me."

★ ★ ★

If anyone had asked, *Are you worried?* I would have answered, *Why should I be?* There was nothing illicit or furtive about our time together, no longer than half an hour. Nothing stealthy or clandestine. But no one asked. Nor did I. Ask myself why I parked on the service road, out of sight. Ask, What's happening here? Though once I did say, "Where are you supposed to be?"

"Here," he said, with certainty in eyes that could as easily provoke, tease. "Today's the day we're moving the urns to the parish house for safekeeping, remember?" I didn't ask him where he was supposed to be again, unwilling to spoil a friendship. That's what we were, all we were. It's simply that we happened to be male and female, mother and minister. Sharing a sandwich or a story.

He taught me a little of clerical lore, the theory that the height of a rector's collar is in direct proportion to the stiffness of its wearer. One afternoon I finally learned all the names for priestly vestments, stole and alb and cassock, and clerics' vanity in particular fabrics and embroidery. We discovered we were on the same religious mailing lists, receiving how-to-be-a-saint junk mail with pictures of miracles guaranteed to stop mailmen in their appointed-round tracks.

And he talked about his roles, wryly, frankly, with no self-pity. "Yesterday I was an administrator. Tomorrow I'll be a mentor, Sunday I'm a lecturer."

"What are you today? Treasurer? Listener? Mourner?"

"Regular," he said. "That's why I come."

"I can't even imagine," I said.

"Yes, you can. It's a service industry."

"Like waitressing, and insurance."

"Like mothering."

He mused aloud at the irony of "Anglican ambiguity," as he termed it, how vocation is different from avocation, how people who feel strongly connected to the liturgy — "like you" — generally appreciated silence, meditation. We laughed over the strangers on the street who yelled, "Howdy, Padre!" to him, and over what he called his Anti-Christ Auto Art, a collection of irreverent bumper stickers. "The best of show are 'The only hell Mama ever raised' and 'Jesus is coming, and He's pissed.'"

"There's something I've always wanted to know," I said gravely.

"Is God dead?"

"A far more serious topic."

He composed his face to match mine. "Hit me."

"When people knock on your door selling

154

magazine subscriptions and light bulbs, do you buy because you're a minister and have to be nice?"

"Come here." He beckoned and whispered in my ear, "I hide in the closet."

He told me about spending Saturdays of his Maryland youth in the JUG basement of Catholic school — "Judgment Under God" — corralled with other models of bad behavior. I told him how whenever I woke up feeling sick as a child that I looked in the mirror and smiled hugely and fiercely, to convince myself that I was well enough to go to school. "Hence four years of perfect attendance medals."

"And untold numbers of infected classmates."

I told him my favorite hymns, and he told me his. I told him my favorite prayer, and he told me his. A baptismal prayer, oddly enough, and he recited it — the sweet request for an inquiring mind, a discerning heart — leaning against a tree, there in the woods, unembarrassed by his audience of one.

So he asked of my children, what they were like, and did, and said. I told him that Mark had once cut open Mexican jumping beans to discover how they "worked," how he relied on duct tape to repair everything from bicycles to tennis shoes. We split a Coke and I told him how Ellen didn't like the way her new-clipped nails felt against bedsheets and that Mark didn't like ironed shirts because they were "crunchy" against his skin. We laughed about Ellen using Wite-Out to give herself a French manicure and Mark announcing at eight, "I'm afraid of dying because there's nothing to *do* all day in heaven."

And as we talked of children, we talked, eventually, of Ceel. Of her childlessness, a condition as chronic and debilitating as an illness, and how I admired her stoicism and longed for her prayers to be answered. "She never despairs," I said. "Never blames. Yet for me it wasn't until I already had a child that I realized how badly I wanted one."

I asked him how he'd come to the decision not to have children, or was it the only road to take in his position, a necessity? Did he ever feel a lack, an absence? "Sometimes," he said. "During a christening, when I hold this perfect little package, imagine the life ahead. And yesterday, when you told me how teaching a child to pump a swing is the hardest thing you'll ever teach them." He quoted me. "You put your legs *out* when you go up . . . now fold, fold!"

He'd raked back his hair, the backward-finger gesture I'd come to know. "It was largely Daintry's decision, I guess. We have a lot we want to accomplish, so . . ." He smiled faintly. "One of those things that seems like a good idea at the time, like cutting open jumping beans. Besides," he said, and gently stepped on a puffball mushroom, "people change. They change their minds."

Beneath his foot the globular mushroom collapsed soundlessly in a small cloud of mustardy dust, a volcano folding upon itself. During those afternoons and conversations, I forgot that he was married and to whom.

And so inevitably we talked of Daintry. We had to; she lay between us.

"Mind if I smoke?" He burrowed through the inside pockets of his blazer and pulled out a cigar. "Daintry won't let me puff in the rectory." I shook my head, watched him trim and light it.

"What's this?" he asked, pointing to a crude wire cylinder weighted at the bottom with stones.

"Mulch in the making. Eggshells, coffee grounds, broccoli stems." I swiped at a hovering yellow jacket and tossed an apple core into the container.

"Won't it draw rats?"

"Bees, mostly. You worried?"

"Worriers do not schedule Jesus film marathons." The previous weekend Peter had arranged for five movies depicting Jesus, from the art house to the commercial, to be shown and discussed at the church. *The Ten Commandments*, even *Godspell*, were expected; the controversial *Jesus of Nazareth* was not.

"You didn't use *Jesus Christ Superstar*." She'd had that album. I recalled it precisely, the brown cover with gold lettering. Singing along, we'd thought ourselves wildly heretical.

"I've given new definition to the term 'bully pulpit,' " he said.

"I admire your courage. I'd never be that brave." Cigar smoke meandered gracefully, hypnotizing me with its bluish flow. "Daintry was." I drew lines in the dirt with a stick. "Once I watched her cut her own hair."

"Haven't you ever cut your own hair?"

I shook my head. "Not like Daintry. She leaned over, grabbed whatever hung down, and whacked off that beautiful black stuff with one chop of the scissors. Scalped herself with an instant shag. We were thirteen. I thought it was the bravest act I'd ever seen, until an hour later. She telephoned a crush who wouldn't give her the time of day. When he answered she held the receiver to the record player so he got an earful of 'Mr. Big Stuff.' "

Peter laughed. "That doesn't sound like a brave Daintry. That sounds like a thwarted Daintry."

I gazed at the lesser hills, footstools to the Blue Ridge. "What have you done to her?"

"What do you mean?"

"She's . . . different."

"Different how?"

I wasn't sure how. "Does she still thump in bed?" Peter looked at me curiously. "No, no, I . . ."

" 'No, no, I' what?" He laughed.

"She used to rock herself to sleep. It reached a point where I couldn't sleep without the noise of Daintry rocking because I spent so many nights with her." I toed a shovel. "We always tried to remember exactly what position we fell asleep in, so the next morning we could see if we'd moved during the night." Ambushed by memory, I looked at him with embarrassment. Like switchbacks of a hiking trail, memory follows an indirect route. "Amazing, what you manage to recall." But his smile was kind, indulging.

"We assigned a different fortune to each color scarab of the bracelet I got for my eleventh birthday. Then we'd ask school friends to pick their favorite stone and we'd predict their future. Entirely invented."

He tapped knuckles to his chin. "You two were close, weren't you? Daintry never speaks of it."

I was quiet for a moment, both wounded and relieved by the revelation. "In the way that girls of a certain age are, to survive, yes. I was a . . . disciple of Daintry's." With the stilled clarity of photographs, visions of us constantly paired flashed before me: wobbling on stilts, counting pogo stick jumps, selling lemonade on the corner, playing croquet at twilight.

I uncapped the highlighter I used for the columbarium's blueprint and waved it under Peter's nose. "Which is better, this or gasoline?" Too close; I left a small streak just above his lip. "We never could decide which smelled better, Magic Marker or gas." How to convey such closeness, the nonsense significance of girlhood's innocent intimacies? That blue was the best color in the whole wide world; that seven and nine were girl numbers, one and three were boys. That wishing for something *not* to happen guaranteed the opposite effect.

"I hated ever missing school," I said. "Not because there was homework to make up, but because I'd miss being with her." I zipped the marker in my backpack. "But it was never the same after I went away to school. We didn't have that intensity of the everyday. You have to know what your friend is wearing, and thinking, and whose initials she's scribbling in her notebook."

"I can't imagine Daintry scribbling initials."

"But she did." Tree bark was rough and uneven against my shoulder. "And when I came home for vacations something had changed. We weren't as close. We were just . . . apart. Different." I tried to recall those homecomings, brief and hurried. At school I'd dreamed of Cullen, and Daintry, what was known and familiar. Yet once home I'd longed to go away again in an inexplicable paradox of wanting both the old and the new, independence and security, safety and free fall.

I closed the cooler as if I might shut the dark underpinnings of the paradox inside it and stood, brushing off the seat of my jeans. "I need to get to work. Not many of these snake days left."

"What days?"

"Because it's so warm still. They're out

sunning, soaking up the warmth for their cold blood and the cold winter."

"Shit!" Peter jumped to his feet, shaking his hand and dropping the cigar. "Bee stung me. Ouch! Damn, it hurts."

"Let me see." He extended his arm, a welt rising on the pale skin of his inner wrist. "Stinger's still there, wait a minute." I pulled out the minute splinter. "Hold on." I reached for the flattened cigar, pinched off the butt end still moist from his mouth, and pressed the damp tobacco against the reddening flesh.

"Home remedy?"

"The best kind. Sorry. October bees are so dogged and territorial. They must intuit the first frost, realize their buzzing days are numbered." Sweat beads had broken out on Peter's forehead. "Give me this," I said, easing off his jacket and pushing him down gently. "Sit a minute."

A plume of smoke curled beside a windowless house in the valley, a thin gray ribbon against the palette of autumn colors stretching out before and beneath the shelf of land. Breathing deeply of the tangy burnt aroma, I pointed to the leaf pile, a tiny distant cone. "One time you asked why we moved. That's why. So I could smell burning leaves again."

Peter cradled his wrist in his other palm. I felt his gaze on me, though I looked straight ahead. I knew that gaze, direct and riveting and interested. "Does Hal know what a romantic he married?"

Though it was only two o'clock, far up the hill the church bell pealed three times, still unregulated to the waning hours of daylight savings. "There's something I haven't changed," he said. "Every spring, those first few days after daylight savings begins and I come across some clock — in the car, on the microwave — and think, *Oh, it's five o'clock, and yesterday it would have been four, and I would have had that other hour.* Isn't that ridiculous?"

But I understood Peter Whicker's wistful, silly, profound melancholy for that lost hour. *That makes two of us romantics,* I could have said.

"Caught you," he said, "goofing off on the job."

I didn't move, sit up from lying on my back. Against the azure October sky snowy clouds billowed in great puffed mounds. "I always believed God lived behind those clouds. They were part of his beard. Bald head kind of rimming over them, fingers on the top of them as he peered over." Waiting for laughter, I tilted my head backward to look at him. Instead he pulled a small black machine from his blazer pocket. "Is that a tape recorder? For what?"

"Taking notes." He spoke into it, repeating what I'd said.

"You're doing it all wrong. See, you're talking into the speaker." I pointed to the tiny microphone at the end of the appliance.

"No wonder my sermons are garbled. Are you listening yet?"

"To what?" I stepped away, conscious of our closeness.

"My sermons."

"I like them."

"Nope. Damning with faint praise is not an answer."

So I asked him how he wrote them, what inspired him: a person, a passage, a piece of music? Were they week-long endeavors or sudden, revelatory blurts? Whether he memorized or used notes. He wrote on Saturday nights, he said: late, alone, in pencil, at a desk. And I could see that, the head bent in concentration, fingers worrying his ear or lip beneath a lamp's pale cone of illumination.

"Use yourself," I suggested. "Things you've told me. Getting punished for throwing rocks down the well as a little boy.

Your own life makes you more, I don't know, personal. Accessible."

He aimed an acorn at the shovel head. "Go on."

"What I want from priests is . . . humanness. I want to know they're human. Then I can connect to you — them."

"*Religio* means connect. Did you know?"

I shook my head. "I'm not good with definitions."

That Sunday in the pew I heard my own words from the pulpit, a sermon about a benevolent God. Peter hadn't used just himself in his sermon. He'd used me.

"Brought you something." He'd found a bird's nest on his way down the hill. Downy feathers still clung to the twigs. "Were you leaving?"

"Going to look for wildflowers. Trilliums, lady's slippers, ferns. It's against the law, but maybe I won't get arrested for transplanting them to a church ground."

"Can I come?" He saw my hesitation. "You might hit the mother lode and need my help."

We crunched deep into the woods, through leaves and sticks, stepping over fallen tree trunks, holding whip-thin bare branches for one another. For twenty minutes I saw nothing but dying weeds, leaves, brilliant-hued vines. Then I heard something beyond our crackling passage, a low trickling gurgle like rainwater in a gutter. I hurried toward the noise and nearly stepped over it: a spring, barely more than a bubble in the soil, shining wetly on leaves and stones. The spring pulsed clear and cold, rising only inches before seeping invisibly into the earth again. Surrounding and sheltering the tiny fountain were fronds of fern, plush moss, waxy galax. And a virtual greenhouse of wildflowers. No longer blooming, but thriving. Peter's mother lode. I dropped to my knees, delighted with the lucky discovery.

He appeared above me. "I thought I'd lost you."

"Oh, Peter, look, a pitcher plant." I ran fingers down the fragile stem of a single-leaved wildflower no taller than my palm, searching, hoping. It was there. Seemingly separate from the plant itself was a tiny fleshy jug springing upright from the moist ground. I gently touched the rubbery curves, the slight opening at its tip. "When I was little, this was the greatest find in the woods. We pretended these were fairy milk bottles. But if you pick it, it's ruined, shrivels into nothing. Because this is the root."

Peter's fingers grazed mine as he touched the little bottle. An erratic spiral of falling leaves died nearby, floating soundlessly to earth. Exaggerated, mingling scents of decay and dryness stung my nose. I thought of Daintry, the other half of *we*. "I've changed my mind about transplanting it. It might die if I move it. Two more weeks and it'll be killed by a hard frost anyway." Somehow September had become November.

"And will you still come to the columbarium when the snake days are over?" Peter asked. "Will you still be here?"

I looked at him, the dark eyes, the disobedient hair. This hopeful, playful, compassionate man.

How would I have answered the question that I'd asked of others: What is it that draws you, appeals, attracts? *Boyish but earnest*, I could have said. *Vulnerable. Funny. Gentle. Ordinary.* And though adjectives were enough, they weren't all.

The way someone listens, I'd have told Ceel if she'd pressed. *Intensely, so that when you're with him he's completely with you. How he tilts his head to talk, leans to listen. Interest*, I'd have said, *interest is more erotic than anything else.*

A single sunlit shaft behind Peter's head

blinded me. I didn't think, *This man is a priest.* I didn't think, *How sorry will I be?* "Yes," I answered him. "I'll still be here."

From Hannah's quote book:
People change and forget to tell each other.
— Lillian Hellman

Chapter 8

"See, El?" We were watching the weather channel. "What did I tell you about that thunder?" Snow was predicted, and the forecast thrilled me. At breakfast I'd said it even smelled like snow outside, an assertion Hal had ridiculed.

"Those guys are always wrong," Mark said. "You said we could go *today*, Mom."

"It's only your permit."

"You *promised*."

I'd planned an afternoon of games and fires and making soup. Cozy, nesting activities. But I had, I'd promised. "Okay, let's go."

Mark zeroed in on the driver's license office in Asheville like a guided missile, leaving me to navigate the triple-story maze of county administration departments alone. When I finally located it, he was waiting to borrow a pen from a woman who was filling out her own form at the imposingly high counter. "Mom," he said, "this is —"

"Have at it," Daintry said, handing him her pen.

"Thanks," Mark said, and sat down at one of half a dozen desks.

"They all look alike, don't they?" Daintry said. "Dingy linoleum, no windows, and a Lion's Club chewing gum machine. Peter and I are on the lam, license-wise. He seems to think getting them changed to North Carolina is on my job description." She rummaged through her pocketbook for change. *Purse,* Kathleen O'Connor had said. *Pocketbook,* my own mother said.

"Price of gum has gone up, though." She inserted a dime into the glass bubble's slot and held her palm open beneath the dispenser mouth. "Our lucky day," she said, checking the assortment of multicolored squares and offering me one. "No licorice, right?"

Daintry pointed to a large appliance on a wobbly card table. "And of course an avocado green coffee percolator straight from the fifties." She took a Styrofoam cup from the stack. "I never had an avocado before I ate one at your house. Your mother put them in salads." She flicked a sugar packet. "You and I fought over those chunks."

"And I'd never had shepherd's pie before yours." O'Connor meals were noisy gatherings, interrupted constantly by phone calls from patients since Jack O'Connor worked alone, had no partner to be on call. "What color are the stools?" he'd ask nonchalantly into the receiver, chewing all the while. He'd hang up, fork another mouthful, and say to anyone who was listening, "If only I didn't have to deal with the parents. If only the clinic were drive-through, and the babies were just handed through the window." An attitude that might have predicted his later downfall. Though perhaps the opinion demonstrated just the opposite: that he cared so.

Daintry wrinkled her nose. "I'm not much of a chef."

I was wrong, then. While I cooked kid-friendly suppers of chicken, spaghetti, tacos, I'd pictured suppers — no, *dinners* — at the rectory as something either glamorous or romantic: risotto with asparagus, peasant soup and chunks of bread.

Daintry filled the cup. "Now's our chance for coffee."

It wasn't the meeting I'd imagined, a musty office basement. But it was Daintry, after all, and we were together. I sat beside her. Mark's head was bent in concentration.

"So he's old enough for his permit?" she said.

I only nodded, attempting no jokes about staying off the road. Somehow I couldn't see Daintry, this new and different version, finding humor in comments I'd heard from other women whose children were beginning to drive. "I hoped he might be satisfied with cruising around with Wendy Howard for a while."

"That decorator's daughter? With the boobs?"

I laughed, lowered my voice. "That's the one. Have you ever seen anyone exude sex the way that girl does? Even the way she stands is provocative. I suggested to Mark one day last week that maybe Wendy's breasts were almost *too* big."

"What did he say?"

"He said, 'I wouldn't go *that* far, Mom.' "

"It's the McDonald's," Daintry said.

"Who?"

"In twenty years some scientist will discover a breast-enlarging chemical in McDonald's hamburgers."

"Could be. We never looked like that."

"Don't be jealous. It's her time to be sexy."

The accusation stung. Was I jealous? Daintry made me feel like a pinched-face disapproving matron. I watched Mark erase an answer and changed the subject. "The last time I was in a driver's license office was to get a blood test before my wedding. Only in Cullen are the marriage license and driver's license office one and the same. The needle sank into the crook of my arm, and I cooled out right in the chair. There really *is* such a thing as smelling salts. They used them on me."

"Did you faint because you were afraid your corpuscles might give you away?"

"VD? Come on."

"Nonvirginal status."

"Hush." I cocked my head toward Mark. "I'm not ready to fall off my perfect parent pedestal yet."

"Please. What is he, fifteen and a half? Mark's probably not a virgin himself. Or maybe he takes after you?" Both suggestions chilled me, but Daintry was grinning.

"What are you doing in here? Alan is waiting out there on the dance floor!"

What I was doing was hiding in the harsh fluorescence of the girls' bathroom.

"He . . ."

"He what?" She was wearing a pink-and-white-striped knit dress and pink fishnet stockings clipped to a yellow gingham garter belt. I knew; I had the identical garter belt.

"He kept putting his face against my neck. Here . . ." I gestured, placing my palm between

173

ear and collarbone. "Sort of, I don't know . . ." I drew my shoulder to my ear as though wiping away the warm dampness of Alan's mouth against my skin. "Nuzzling me."

"He wants you to turn your head," Daintry explained patiently. Not scornfully, not derisively, simply imparting information. "He wants you to turn your head so you can kiss. So you can make out."

"While we're dancing?" Diane Walker glanced at me from the mirror where she was applying eye shadow to a lid already bruised with blue.

"It's the last dance," Daintry said, as if that explained everything. "He won't get another chance."

So I'd turned my head and, with Alan's hand at my back, let myself be led to a darkened corner crowded with folding chairs. To make out.

"Don't you read the papers?" Daintry said now. "You're as bad as Peter. Or as innocent. I keep pushing him to lead some sex seminars for parish teens. It ain't *all* about God."

I thought of Peter. I knew what it felt like to be pushed by Daintry O'Connor. *Go on, chicken.* "Go on," she'd said. In our roamings far beyond the neighborhood, we'd come upon an abandoned house, derelict and condemned, one spring afternoon.

I didn't want to be there. I wanted to be at home forcing Ceel and her after-school playmate to turn a frazzled length of tow rope against the driveway so I could learn to run *into* the circling rope instead of beginning like a novice, a baby, with the rope held lightly at my ankles. But Daintry wanted to play Lewis and Clark and explore. Daintry won.

At the house's foundation I poked around wild jonquils bent beneath soda and beer bottles hurled into the lot by passersby. I couldn't decide whether to use my hands to pick flowers — I'd already cashed in my daffodil allotment at home — or take the bottles to trade in for nickels. Daintry and I were saving to buy one of the blue Easter chicks baking under a light bulb at the five-and-ten. We were always saving something — Blue Horse seals and Icee points carefully scissored from sticky, empty cups, even our mothers' Green Stamps, complaining that they never fit the squares of the S&H books.

Daintry called to me from the rotting porch, and I looked up, hoping she was ready to go. She'd already mastered jumping into a circling jump rope; had demonstrated it on the playground that day at school. "Cinderella, dressed in yellow, went upstairs to meet her fellow," she'd chanted, black hair flying in perfect Pocahontas braids. When had she learned to jump in like that? And where was I when she did?

"Look, Hannah." The door to the weathered house was intact and locked, but above the handle was a mosaic of stained glass. I had to admit it was wondrous. We'd never seen stained glass anywhere but at St. Francis.

"Let's take some home," Daintry said.

"How?"

"Break it, dumbo."

"But —"

"Nobody lives here anymore. Nobody wants it. Quit following the rules. I'll do the blue," Daintry directed. "You do the red." She handed me a broken board; there were plenty lying around. "One, two . . ." She saw me falter. "Go on," she said. *"Go on! Three!"* I struck the pane, shattering it with a sickening twinkle. I looked up from the shards at my sneakered feet, horrified to discover that Daintry had held back. "Gotcha last," she said, laughing, and smashed her board into the blue glass.

"Look what Daintry and I found." I showed my father that night.

"Where did you get that?" he asked.

"That old house nobody lives in near the Freeman place."

"That house belongs to Mr. Freeman, too," my father had said sternly, and made me call up the owner, confess what I'd destroyed, and offer to replace the window.

The gum coating had melted in my hand, green as the glass. "Did you get punished for breaking that window on the Freeman property?" I asked her. "The stained glass?" I was sure she didn't remember making me; people don't recall traits and gestures that are second nature.

"Hunh," Daintry said. "You made me help pay for it."

I laughed.

"What?"

"You made me, I made you. Even steven."

Her eyes flickered over the cup's rim. "But tell me about Hal. He wasn't the first, was he. Who was? One of those cookie-cutter khaki-clad frat boys?"

I thought of Hal in those days, when I was crazy for him, craved touching him, threading my fingers through his coarse-textured hair, the color of tallow. How, knowing his class schedule, I'd take an indirect route to my own class just to cross his path. Whatever Hal was, he wasn't Daintry's to denigrate. "I married one of those cookies, and he was a cute cookie, too. We couldn't all date the editor of the newspaper. Why, is this a lemon squeeze? Was Ford your first?"

"No," she said, snapping the wooden stirrer in pieces. "So what's Hal like? I was gone by his era."

"Not *gone*. Just . . . inactive."

"No, Hannah." I heard pity in her voice, yet something else: regret? Wistfulness? "I was definitely gone by then."

Mark was giving his best gangster expression to the instant photo machine. "Why did you?" I said. "You left me. Again."

Daintry's eyes hardened. "That TTF stuff, true tried friend," she mimicked the sorority password. "Such crap."

Her derision, the swift change of tone, was startling. "I know it was crap. Everybody knew it was crap. We howled about it. We howled that the Tri Delts got into coffins during initiation to be born again, or that Chi Os had to recite the Greek alphabet. But who cares? It was just someplace to hang your hat, to give you a sense of —"

But Daintry finished my sentence — "Identity" — and I wondered whether only I was aware of the irony, that for so long my sense of self had been linked to her.

"Do I look like a thug?" Mark interrupted, waving his newly minted permit beneath my nose.

Daintry smiled up at him. "Your mother and I took driver's ed together."

Of course we had. Our birthdays were close enough to place us with the same schedule and teacher and car with its STUDENT DRIVER rooftop warning. Daintry's birthday was in May and mine wasn't until July, but then again, there wasn't much she didn't do before me, from cussing to kissing to starting her period. Whether it was *nookie* or *fuck*, it was Daintry who knew it.

"Do they still have teachers from the high school as instructors?" she asked Mark.

He murmured a response, but I was watching Daintry. She sensed it, she knew it. The whole town had known it. The class president and the teacher. The valedictorian and the teacher. Black-haired Liat and Mr. Simpson, the copper-haired drama coach.

Mike Simpson taught drama at the high school and moonlighted as a driver's ed instructor. He was in his early thirties, slight, with springy auburn hair and blue eyes that took in both road hazards and our reactions to his risqué double entendres and innuendos. "Any space for me in your mutual admiration society?" he asked us. He was funny, high-spirited, full of theater anecdotes and inquiring glances. He was also married, with a toddling child.

Teachers were normally feared or ridiculed and scarcely considered outside the classroom. Freshmen weren't permitted to try out for plays, so Daintry and I had no classes with Mr. Simpson. Navigating three-point turns on the Cullen streets, its four stoplights, the one venture all the way to the interstate, had been odd, wonderful, and not simply due to the novelty of driving or the hope and dread that Mr. Simpson might slam his foot to the famed passenger brake the cars were equipped with. He was charming and candid with us, joking and talking as if we were equals. "Call me Mike," he said.

I admired Mr. Simpson, appreciated his driving tips and his ease with us, though I could never bring myself to call him Mike. But Daintry called him that, and more. Daintry O'Connor had loved Mike Simpson, and he'd loved her. Or so the rumor went. Not then, but later, during and after he directed her in *South Pacific*.

Like other outlaws — Ceel and her liquor forays — they'd driven to South Carolina, a "no tell" motel, it was reported. Boldly, brazenly, in the student driver car, no less. Play practice indeed. In a town the size of Cullen, as conservative as Cullen, a student's affair with a married teacher was the white-hot stuff of scandal.

The gossip reached me hours away at Wyndham Hall. As I tried to concentrate in a study hall basement where the only white-hot excitement was the classmate who dropped a lit match into an overflowing trash can, vivid images reeled through my brain. Steinbeck's implied sex in *East of Eden*, open on the desk before me, couldn't compare to the explicit sex I created mentally. Daintry's long legs wrapped around Mike Simpson's back. Her black hair caught in his mouth, his hands clutching breasts and buttocks in a scenario I concocted, sequestered in study hall and, indeed, a long way from being anything but a virgin. Visions that thrilled me. Of course I believed it. Of course it would be Daintry. Who else?

I might have asked her outright for the truth. But whether fact or falsehood, it somehow parted us further. That she'd progressed so far beyond me, capable of an affair. Capable of secrets. Capable of a life that didn't include me. I didn't care about the rumor. I cared that I couldn't trace the moment of separation, how we'd moved from roller skates to Barbie wedding dresses to minor vandalism to two different people.

"Can I drive home?" Mark asked. I nodded and gave him the keys.

Daintry drew her fingers down the surface of the scarred wooden desks where we sat like classmates. "Hannah . . . do you still have the desk?"

"Yes," I said. "I brought it to Rural Ridge."

"Is it still white?"

"The drawer pulls are blue."

"Yes," she murmured. "They were blue then, too."

She didn't need to explain. The desk was a gift from Santa the Christmas I was ten. It had been splendidly, abundantly arrayed with stapler and brads and construction paper, blotter and pencil cup. I adored the fabulous newness of it all, as had Daintry.

"Remember how we left it, didn't touch a thing, pick up a single pencil the whole Christmas vacation?" she asked.

I nodded. For we'd been reluctant to disturb its tidy, ordered appearance and arrangement. Intuiting, bound by an unspoken understanding that once the box of gold stars or the jar of sweet-tasting paste — just as at school — was opened, once the pencils were marred with toothmark dents

182

or the plastic wrapper was removed from the solid bulk of college-ruled paper, the desk, the tableau of perfection, would vanish into something ordinary and old and used.

"Do you still have the lazy Susan?" I asked. For I'd loved that, the broad wooden turntable laden with sugar bowl, salt and pepper shakers, vinegar, in the middle of the O'Connors' kitchen table. I loved its slow, silent spinning, the cozy jumble of jars, the ease of reach, when my own kitchen table was cleared after every meal. "Do you?" I asked. It was so easy, too, lured back like filings to a magnet, to recall how I'd loved her.

But Daintry only laughed, as though ridiculing the idea that my desk and her lazy Susan were comparable. "Congratulations, Mark," she said, slipping a twenty-dollar bill from her wallet. "This is for your first tank of gas." Mark whooped and took off down the corridor.

"Thank you," I said, "but that was too much. More than his allowance. I hate for my children to be so enthralled with money."

Daintry's gaze was pure assessment. "Don't you know anything, Hannah? That's what everything's about."

"It wasn't for us."

"Sure it was. Don't you remember making Creepy Crawlers and selling them at school? And don't forget Saturdays at the factory, the vending machines." Often my father took us along when he went to the plant on weekends, emptied of seamstresses and cutters. Daintry and I would wrap ourselves in belts, hundreds of identical lengths, snitch gum from open packs left on sewing tables decorated with pictures of children grinning before studio backdrops of gushing waterfalls. Stomachs against the cold cement floor, we slid yardsticks back and forth beneath the row of crackers and candy and soda machines, hoping to find dropped coins.

Until we'd aged sufficiently to earn a paycheck, when the summer before our high school senior year we'd worked on those belts and buttons as employees in the plant's discount outlet. For eight hours a day we rebuttoned and rebelted and rehung dresses women had driven from around the state to try on and discard in the changing rooms. On breaks we ate barbecue potato chips from the same vending machines we'd once searched beneath and mourned the amount of our hourly wage.

Daddy had finagled the drudge jobs for us. Because I'd asked him to. Because I'd sensed my widening separation from Daintry and believed proximity alone could restore our indivisibility.

Mark buckled his seat belt. "Did you check out her car? A Lexus. She's cool."

A Lexus. How far we'd come from our mothers' cars that summer of driver's education. Both were old, clunky station wagons. My mother's was faded blue, Kathleen O'Connor's had fake wood panels peeling away in strips. Those, at least, were comparable. "Cool because of her car?"

"Sure." Revving the accelerator, he grinned and said, "Gross show of power."

From Hannah's quote book:
Not happiness, but intensity, was what she craved.

— Mary Stewart

Chapter 9

At ten that evening I moved through the house collecting the multiplying clutter of daytime: pencils, glasses, stray shoes. The television was tuned to the sports channel. The mail was scattered on the kitchen table. The coffeemaker was prepped for morning. Hal had come home earlier than I for a change; it was obvious in the mundane domestic details of our semiseparate lives.

"Breakfast is the only time you're here anymore," I'd said to him that morning. "What time did you come home last night?" I'd gone to bed leaving only the hall light burning.

"Late, after eleven. I stayed afterward to talk with another board member," Hal said. "And I have a curriculum meeting Thursday night."

Beyond the window, spooked doves fluttered clumsily away from a pie plate of bread heels, leaving an aggressive bluejay selfishly and wastefully scattering crumbs. "How many committees are you on?"

He swiveled, piqued. "I'm good at this, Hannah. Can't I have a creative outlet? You have your columbarium." I was silent. "Bring home the flathead shovel," he said. "I'm starting a new section of your wall."

Not my *wall*, I'd thought. Hal had ordered three containers of Tennessee fieldstone, declaring his intention to build a walled garden in our yard near a stand of rhododendron. Walling me in as Daintry walled me out.

Now I put glasses in the dishwasher while Hal ate ice cream from the carton. "Where was Mark until nine tonight?" he asked.

"At the mall with Wendy Howard." Doesy had poked her face through the hemlock hedge. *"Haaayyy! Mark and Wendy sure are spending a lot of time together. Maybe they're having a little thing! Isn't that cute?"* "Wendy's supposedly grounded, but Doesy's definition of grounding is to not let her use the phone between four and six in the afternoon."

"How do you know?"

"She told me."

"Humor her. She loved Asheville Academy and she's loaded."

"What does that have to do with the Academy?"

"Hannah," Hal said wearily. "Private schools always need money. And if Peter Whicker has his way, we'll need more. For someone who's a nonvoting board member, he's a nuisance."

"Why?"

"He wants to personally appoint a new member to the scholarships committee. *And* he wants a significant portion of scholarship funds to go to students based strictly on race."

"So?"

"So St. Martin's gives several thousand dollars to the school annually, and Peter . . . well, the rector controls that money, indirectly. It's a delicate situation. He's controversial."

I might have contradicted him, suggesting Peter Whicker wasn't controversial but committed, dedicated. But I said nothing, unwilling to be drawn into a discussion of Peter's traits and protecting something I wasn't sure of. Our conversations, our companionship. Our privacy. "Use a bowl, Hal. You're dropping ice cream on the floor." I pointed to the melting droplets with my new sandal — comfortable contraptions that looked as if they'd been made of old tires and that I suspected I'd bought precisely for their unapologetic ugliness.

Hal studied the shoes. "Hannah," he said with amusement, "what *moved* you?"

I sponged away the mess myself and began undressing on the way to our bedroom. Tossing a flannel shirt over a chair, knowing I'd wear it again tomorrow, I remembered those years — years! — I chose a shirt in the morning simply because Hal hadn't seen me wear it recently. Incredible the lengths one went to, that early and undeviating desire to please.

"Hal," I asked as he turned back the sheets, "do you ever wonder about certain couples, how they wind up together?"

"Such as whom?" His words were drawn and distorted by a deep yawn.

"You know who I mean. The ones you watch saying 'I do' at the altar, thinking all the while: *Never. It'll never last.* For no particular reason, a hunch. Couples you meet later, too, already marrieds who seem complete opposites. Like . . . well, like Peter and Daintry. They seem so" — I groped — "unsuited," regretting my prim choice of words. "Maybe she's hell in bed."

Hal frowned. "How do you come up with these things? Your train of thought is astonishing."

"I was joking." I opened the mystery Ceel had recommended and turned automatically to page one hundred. *"The sex scenes are* always *on page one hundred,"* Daintry had said. The soft-core porn we scavenged from Geoff's room proved her correct more often than not. I scanned the page, and though it didn't exactly qualify as sex, a male character was stripping to skinny-dip. *Hanging hog,* the author described the lawyer who was looking for a playmate for his *meat puppet.*

"Ever heard this expression for penis?" I asked Hal, and repeated the phrases aloud. "Why is it that the female body is tagged with all the foul words and men get all the hilarious ones?"

Hal didn't take his eyes from his own book. His fingers moved unconsciously over his chest, playing with the frizz of sprouting hair, then traveled to his navel and circled its fleshy cavity.

I propped the book's spine solidly on my rib cage and tried to concentrate. But it was happening again: my heart slipping out of patterned sync. As I'd once watched my belly undulate with the restless movements of my unborn children, I watched my chest, convinced it was lurching with extra beats, urgent irregular pulses. "Hal. Look at that."

Still he didn't turn his head. "At what?"

"The way my heart's beating. Look, the

book moves. Should I worry?"

"Mmm." No verbal violence marks a marital drift. There is only that slow segue into indifference.

My heart banged again, captive in its rib cage prison. When Daintry and I were eleven, a science assignment required us to memorize the path of blood through the heart, a complicated journey through atriums and ventricles. Right, left, upper, lower, entrance, exit. Though Daintry mastered it quickly, my brain refused to cooperate. I couldn't picture the convoluted route or grasp the terms. "Listen," she'd said, "just learn it this one time and you'll never have to know it again."

"Is it the moon between the sun or the sun between the earth?" Ellen had recently, similarly fretted, frustrated with the difference between solar and lunar eclipses. "Which is in the middle and what makes the shadow? I don't understand how it works, and the test is tomorrow."

"You don't have to understand it," I told her. "You just have to memorize it. Learn about eclipses just this one time and you'll never need to know it again." Hal had shot me a disapproving look. And I, who didn't understand the workings of my heart, should have known better, too.

Hal yawned deeply, then again. And again. He idly scraped a paper bookmark down his jaw, once, twice. The rough stubble rasped. Who can chart the moment when a habit or tic or fault moves from endearing to unnoticed to infuriating? It's as unremarked and unobvious as the transition from mentor to nemesis.

"I saw her the other day."

"Who?"

"Daintry."

"Mmm."

"She offered outrageous things to Ellen for her birthday, gave Mark twenty dollars. And all the while she's cat-and-mousing me."

" 'Cat-and-mousing'? I repeat: Your trains of thought are astonishing."

"She told Ellen that Wyndham Hall had hair dryers in the bathrooms."

"Probably to avoid blowing fuses."

"There weren't hair dryers at all, and you've missed the point. Don't be so logical."

"What do you want me to be?"

"I want you to be . . . on my side."

His eyebrows lifted. "Is this about sides?"

"No, it's . . ." What was it? "Daintry made Wyndham Hall sound as though it were some exclusive rich-girl school. You know what I mean."

"What is it between you and Daintry? Some kind of love/hate thing?"

I shook my head. Love/hate was for summer or siblings or holidays. What was between Daintry and me had too many components, too many nuances. Too much history. "You can't package a relationship like that. It's not that simple. It's not that black and white."

Hal merely sighed, content with his calm rationale. He snapped the elastic of his boxers, wormed his hand inside, and re-arranged his genitals. The blankets moved as though moles were tunneling.

Stop that! I wanted to shout, struggled against reaching out to grab his hand. *Oh, you don't know,* I pleaded silently to some invisible entity who might contradict me. *You just cannot know. There comes a night you think you will scream from the sheer flat line of predictability. If he does it once more, picks at his chest or navel or chin one more time. Or if he does nothing at all. Simply scream.*

"Obliquity," he murmured. "Know the definition?"

Yet there was the time I'd have taken his hand, said, "Let me help you," with invitation. Now there was only that lackadaisical reach of hand to hip as one or the other of us tried to decide whether we felt sufficiently sexy to screw. There was no gauging the sexual shifts from furtive and frantic, to tender and easy, to social joking about Halley's comet frequency and getting lucky. Now there was only Hal closing his book, cutting off the bedside lamp.

"Watch what you put the electric blanket on," he said. "I got hot last night." Now there was only bedtime appliance instructions. It comes to this.

"Love you," he said.

"Me too," I said, automatic as the sex scene check. It's no one's fault. Of course I loved him, too. I loved his patience, his serenity, his logic, his steadfastness. No, I *admired* them, as I admired much about him. But admiration is a distant cousin to love.

Love. "I absolutely love your husband," an Asheville Academy teacher had told me recently. "Don't you?"

Love. "Did you notice how Ed Jordan couldn't keep his hands off his new wife?" I'd asked Hal after a party in Durham. "He didn't let her out of his sight. Talk about true love."

"That's infatuation," Hal had returned noncommittally, "not love. Which would you rather have?"

Love. "Mark loves Wendy," Ellen had

whispered to me through rubber-gloved fingers while we scrubbed terra-cotta pots with bleach before winter storage. In the driveway the two teenagers were washing the car, and I looked up in time to see Mark flick a soapy rat-tailed rag at Wendy in shameless, timeless flirtation. "Mark needs a Wendy fix," Ellen said, and giggled.

"That's not the same thing as a you fix," I said as Wendy squealed obligingly and lunged for Mark, equally shameless. *Don't be jealous. It's her turn to be sexy.* "It's different."

"How?"

"A you fix is about love. That's . . ."

Ellen had stripped off the gloves, on to other matters. "My hands stink."

Love. "They get along well," Mark had observed of a classmate's parents as we drove away from their house. I knew what prompted my son's comment. As the couple chatted with us they'd stood with arms entwined, hands in each other's back pockets, smiling at each other more than at us. There'd been a kind of wistful envy in Mark's tone of voice. I reached across the seat and patted his thigh, for which small affection I was rewarded with a scowl. I also knew that the pair was in marriage counseling. That twining and touching and smiling was therapist-prescribed behavior. I knew the look of a couple making a concerted, demonstrative effort at reloving. You had to be married to recognize it.

Hal's leg jerked without warning, a nightly routine of twitching with slumber's unwinding. I braced for the next nocturnal jolt, his limbs bolting with inconsistent spasms. I'd tried speaking aloud to him, even laying my leg heavily over his. Nothing worked. How did it happen, the slide into same-house separation?

"How do you know if you love someone enough to marry them?" I'd asked my father once, at Mark's age, perhaps. Asked with all the sincerity I'd once asked how he could sleep every night, wasn't he afraid our house would burn down? I'd sat on the stoop in the velvet dampness of a summer night, chin upon my nightgowned knees.

"When you can't stand to be without someone for a single day, when it hurts your heart to be away from them even for an hour, then you know," my father had said, equally sincere. He hadn't lived long enough for me to ask him how you kept it that way.

Unable to sleep, I rose, fumbled through the blackened house, and switched on the outside floods. Checking, scanning, hoping for the first flake. Nothing. My old wives' prediction for Ellen had come to nothing, like my attempts with Daintry. The spotlit glare illuminated only the sad battered bird feeder lying on the ground where it had dropped unnoticed, as if finally yielding to the invisible weight of neglect. The cedar shake roof had fallen off, the glass side panels shattered.

Hal's corduroy pants were crumpled before the louvered doors of the washing machine. Apparently he couldn't be bothered to put them in the hamper like everyone else. The dull olive nap of the fabric was dotted with burrs and tiny seed pod triangles. My husband was constructing his rock wall with the same thorough perfection he brought to any task. At the sight of the stubborn hitchhikers I felt a sudden spasm myself, a lurch of love. Of course I loved Hal. Surely. Inadequate, inarticulate, mis- and overused word with no definition, but the right word all the same.

"What do you tell them?" I'd asked Peter when he'd come to the woods after a marriage counseling session. He'd looked tired, beaten. I couldn't touch him, but I could talk to him. " 'Don't go to bed mad'?"

"That old shopworn dictum." He laced his fingers. "There's a scientific reason

197

people in the throes of romance are dreamy, think life is perfect. Our bodies literally release a chemical when we fall in love. The euphoria hormone. It only lasts six months."

I sat beside him, grubby hands tucked inside my folded knees. "But what do you tell them," I asked again, "later? Afterward?"

Peter creased a leaf along its spine and folded it neatly as a letter. "They don't want to hear what I say. That after a certain time, loving is an act of will. It's . . . work." We were both silent a moment. "The truth is, people don't need marital counseling *before* they're married. They need it *when* they're married." He'd sailed the leaf away. "Do you suppose I could change that rule, too?" Since then we hadn't spoken of marriage, or of Daintry, or Hal.

I brushed at the clinging pods on Hal's pants and thought of another pair, Peter's. He'd wanted to help plant the bulbs.

"No," I'd told him. "You're not dressed right. It's dirty work."

"I won't get dirty. No one will know." The reference was innocent, but the words rang between us, fraught. "Because I'll do the shoveling," he said quickly, stooping, moving with that restless energy, "and you'll put in the bulbs." But his trouser cuffs had gotten soiled, and I'd worried over them, kneeling to scrub the stains with my shirttails as Peter stood above me. Like other physical gestures — his hand at my waist or elbow, the touch of fingers when I gave him an apple, my palm over the small welt of his bee-stung finger — it had felt an intimate act.

Had Daintry noticed the stains? "Did you get those bulbs planted?" she'd asked. Casually or pointedly? I tried to remember.

Love. "She's cool," Ellen had said of Daintry. "I love her."

Love. "But it was different from you and Daintry," Ceel had said. "I *loved* Geoff."

Love. "You've always loved those PKs," she'd said.

Love. "That's not love," I'd said to Ellen, "that's . . ."

One night years ago as I read to a five-year-old Mark, he'd pointed to a word and without fanfare simply uttered "ball." I'd gasped at the wonder of it, the absolute unexpectedness. At breakfast the page had been unintelligible squiggles of ink, by nighttime it was *ball*. "Mark's reading!" I'd exclaimed to his kindergarten teacher. "How did you do it? When did you start teaching them to read?"

She'd smiled at me, responded mildly.

"No one knows how people learn to read. If we did, there'd never be anyone who was illiterate."

Wasn't it the same with love? If we knew what it was that attracted us to other people, there would never be any infidelities. Or love. People speculate, "What does he see in her?" and vice versa. There's no formula for attraction. Nothing as simple as moons and suns, aortas and atriums. Sometimes it isn't the way someone looks, that they're funny, or prodding, or hopeful, or intense.

I put my husband's pants in the laundry hamper, as I'd done a thousand times. *"You're so married,"* Daintry had said. Sometimes it's as simple as this: He's not what you already have.

From Hannah's quote book:
What is the past, after all, but a vast sheet
of darkness in which a few moments
picked apparently at random, shine?
— John Updike

Chapter 10

"It's the gin," Mother said.

"I used vodka," Ceel said.

"Did you buy any extra ornament hooks?" Mother asked me, and secured the final word in the debate over which liquor, added to tap water, produced the more rigid, topple-proof stems when forcing bulbs: "Gin works much better."

I stepped into a familiar role of diplomat. "What does it matter as long as they're standing?" Ceel's narcissi were triumphs: frothy white crowns on foot-high stalks springing from rocks and water. And gin. Or vodka. "Thanks for saving one bowl for me."

"I ran out of moss," Ceel said. "But I figured you'd know where to find more."

Hal grunted from behind the tree where he was attaching lights. "All done. Have at it while I have at vodka *and* gin. Ben?" he called to the kitchen. "Whatever you're fixing, do it double."

"Wait!" Ellen said. "We need music before we start hanging ornaments. And where's the *White Christmas* video? Everything has to be just right." Like a countdown to launching, Ellen had been crossing off the days to this Friday night of vacation's beginning. The night the tree was put up and the house decorated was on a par with Christmas Eve in Ellen's holiday scheduling. It wasn't Christmas proper until the house was cozied with red and green clutter. She'd arrived home from the half day of school giddy with freedom and festivity. But her smile sagged with disappointment when she saw the den, unchanged since breakfast.

"Where are the boxes? I thought you'd have everything ready. You haven't even brought out the ornaments and stockings?"

I understood expectations and their debilitating effects. The first Sunday in December Hal had expressed similar dismay at supper. "You haven't gotten an Advent wreath for the table?" It seemed less a question than a statement of my inadequacy. So I'd fashioned a circlet of greenery from tree lot trimmings and scavenged the attic for the four leftover purple candles, only to find them melted into a waxy clump.

Even Mark had directed a Christmas complaint in my direction. "You're trimming the tree on a night I have to work?" He'd gotten a vacation job in the kitchen of Honey Hams.

"But you told me it didn't matter to you when we decorated, Mark." It took an act of Congress to coordinate the evening around holiday hubbub, selecting the tree, making certain Mother, Ceel, Ben, Ellen, and Hal were available and included. Mark had shown no interest in participating. "You said to do it whenever we wanted."

"I can't believe you'd do it without me," he'd insisted. "At least get some icicles. Everybody but me thinks icicles are tacky."

"There's a big blank spot on the right," Mother said now. She walked over to examine the black hole. "Four bulbs are out. You should have checked the strand before they went on the tree, Hannah, and bought extras."

I sighed. It was hard to say what induced the greatest guilt: children, husbands, mothers, or Christmas itself. I thought I was prepared — shopped and wrapped and packed and delivered and mailed — covering every base in that blitz of activity and readiness. Making time to enjoy the short days beforehand.

"Did you put that soup on?" Mother was saying.

"Mark brought some ham from work and I thought we'd just have sandwiches."

"No, we need something warm. It's my homemade. It'll be more filling."

"Sounds good to me," Hal agreed with her. I put down a fragile hand-blown globe and went into the kitchen. Obeying. Capitulating. Again.

"Church is at ten," Mother said.

I reached across the platter of eggs and bacon for Hal's hand. It was early in our romance, and we were visiting Cullen. "Let's be lawless. Stay home together and read the paper, take a walk." I sensed my mother's frown and ignored it, silently challenging her to interfere.

"I'd like to go to church," Hal said. "Really."

"We'll need to leave right afterward to get back to school. Don't you want to laze around here, the two of us?" Hal smiled, indulging my wheedle.

But after breakfast Mother followed me to my room, closing the door for privacy. "Hal obviously wants to go to church with us, Hannah. You ought to be glad about it. And if you can't be glad, at least let him do what he wants to do."

"He can go with you, then," I said tersely, in the tight grip of defiance. "I'm staying home."

Her double reflected in the full-length mirror,

she stood at the door and delivered her parting shot: "Fine. That's between you and your God."

And I had gone, of course. The good daughter. The good girlfriend. Dutiful. Faithful in several senses of the word.

"I want to do the angel at the top," Ellen was saying. "Daddy says if he and Mom ever fight, the angels will cry."

Ceel looked at me curiously, but Ellen pulled on her. "Did you hear me in the Academy show, Ceelie? I sang *aingells,* not *aingulls,* just like you taught us in choir."

"I can't believe Peter Whicker substituted a come-as-you-are afternoon service for the Christmas Eve pageant," Hal said. "He's made more decrees than Caesar Augustus."

I bit back a defense for Peter's idea and teased Ellen, "Remember when you used to say, 'Christ the sailor is born'?"

Ben shuffled CD cases. "What about carols instead of this?" A jazzy version of "Rudolph the Red-Nosed Reindeer" — Ellen's selection — was blaring from the speakers.

"Hey," I said, more diplomacy for the sake of Ellen's ritual. "I need a tall man. Put this crystal snowflake somewhere safe and high, will you?"

"Is that your favorite ornament, Mom?

Everybody has to have a favorite," Ellen said. The conversation fell to favorites, and I relaxed as the tree filled with finery. I knelt at the ornament box and carefully extracted a crumpled construction paper wreath whose unevenly scissored center held a photograph of a five-year-old Mark. Once the wreath had been adorned with macaroni curls painted red. Attic mice had nibbled away the pasta, paper, and even the clotted glue, so that only a mangled paper circle remained. But Mark's beaming kindergarten grin was intact. "Oh, look. This needs a special place."

Mother peered over my shoulder. "That reminds me. I brought your baby book. I cleaned closets and thought you might like to have it."

Her easy indifference surprised me. "You don't want it anymore?"

"Where is it, where?" Ellen asked. "I want to see how Mommy looked."

"In your room with my things," Mother said. "I'll check on the soup. Who's hungry?"

"I think we're about finished here," Ben said.

"Don't plug in the lights or put the presents out until I get back," Ellen said.

". . . is my two front teeth," a kiddie voice

croaked and lisped from the speaker.

"Was that the doorbell?" Ceel asked.

"I'll get it," Hal said. But he didn't need to. Our door opened with no more introduction or hesitation than it had three decades earlier. *You and me are going to be best friends.*

"Anybody home?" Daintry said.

"All of us," Hal said. "Come in. We've just finished decorating the tree. Let me have your coat."

"I just wanted to drop off a Christmas present for you and Hannah." She unwrapped a fringed black shawl, revealing the red tin bucket filled with heart-pine fatwood she held. "I can't stay."

"Thank you," I said, summoning gratitude to cover my embarrassment. Because though I'd debated buying a gift for Peter and Daintry, I worried the gesture would look odd, suspicious. Now the lack of reciprocity seemed worse. "You shouldn't have."

But with her next sentence, Daintry eliminated any pretense of personal selection. "Peter likes to give presents to parishioners." She set the bucket on the hearth. "So many people have gas logs these days. I knew somehow you'd be purists."

Hal was delighted with her prescience. "We always need kindling."

Daintry looked carefully around the room. "But you don't have a fire tonight."

The observation struck a chord with Ellen. "Yeah, Mom," she said, a new refrain of reproach. "And you didn't make popcorn for us to string."

"It's been so warm . . . ," I began.

"Thanks so much for the narcissus, Ceel," Daintry said. "I usually burn a gardenia candle in our bedroom at night, but don't need to with that divine fragrance."

"Do you like our tree?" Ellen asked.

"It's wonderful. Maybe you could come help decorate mine and Peter's. We always wait until Christmas Eve to put it up."

I knew that. Knew he'd already picked it out himself. He'd asked me which tree lot had the freshest trees, the lowest prices. I'd met him in the church courtyard as I was making one of several trips back and forth from the columbarium to my car, loading tools — buckets, rakes, shovels, clippers — no longer needed. He'd been shopping in Asheville, fruitlessly.

"*Can I be you and you be me?*" he asked, cramming a wicker basket in the corner of my trunk. "*If you'll buy my presents, I'll clean your columbarium. The only gift I came home with was an idea for a sermon. A cosmetics clerk asked me if I'd like a whiff of 'Eternity.' I think I*

208

can do something with that."

"No 'Gift of the Magi'?" I said, helplessly thinking of his pocket watch and Daintry's possible gift to him. Hating my vulnerability.

"Overdone."

"Peter," I said from the dim recesses of the trunk, where he couldn't see my face, "I was kidding."

He was silent, and then I felt a tug on the hem of my sweater. I straightened slowly, so as not to bump my head. "I'm sorry," he said. "I was thinking of myself."

"No, no, it's my fault. It's that —" I thought of the Christmas cheer raging away everywhere else, canned carols and artificial garlands and festooned storefronts. "I put everything to bed today."

"What?"

"For the winter. Heaped mulch around every little shrub and perennial. It made me, I don't know, melancholy. That's all."

He looked at me, and for a moment I thought — feared, hoped — he might take my chin in his hand. "Hey," he said quietly, "There's a sermon there, too. A better one. You've given me a Christmas present."

"No, no, you can't —"

"Hannah," he stopped me softly, "I know."

"Soup's on," Mother called from the

kitchen. "Come now while it's —" Framed in the doorway, she stopped as if tethered when she saw Daintry. A single drip from the ladle she held fell soundlessly to the floor.

"Hello, Jean," Daintry said. My mother's first name from Daintry's lips was shocking. As if they were equals. As if Daintry were challenging her to correct the presumed informality.

"Daintry," Mother said. Then again, softly: "Daintry."

"You didn't know I was living in Rural Ridge?" There was something knowing in Daintry's tone and smile. Triumph? "Hannah didn't tell you?"

Whatever it was that had halted my mother vanished. She straightened. "I believe she did, come to think of it. I simply wasn't expecting to see you."

Daintry nodded, granting her that. "No doubt. I just stopped by with a gift."

"How nice," Mother said, Emily Post herself. "Why don't you stay and have dinner with us? I'd love to hear about . . . your family."

Daintry twirled an earring. "I'm sure Hannah can tell you." Neither woman moved to shorten the ten feet between them where I stood, the midpoint between two poles in my life — and polar opposites — pulling and pushing and molding me. In the charged air I smelled fear and antagonism and secrets withheld.

"Tell me," I begged. "Tell me how." Twelve magazines lay on the carpet in three rows of four, a stepping-stone square in the middle of the O'Connor living room. We were playing Black Magic, a reasonless, ruleless game I didn't understand.

"You have to be in cahoots," Daintry said, "then you know the secret." The secret was driving me wild. She stood, arms across her chest, impassive and immovable. I stared at Reader's Digest, Southern Living, Life, Good Housekeeping, *Heather's* Seventeen, Time: *politician and celebrity faces, an ocean liner, a soldier in uniform, a steaming casserole.*

"You can do it, you're smart," Daintry said with that tone of encouragement and challenge and absolute authority. "Figure it out." She stepped on a magazine. "This one has it, but this one doesn't."

"Doesn't have what?"

"It. Black Magic."

"But what's 'it'?" I nearly shrieked with frustration and exclusion. Daintry's expression was serene. "Somebody had to tell you *the secret!"*

"No," she contradicted calmly. "I figured it

211

out." *She kicked a* Highlights, *my contribu-tion.* "This one doesn't."

"This is boring. I quit."

"Boring because you don't know the secret. You don't know how to play."

"It's not even a game unless you have someone who doesn't know how," I said. I'd wit-nessed enough of these matches to figure out that much. "I'm leaving."

"Go on then, baby."

". . . kissing Santa Claus!" a chorus of ju-venile voices screeched from the speakers.

Mother winced. "Isn't that side over yet?"

"I like this music," Ellen objected.

"You know, Ellen, your granny used to object to me and your mommy playing just that kind of Christmas music," Daintry said. *Your granny.* Had the words not seemed so purposely cutting, I'd have laughed. It was there again, that striking assumption of intimacy and connection. "I was admiring your handiwork on the tree," Daintry said. Would she never leave?

"Ellen loaded the midsection with her fa-vorites," Hal said.

"Daddy! Besides, after I go to bed Mommy J changes all of them." Daintry smiled as if unsurprised.

Ellen pawed through the box of orna-ments. "Nothing's left but the duds."

212

"The rejects," Daintry said.

"Yeah," Ellen agreed.

Daintry bent over the box. "Who cares about shiny balls, right?"

"Right. Bo-ring."

Like an anthropologist observing mankind of another era, a mummy being unfurled, I watched with objective fascination as Daintry turned the full force of her charm on my daughter. Then she plucked something small and dark from the castoffs and the ignored; extracted something from the jumble of armless Santas and wingless angels. "But here's one."

Ellen waved it away. "That ugly thing. It's Mom's."

"Yes," Daintry said, "I know." She held out the ornament, dangling by thin sewing thread from her index finger. It was a crèche, chipped and cheap and plastic. Mary and Joseph were poorly painted vertical blobs, the manger was a veed cradle on spindly X legs, the shed's slanted roof was grooved to look like wood. Derided or ignored, the ornament was nonetheless priceless to me. It had been a gift to St. Francis Junior Choir members, and I'd preserved it since girlhood.

"How did you know?" Ellen asked.

Daintry walked to the tree and carefully

hung the crèche on an upper branch. "Because I had one exactly like it."

"Plug in the lights," Hal said. "Let's see how the finished product looks."

The tree snapped with sudden illumination, a polka-dotted burst of bright red bulbs.

Daintry clapped, laughed. "Surprise!" Ellen crowed at her reaction. "I bet you don't know anyone else in the whole wide world who uses all red lights."

"You'd lose the bet," Daintry said. She swept her shawl about her shoulders, then paused. "But aren't you going to turn out the rest of the lights in the room? See how it looks with just that red red?"

Ellen gaped. "That's what I do before I go to bed. How did you know?"

"Some things you just know."

"It's the double letters," she said six months later. We were making a topographical map of North Carolina for school.

I looked up from the cardboard I was cutting. "What?"

Daintry squeezed two droplets of green food coloring into the doughy mixture of flour and water. "Black Magic. Good Housekeeping has it, Life doesn't. Seventeen has it, but Time doesn't. And headlines count, too." She screwed the cap carefully on the green bottle. "Would you have ever guessed?"

"Give me that mixing bowl. The Piedmont isn't all green. Add some brown."

She laughed.

I walked to Ellen and wrapped my arms around her shoulders as though my embrace could protect her from this intrusion. The night had been marred.

"Perhaps we'll see you at the five o'clock service Christmas Eve," Mother said.

But it was Daintry who would have the last word. "No, I don't expect you will. I've always thought that family service is like a circus."

I watched my mother's mouth tighten. *Can I go to the midnight service with the O'Connors? Please, please, please? They invited me. Why can't we go to the late service?*

"Oh, and Hannah," Daintry said, hand on the door, "I was wondering if you'd be in charge of organizing appointments for the pictorial directory."

"What?"

"It was my idea, to have parishioners' photographs taken for a pictorial directory. So we can all have names to go with faces."

"I . . ." I hated the idea.

"Since the columbarium is finished."

"It . . ."

"You have plenty of time now, don't you?"

Mother spoke up definitively, answering for me. "I'm sure Hannah will do a wonderful job. Whatever she does, she does well."

Daintry tapped her chin with one finger. "I'm sure of it, too." She looked at me. "I'll call with the details after Christmas." The door closed behind her.

"Can I put the presents under now?" Ellen asked.

"Let's eat," Hal said. "I'll have soup *and* a ham sandwich."

But Mother hadn't moved. "Why didn't you tell me the O'Connor girl was living here?"

"Her name is Daintry, Mother. And she's doing a little more than just 'living here.' "

"She didn't take her husband's name? Or one of those slash names?"

Ceel laughed. "No."

"What does she do?"

"Manages an Asheville stockbroking office."

Mother wasn't impressed. "A pictorial directory," she mused, Daintry dismissed. "Dreadful."

After dinner was eaten and cleared; after Ceel and Ben departed; after Hal and Ellen and Mother had gone to bed, I sat on the sofa before the tree. Sat in the silent room darkened but for the eerie glow of red against the black branches and held the baby book Ellen had forgotten in her trimming glee. The baby book Mother no longer, seemingly, had any need to keep.

I might have flipped through its pages. Might have looked at the pictures cataloging all those events of childhood. But pictures hold only moments, fractions of seconds preserved in toothy smiles and flashbulbed eyes made feral with pinpoints of red. Within the stained satin cover were snapshots of birthday cakes and Christmas mornings and beach vacations. There were before and after grins of braces and haircuts, glasses and contacts. Yet as a photograph of an impulsive hug isn't evidence of intimacy, a relationship can't be documented in a split-second, freeze-framed rectangle. The album I held couldn't capture the unguarded, guileless, myriad moments of a childhood friendship. There were no pictures of chalked hopscotch grids or giggled telephone pranks or backyard forts.

Nor were there sounds within its pages. Of banged "Heart and Soul" on the organ, or arguments over whose turn it was to play the right-hand melody. No *one potato two potato three potato, four.* No tuneless plinking accompaniment to the jerkily twirling ballerina that sprung up when I opened the lid of her jewelry box, or tinny "Edelweiss" when she opened the lid to my music box from Switzerland. No churning of the rock tumbler we left grinding night and day for a month, waiting to unplug and silence it and discover ordinary rocks transformed to smoothly patinaed jewels. There was no coin, the first sandwich quarter made of copper and silver that we saved as if it might be the only one minted, taped to the pages. No pictures of our private industries, damming the creek behind our houses as if we might actually control its ceaseless flow. Playing — and cheating — on a Ouija board in a dark closet. Scissoring a stack of home-made thousand-dollar bills for a week-long Monopoly marathon. There was no room on its pages for jars filled with grass and earth, our earnest efforts to make lightning bugs and caterpillars and June bugs and earthworms feel cozy in captivity.

There were no pictures of Daintry and me beneath a red-lit Christmas tree, our arms and legs radiating like spokes as we lay among the presents, looking upward into the furry branches. "A book, easy," we'd say, pressing and guessing at the contents; or peeking outright as I gargled an entirely fake cough to cover Daintry tearing an entirely unaccidental rip in the wrapping paper. And no picture of my disappointment the Christmas we pledged to ask for wispy-haired trolls so that we could play with them together. "Let's see yours," I said Christmas afternoon, proudly displaying my brown-skinned, bug-eyed midgets.

"Oh," Daintry said, barely glancing at my toys, "I changed my mind and asked for art supplies instead. Look at this book on van Gogh."

Traitor, I'd thought, hating my ugly trolls.

There was no photographic record of us memorizing those poems for fifth-grade assignments, no sounds of childish chanting or of our chest-beating moans when we discovered "The Highwayman" a year later. There was no box of Luden's cough drops, candied medicine that was good as currency those elementary days. No copy of the songbook we purchased together at the school store to share during assemblies. Gone, gone, in a blink of unrecoverable time. Nothing at all to prove the sweetly squandered thousand thousand moments of pure happiness. Unadulterated. Un-adult. Oh, Daintry. I drew a deep breath, gasping in a smothering sadness for all the lost spontaneous joys, the trivial thrills of a girlhood shared. I leaned forward and placed the album on the table beside Ceel's narcissus. In the glass bowl the delicate white roots twined inseparably throughout the pebbles.

"Mom?" A draft of cold air gushed in as Mark closed the front door. He shrugged off his coat and sat down beside me. "What are you doing, staying up to check on me?"

Mark had been on a short rope ever since he'd come home reeking of smoke several weeks earlier. "It's not me," he'd said. "Wendy and her friends smoke, and I was just in the car."

But a week later I'd discovered something more worrisome than lingerie magazines under his bed: a heavy STOP sign. Hal was livid. "Stealing government property is a felony." Again Mark objected, claiming that the sign had been lying on the side of the road.

"Mark," I'd told him later, "whenever you're with friends who are doing something you don't want to do, blame it on me. Say, 'My mother will kill me.' 'My mother won't let me.' 'My mother will punish me.' 'She's a . . . witch.' You can blame it on me."

"All I smell is syrup glaze," I said to him now.

"Wendy calls me her 'honey funk hunk.' "

Dear God, I thought, and said, "Settin' there jes' lak a spider."

"Huh?"

As if Mark would know *Gone With the Wind*. As if it would deter his attraction. As if he could ignore his sexuality even as I, decades older and supposedly wiser, was experiencing the same powerful pull myself. "Never mind. I was just enjoying the peace."

"You ought to see how the windows look from outside. Like a nuclear meltdown."

"Oh, admit it. You love the red bulbs."

"You decorated without me."

"You know what, Mark? My first year at Wyndham Hall, the only thing that got me through December exams was thinking about decorating our tree, having everything be normal and usual and exactly the same. And when I came through the door, there it was, done. I didn't know whether to sob with hurt feelings or stomp around being furious." Mark picked at the beginnings of a hole in his jeans, listening. "And guess what. Go ahead, it won't kill you. Say, 'What?'"

He gave me a grudging smile. "What?"

"The tree was beautiful, and Christmas came and went, and I lived. I got some things I wanted and some that I didn't, just the same as every other year." I stuck out my tongue at him. "Nyah."

He shook his head as if he were the mature one. "Mom, you are so strange."

"Maybe." I stood and walked over to the tree. "What do you think?"

"It isn't finished."

"Sure it's finished. Right down to the — up to the — angel on top. Or do you think it should be a star? We could have a good family feud over that issue."

"The *icicles.*"

"But you can't even see the branches when they're covered with those stringy things."

"Thanks a lot." His lips were set in a thin line of stubbornness. Or hurt. I peered closely at him, and something inside me tumbled and gave way.

"Actually," I said, "I was just saving them till you got home." I took a paper bag from beside the ornament box. No one had thought to look into it between decorating and dinner and . . . Daintry. I handed him two slender cellophane-wrapped boxes. "After all, they have to go on last, right?"

He grinned, hugely pleased, and slit the plastic. "You didn't forget."

"I didn't forget." It wasn't only Ellen who needed ritual. I leaned to switch on an end table lamp.

"No!" he nearly shouted, then lowered his voice for the sleeping house. "No lights."

Like a waiter's napkin, the icicles draped

Mark's forearm in a silvery cascade. As they swayed soundlessly he held up his free hand to stop me from saying more. "I know, I know. Put them on one by one, branch by branch. Only at the ends. No clumping, no tossing. Take your time. Careful, careful." He separated one limp strand of tinsel from the mass and hung it delicately on the closest bough. It twinkled a solitary metallic red. "Your turn," he said solemnly, and held out his arm to me.

"Mark," I said, equally serious. "You're doing this all wrong. Totally, *heinously* wrong," I repeated, using one of his own overused adjectives to show him I meant business. "Now watch," I said, and scooped up a dozen foil ribbons, "'cause I'm only going to show you this once." I took two steps back and pitched the strands toward the tree. "Icicles have to be *flung* for the proper effect." I pointed at the helter-skelter landing of the silver strips. "Now you try and let's see if we can get this right."

Mark laughed. He began to carefully put down his burden of perfectly aligned icicles, but I touched his arm. "Nope, uh-uh, like this," and shook his arm so they fell to the sofa in a tangled lump. We stood over them, eyeing them and each other.

"You know," I said, "we could make a swell tinfoil ball."

"Nah," Mark said. "I. Wanted. Icicles."

We fell on them like famine victims. Twirled them in our fingers and grabbed them in our fists and flung them inanely toward the tree, mindless of where or how or if they landed. Clumps of red-burnished silver dotted branches like mangled birds' nests. Backs to the tree, we tossed the icicle threads over our shoulders in unison, spilled salt and superstition. We clapped hands to our mouths in silent hilarity as we tied a bow round a Santa's beard, handcuffed an angel with an icicle bracelet, tinsel-lynched a reindeer ornament to a branch, used slivers as makeshift dental floss in delirious spontaneity. It rained thin metallic silver with our wasteful, careless, free-falling pitches. Mark threw overhand, I threw my best like-a-girl underhand, he went in for a layup with a crimped handful. The tree was a crazy web of shimmering foil, dripping and strewn with our unorchestrated handiwork.

We must have looked mad, leaping and bobbing in that strange fiery light before an indoor tree. We were twin banshees, a dervished duo enacting a pagan ceremony before finally collapsing to the floor, panting with laughter and exertion. And for everything else I'd remembered that night, I couldn't recall when I'd felt so free and foolish.

I reached out to pick a silly silver string from Mark's hair. "Forgot one," I said, and handed it to him.

Our fingers touched as he took it from me and hung it carefully from a branch empty of sparkle. The single icicle swayed gracefully, as if some slight breeze, a breath, had set it in soundless motion.

"There," Mark said. "*Now* it's Christmas." He crossed his arms behind his head and lay down, snug within the presents beneath the lowest boughs. Just as Daintry and I used to do.

From Hannah's quote book:
Like a relapsing fever . . . the familiar ache
of age and sadness and wisdom.
— Norman Mailer

Chapter 11

"You should wait to take down the tree," Mother said over my shoulder.

I pulled the ornament box closer. It was late morning of New Year's Eve, and Hal had gone to the Academy with Ellen as eager company. The vacated school was a paradise for her, a life-size setting to play Teacher, where she scribbled assignments on blackboards and instructed imaginary students. "Wait for what?"

"Epiphany."

"When's that — January fifth or something?"

"You know very well when it is. We've hardly had time to enjoy the tree."

"You're getting ready to leave," I reminded her.

"It's a sin, what's become of Christmas. Stores decorated before Halloween. Whatever happened to Advent?"

"The tree's a fire hazard. Needles have

226

been dropping to the floor for days." I unhooked a Snoopy on skis and freed a wicker pram twined in tinsel. "Besides, it's bad luck to leave it up over New Year's."

Mother stooped and lifted out the tiny plastic crèche from the cardboard dividers where I'd already packed it safely away. She turned it over in her hand. "Hannah . . ."

I unhooked a stuffed mouse. "Yes?"

She replaced the ornament efficiently, clasped her elbows, and looked around distractedly. "You've done a nice job with the house. I wasn't sure whether this move was the right thing for you and Hal."

"Daddy always said it was never the right time to change jobs or buy a house or" — I paused — "have a baby." *"Don't tell Mother about the latest rejection from the agency. I don't want to say anything until I have a baby in my arms,"* Ceel had said, adding, *"If that ever happens."*

"You do have those beautiful boxwood out front," Mother mused as if still deciding whether the house was worthy. "You and Hal don't have plans for New Year's Eve?"

I shook my head. "Is that okay?"

"No, I mean yes, I mean . . . I just assumed you'd want to celebrate in some way. Your Christmas presents to each other seemed . . . odd." She gestured to the window where my gift from Hal was already in use: a sleekly modern squirrel-proof bird feeder. "Not very romantic. Have I ever told you about your father's Christmas present to me the first year we were married?" She had, but I let her tell me again. "We were so poor. Christmas morning I unwrapped the gift and it was this big, green, ugly sewing box. I burst into tears holding it. After that we always made sure to give each other something even a tiny bit personal."

I thought of my back-rub coupon book for Hal on our own long-ago, poverty-stricken Christmas. This year my gift to him was a handheld computer dictionary, though it had been weeks since we'd challenged one another with definitions. Weeks since we'd even read together in bed. It was just a hectic time, we'd told ourselves, but our lovemaking seemed stratified now, easily, painfully assigned to category: Saturday night sex; bottle-of-wine sex; sex as sleeping pill. "But you still use that sewing kit, don't you," I said gently.

Mother straightened. "You know," she said, pointing on her way back to the bedroom, "that picture is hung too high on the wall."

I sighed.

Five minutes later she called to me again. "Hannah?"

I stopped in the doorway of Ellen's room, messy with Christmas loot and Mother's packing. She stood at the window, gazing outside. It was unusual to see her paused, stilled with inactivity. I disliked those rare afternoons as a child when I arrived after school to a quiet house and found my mother napping, stretched out on her bed like a corpse. An arm was thrown across her eyes, and its underside was a startling fish-belly white. Small snores leaked from her slightly gaping mouth, and I would watch, simultaneously fascinated, frightened, and repulsed. She seemed distant, her parental authority diminished by unconsciousness. Yet she was somehow naked as well, helpless and vulnerable in slumber.

"Mother?"

Roused from whatever reverie she'd been lost in, she started, and her head jerked in my direction. "Oh, I . . ." She walked to the bureau and began busily gathering toiletries. "Where did Mark go?"

"He's at work, why?"

"I wanted him to pick up a crate of fatwood kindling for me from that roadside store."

"You have gas logs." *"I knew you'd be pur-*

ists," Daintry had said.

"I was thinking of using them for Christmas presents next year, tied in bundles with plaid ribbon."

"*Next* year? Who's rushing Christmas now? 'Whatever happened to Advent?'"

Mother crossed her arms defensively. "Fatwood is better when it's aged. Besides, that's not rushing, that's preparation."

"Like Advent?" I laughingly suggested. "Daintry will be pleased you thought her idea was a good one. Imitation being the highest form of flattery."

"A better idea than that parish photograph directory," she said brusquely. "Are you going to help?"

"I don't know."

"You still let that girl boss you around."

I was stung. "What is it you have against her?"

"Geoff O'Connor broke Ceel's heart."

"I was asking about *Daintry* O'Connor."

Mother zipped the side compartment of her bag. "Did I tell you about Paul Sullivan?"

"Yes." No doubt the earlier reference to my father had reminded her. Paul Sullivan, a jut-jawed pillar of St. Francis — usher, lay reader, senior warden, Every Member Canvas head — had dropped dead a month earlier while swinging a nine iron, killed without symptom by his own heart at fifty-four. A death too similar to the "no warning" circumstances of Daddy's.

Sometimes Ceel and I talked of dying, macabre conversations in which we speculated whose genes we'd inherited. Whose thin hair or blue eyes, bowlegs or small shoulders — and whose death sentence. Would we be genetically blessed with our mother's good health and longevity? Or doomed to our father's fate, felled by a stroke at fifty-five? "Don't you dare die first and leave me to gum chicken salad alone," she'd warned me with utter seriousness. And with each conversation, the limit of age with which we agreed to be content — satisfied with having lived long enough — expanded.

"Sixty. If I can live to sixty it's okay," we blithely swore. And then, "Sixty-five, just to sixty-five." And later, greedily, *seventy,* we openly begged each other, and privately, God.

Surrounded by Ellen's juvenile possessions, Mother's face looked etched with age. Memories leave their markings. "Paul was such a good Episcopalian," she said.

"You and your 'good Episcopalians,' " I teased her. "You're such an Episcopal snob.

A murderer could be forgiven as long as he was Episcopalian."

"Murderers can be forgiven."

I plucked at a loose thread on Ellen's quilted bedspread, unsure whether to trust my voice. "What did you think of our minister?"

"He seemed nice enough. No point in getting attached to an interim rector, though."

The thread stretched, snapped in my fingers. Mother fetched her shower cap from the hook on the door. "What about that Doesy Howard? She seems nice."

"Oh, Mother."

"Oh, Mother, what?"

"There's no . . . *basis* there. We have no common ground."

"What kind of common ground do you need?"

What indeed. "Did you see the Thursday paper featuring Daintry front and center in the business section?" I said instead. I hadn't shown the article to anyone over breakfast that morning. It hurt to mention it now, but I was powerless not to, the way a tongue seeks a raw ulcer despite the pain. "Holiday filler," I joked feebly.

"I never read the business section," Mother said, dispatching the topic. Though not entirely. "Doesn't surprise me a bit. She could do anything she put her mind to." The tone was neutral, not complimentary. "Mark seems like an awfully unfocused child."

I bridled, though I had no intention of sharing my concerns about Mark's recent misbehavior. They were trifling infractions, likely, typical teenage stunts. My private New Year's resolution was to distract him from Wendy Howard. Wean him away, a baby from a bottle, though it was hardly an apt analogy. *"He's probably not even a virgin anymore,"* Daintry had said. "Mark's almost sixteen, Mother. He's supposed to be unfocused. Comes with the chromosome."

"Does he have a sport?"

"Having a sport" was a trait Mother had long espoused, as though an aptitude for golf or tennis or baseball could simply be decided upon and claimed for life. I thought of the single Cullen tennis court paved with highway asphalt, whose cracked and buckled surface sent balls careening crazily and defeated any hope of actual play. *"Best place for smoking on the sly,"* Daintry had informed me one humid summer evening as we listlessly lobbed balls over the swaybacked net.

"Remember that summer of back-to-back tennis camps you insisted I go to?" I reminded Mother. "It totally backfired. I hate tennis. I hate competing."

She fastened earrings to her lobes, wincing as spring snapped onto flesh. Her expression was thoughtful. "Did I ever tell you . . ."

"What?"

"You were about twelve. I was picking up Sunday school materials at St. Francis and you stayed in the car sulking about something. I mentioned — or complained — to Father Edwards how you refused to try out for the junior high basketball team, or cheerleading." She snapped her fingers, retreated to the bathroom again, and reemerged with a toothbrush. "Almost forgot this."

Though she moved with her usual brisk efficiency, I sensed a stall. "So what did he say?"

"He said, 'Jean, leave Hannah alone and let her read. That's what she likes to do. It's what she's good at.'"

A warm rush of appreciation and gratitude for Father Edwards, the dreamy, portly minister of my confirmation and wedding ceremonies, filled me.

"Well. Trying to get you interested in sports was a losing battle at that point. Daintry O'Connor had you under a spell."

I laughed. " 'Spell'?"

"She was like the Pied Piper. You were fixated on that girl."

The vehemence surprised me. "I thought we were fixated on each other."

"Are you serious? She never needed a soul!"

"Maybe Daintry didn't need me, Mother. Maybe she just *liked* me." I didn't like the turn in the conversation. "*She* didn't have a sport."

Mother slid one slipper toe into the other and tucked them in her bag. "She should have. She was certainly competitive enough."

I rose. "How about a turkey sandwich for the road?"

Mother knelt and looked under the bed. "I want you to do something for me."

"What is it?"

"Persuade Ceel to drop these adoption attempts."

The day before Mother's arrival, Ceel had come over bearing a bulky album. "I brought something for you to see," she said with uncustomary shyness. "Our portfolio. Minus the five-page autobiography that I'll spare you from reading, and spare me the embarrassment."

I flipped slowly through pages stiff with

glue and photographs, some of which I myself had taken of Ceel and Ben. Pictures of their house; of Ceel in the kitchen, holding baskets of flowers; of Ben at school, directing carpool with his megaphone; of the two of them hiking together along a wooded trail; bundled in scarves on a sled, their smiles white as the snowy scene that surrounded them. Wonderful pictures, captioned in Ceel's handwriting with exclamation points of enthusiasm. Wonderful pictures, and heartbreaking.

"Here's the killer," Ceel said, and pointed to the final snapshot. Sporting helmets, knee and elbow pads, she and Ben were Rollerblading through the Academy parking lot. "That's a grimace, not a smile."

"Since when have you taken up Rollerblading?"

"Since the agency powers-that-be suggested we include activities in the portfolio that appeal to teenagers. That's who the mothers are — teenagers, and they're the ones who pick the parents."

"As if a sixteen-year-old could make that decision. That teenager could be Mark!"

Ceel nodded. "Except that Mark probably would have nothing to do with it. If the daddies were involved, the teenage mothers wouldn't be giving up their babies in the first place, right? Or even be pregnant." She closed the book. "The agency gives each mother three or four portfolios — the next-in-lines, and they decide on that basis." Though she shrugged, her accompanying smile held a measure of admitted defeat, of yielding to the necessary. "I'll do anything they tell me to do. Anything. You do what you have to do."

"Is that related to 'People do what they want to do'?" I was quoting one of Mother's oft-repeated maxims. Yet it was never intended as a nugget of wisdom, but as a comment on behavior instead. People did what they *wanted* to do, not what they *ought*.

"I'm mailing it tomorrow," Ceel had said. "Keep your fingers crossed."

Somewhere in a cubicle or hospital bed, Ceel's painstakingly created album was being perused and debated. "Adoption is different these days," I said to Mother now, knowing she could cite a roster of adopted children who had grown into adults with addictions and instability problems. "The people in charge know much more about the children they find homes for. Look at the O'Connor children. They were adopted and look how they turned out. Every single one, extraordinary."

"Since Jack O'Connor handpicked them

I'd call it something other than adopting. Cream of the crop."

"Oh, Mother, what can you do, compare Apgar scores?"

"What's that?" she asked. I shook my head. A pointless conversation. "I'm just trying to do the best for my child."

"Mother. Jack O'Connor was trying to do the best for the children he found homes for, too."

"Do you see much of her?"

"Who?"

"Daintry," she responded impatiently.

"I've tried, but . . . I don't know. She's aloof. Maybe it's me, expecting too much."

"You've never had any trouble making friends."

"Mother, this isn't a fifth-grade problem. It's a genuine . . . impasse. There's an unresolved feeling to every conversation between us."

"Impasse? Don't be dramatic."

"We're . . . different people with different interests now, like you and, well, Daintry's mother."

"I never let Kathleen O'Connor make me feel inadequate in any way," Mother said curtly, correction and negation both. She looked up quickly, then away to the window again, the fir-studded slopes. "Hannah," she began, "there's something I ought to tell you." My stomach knit.

"Daintry . . . ," she began, faltered. "You and Daintry were . . ."

"Best friends."

Back to me, she straightened her shoulders. "Before sixth grade began I went to the principal and requested you and Daintry be put with different teachers. I wanted to separate you."

I laughed, relieved. "That's just the kind of demand that drives the administration wild at Asheville Academy. Intervening mothers."

"Mothers have to be advocates for their children."

I rolled my eyes at the trendy terminology. "Also known as favoritism."

Mother sat on a tufted stool and took my hand. "Daintry made you nervous the other night when she stopped by, didn't she? Don't be so thin-skinned around her."

"I thought she was making *you* nervous."

"Daintry and I . . . There's something between Daintry and me."

"Join the club."

Her head jerked up. "What?"

"Nothing."

"Oh, I . . . I thought she might have told you."

"Told me what?"

She stroked her neck, looked in the mirror, smoothed an eyebrow with her baby finger. "You'll do most anything for the welfare of a child."

"So you said." I waited.

"Just before you both went to Carolina," she said slowly, then gathered speed, "you were visiting that school friend in Shreveport. Your luggage got lost, I remember." Her throat moved faintly with swallowing. "Daintry and I had lunch together at Jack Horner's — remember Jack Horner's?" She rose and pushed the stool back under the dressing table. "They fixed the best hot dogs in Cullen."

"Why did you invite Daintry to have lunch?"

"I was writing old friends, asking them to send recs to their sorority on your behalf."

"Yes." I knew about alumnae recommendations, had heard plenty read aloud during cut sessions.

"I suggested to Daintry that she go through rush."

"She probably would have gone through rush anyway. Everybody did." For we'd done that together, too, exhausting evening parties of chatter and punch and do-you-know. Comparing houses and judging sisters afterward, even as those houses and sisters were comparing and judging us. Exclusion, I came to discover, depended on frighteningly trivial details. Find me a creature in nature crueler than a human female.

"Description?" the rush counselor asked, opening a cut session.

"She had on those big, red-rimmed glasses," someone volunteered without looking up from the needlepoint cummerbund she was stitching for a boyfriend.

"Positive comment?"

Silence. Slight, damning giggle.

"Negative comment?"

Audible sigh. "This is the third round and she didn't remember my name. Cut."

"No . . . No. She wouldn't have," Mother went on. "Daintry couldn't afford to join a sorority. Tuition, textbooks, living expenses, all that was more than Jack O'Connor could financially handle. Small-town pediatrician, sole practitioner, and most of that gratis. He'd already put two children through college, and still had two to go."

"But she pledged with me." For we'd made it, Daintry and I, granted admittance to those cloistered confines of belonging. After an intense and endless night of discussion, my fear of rejection was unfounded. We were both issued identical bids and joined the same sorority.

"Yes. I was the one who paid Daintry's dues and fees that first year and . . ."

"Why?"

"Because I'd asked her to, well, take you under her wing. Look after you. Go through rush with you."

My face went slack.

"You know how Daintry was," she continued. "Charismatic and popular. A natural leader."

I didn't hear what Daintry was. I already knew what Daintry was. What I heard was how my mother had guaranteed my social security. "Let me see if I get this straight." I watched my clenched fingers whiten at the knuckles. "You paid, she pledged, and I held on to her coattails. You cut a *deal* with Daintry O'Connor. Does that about sum it up?"

"That's a negative way of looking at it."

" *'Look after me'?*" Disbelief made my voice shrill. On a journey to nowhere I strode across the room and back.

"Just for that one year." My mother's voice asked for understanding, but I heard nothing but her addendum. "You were in thrall to that child."

"Who cares? I was happy."

Mother's face was stricken. "It was subservience! You were her slave! One of the reasons we sent you to boarding school was to get you out of Daintry O'Connor's clutches."

"And then you purchased her clutches again."

She set her jaw. "Would you rather I hadn't told you?"

I ceased pacing abruptly, fighting for control and for comprehension of my mother's calculations. "What were you thinking? Was Daddy part of it?"

"No. I used money of my own. I told you what I was thinking. You have to be an advocate for your child."

"You call that stunt *advocacy?*"

"I can appreciate how knowing this might be an awkward position for you, but —"

"*Awk*ward?"

"Stop repeating what I say. You *still* let her get to you."

"Don't. Do not talk to me."

"There are things you do for people that seem right at the time. For people you love. Something that presents itself as a perfect solution. And I'm not sorry. I'm not."

"I want you to go now."

"Hannah —"

"I need to get all this Christmas crap out of the house," I said, certain I would strike her if she dared utter a word about my language.

She stood. "It's water over the dam. Past history."

Not when the past was so vibrantly affecting the present. *Don't you know anything?* I could have said to my mother, just as Daintry had said to me.

Needles pricked my arms and dug under my nails as I pulled light strands from the tree. Daintry O'Connor agreed to be a protective watchdog in a bargain between daughter's mother and daughter's friend. My fingers shook with both anger and shame.

As roommates that freshman fall something was restored between us. Together we'd shopped for bedspreads and hot plates, navigated the perilous waters of drop-add, ate wormy ramen, endured a suitemate who played Bette Midler day and night. Had it all been only a purchased facade?

I coiled the cord tightly, yard upon yard of light bulbs dulled with daylight and streaked with silver tinsel, then moved around the room swiftly and methodically clearing decorations — wire reindeer, angel candlesticks, porcelain Santa basket empty of peppermints. From the mantel I un-

hooked stockings, homely St. Francis ba-
zaar offerings from decades earlier, all glued
rickrack and irregularly sewn appliqués.
The O'Connor stockings, products of their
mother's time and talent, were beautifully
needleworked with elves and Santas and angels sprouting downy wisps of angora yarn
as hair and beards, gilt thread trimming
wings and slippers, jet beads for eyes.

Without a glance at gay greetings grown
stale, I emptied a basket of cards. *"Look at
this,"* Mother had said one Christmas,
holding out the O'Connor card. *"She put
apostrophe s on their name."*

"Look at this," Daintry had said to me in
South Building. We'd gone to check our
class files, count required courses. She'd
pointed. *"My projected QP is 3.2. Yours is
2.3."*

From the fireside tin bucket I plucked
Christmas matches from splinters of
fatwood: Daintry's gift. Searing, unexpected grief buckled me to the hearth. Grief
for what once was: an uncomplicated
friendship.

After that single semester as initiated sorority sisters, Daintry simply exited. She
went inactive and moved into an apartment
alone. It was said she'd taken a job in the
alumni office. Now and then her name

would appear in the campus newspaper or on a poster tacked to the Student Union bulletin board, connected to some campus activity or movement, running for Student Council office, an organizer of some panel discussion. I'd glimpse her strolling Franklin Street on a balmy Saturday, hurrying across the Pit toward the Student Store, even on one frigid March night among hundreds of spectators massed outside Greenlaw Hall during the streaking craze. As she'd done at Cullen High, Daintry pursued what she wanted with remarkable single-mindedness, making a life for herself and moving beyond me, out of reach. Until that afternoon in the graduate library, when she'd found me and taunted me with lines from my own book of quotes.

"*No, Hannah,*" she'd said that day in the driver's license office. "*I was gone by then.*" Now I knew why.

But for storage boxes, the room was devoid of Christmas, returned to the regular. And I was glad. I would not be crushed, humiliated; refused to be. I was glad I hadn't known, even grateful. I took down the wreath, separating the velvet bow from the boxwood branches to preserve for next year.

But it was all futile activity. I pressed the heels of my hands against my eyes again, hard, until dizzying ribbons of color streaked the darkness behind the lids. I kneaded my face, pulled my hair back tightly as though pain equaled erasure. Of Daintry showing me the correct organ knob, Daintry telling me to use rubber bands to hold up my knee socks, Daintry *tsk*ing over my outie belly button, Daintry elbowing me at confirmation classes, Daintry persuading me to "suicide" a sorority on bid night. And Daintry in her present incarnation: regal, chiseled, capricious.

I added the bow to the pile of Christmas trappings and looked around. Christmas was finished, dismantled. Nothing remained to do but empty the trash.

Outside near the border of shrubbery, Doesy's paper-bag luminaries lay flattened by a careless driver. Wendy, no doubt. Several had blown into our yard. I picked one up, then another, and as I stooped something glinted, catching my eye. Beneath the feathery hemlock boughs, conveniently evergreen, was a stash of empty airplane liquor bottles. Vodka, rum, bourbon. Perfect miniatures of their bigger brothers.

Doesy came outside, dressed in spandex and sweatshirt. "I was just on my way to the fitness center. What are you doing under there?"

I showed her two luminary bags I'd filled with the bottles.

"Goodness! Litterbugs."

"Doesy, these aren't highway litterbugs. These are . . ." I chose my words carefully. "Could they be Wendy's?"

Hand on the car door, Doesy halted. "Well, let's just ask her, shall we?"

"But Wendy's not going to just admit that she —"

Doesy leaned into her car and blared the horn. Wendy appeared in the doorway, languid and slouched, a cropped sweater above low-riding jeans exposing her navel to the December chill.

"Mrs. Marsh has found some liquor bottles out here. Do you know where they came from?"

Wendy's eyebrows raised in innocence. "Beats me. They aren't mine." She shrugged and closed the door.

"See?" Doesy said.

"But —"

She climbed into her car without a backward glance. "My daughter has said they aren't hers, and I choose to believe my daughter." The window glided down. "Ask Mark. Don't you remember what you were doing at his age?" Gravel shot defiantly beneath the Jeep's tires as she accelerated from the driveway.

I stood, dumbfounded, debating my choices of what to do next. The day stretched empty and silent before me, yet crowded and noisy with revelation.

The columbarium. I hadn't been there since the children's vacation and the onslaught of holiday activities. Stillness, quiet, mine.

Unsure whether to take the bags by the recycling center — a darkly comic effort at good citizenship — or confront Mark with them, I was still holding them when I reached the columbarium. The teak bench I'd ordered had arrived, a slatted two-seater with a curving back, and I sat down on it, calmed and pleased with the way it looked even without any greenery to soften the legs.

"Kind of a lonely way to spend New Year's Eve, isn't it?"

The bare tree branches behind Peter radiated from his head like his own crown of thorns. Or stiff Medusa snakes. "Depends on your definition of loneliness."

He sat beside me and gestured to the paper bags. "It's too late and too cold for picnics. What are these?" I unwound the necks and showed him. "You've been drinking on the sly down here and didn't invite me. No, you've started celebrating New

Year's early and didn't invite me." His eyes were rueful. "Daintry says I have the highest need for inclusion of anyone she's ever known."

Inclusion, exclusion, Daintry. Familiar topics. "We used to spend New Year's Eve watching TV together. Eating popcorn. Burning saucepans to fix popcorn. One year we made confetti with a hole puncher. Do you have any idea how long it takes to make confetti one polka dot at a time?"

He smiled. "Would you like to come over and spend New Year's with us? I'd need to check," he went on, "and I know you'll want to ask Hal, but —"

"Peter." I put my hand on his arm. "I don't think that's a good idea."

In the dimming afternoon light his collar gleamed palely. "Tell me what's wrong."

"I found these hidden under bushes beside our driveway." There was no point in mentioning Doesy or Wendy. "I just wonder what . . . children are doing. Mark doesn't talk to me much these days."

"Wasn't there a time when you didn't talk to your mother?"

My mother. Halfway home by now, unburdened of confession. "Yes." I sighed and pulled at a tag wired to the arm of the bench. "Growing up is hard."

He laid his arm lightly along the back of the bench, behind me. I was conscious of its placement, knew that proprietary gesture. "You mean growing up *was* hard."

"No," I said softly, looking at him, at all he didn't know. "I mean *is*."

"But that's not it. Something's hurt you."

"No."

"Some*one's* hurt you. Haven't they."

No. Neither. *Both.* I didn't answer.

"Don't let it, Hannah. Don't let them. Let it go. Let. It. Go."

"Turn the other cheek? Are you *counseling* me?"

Then he did, literally, turn my cheek with the flat of his palm, fingers at my ear. "Don't be sarcastic." I wouldn't meet his eyes. "Look at me. Someone pushed the Catholic Church in my face for so long that I left it just to hurt her. That's why I jumped the fence. Just to hurt someone."

"Who, Daintry?" Peter said nothing. "Who was it?" Prying, testing, pushing him to prove something.

He drew a hand across his forehead. "My mother."

Gray glinted at his temples, silver I'd never noticed. It had hurt him to admit it, and I'd hurt him by asking. "So you atoned by becoming a priest?"

In the chill late afternoon gloom his breath escaped in puffs. "It doesn't work that way. Don't make me tell you that. I forgave her, and she forgave me."

I knew it; had said the identical words to Ceel about the reasons for her childlessness. *It doesn't work that way.* Payback and retribution aren't valid. Ashamed, I cupped hands to my face, warming the cold knob of nose. "I'm sorry. Sorry for pushing, for the sarcasm."

"Hey. I forgive you, too." He tugged my fingers down, folding them inside his own warm hands skin to skin. "And I've missed you," he said, then leaned and kissed me. And in the windless cocooning silence, I leaned and kissed him back.

From Hannah's quote book:
To be young. To be young. There is nothing else like it: there is nothing else in the world.
— William Faulkner, *Light in August*

Chapter 12

Daintry and I were standing against the wall in the St. Martin's parish hall, watching what passed for a Shrove Tuesday pancake supper. Leaning, rather, as though the noise and activity had shoved us there. Plates of pancakes swimming in syrup were pushed through the same kitchen window as dirty dishes. Long tables were littered with remains of dinners. Children clamored for attention as parents roamed the room, looking for vacant seats. People pawed through silverware and spilled sugar and coffee on another messy table. Teenagers were running the show, tossing Mardi Gras trinkets, juggling, vying for the microphone to perform a song or joke. "Keep it clean," I heard Peter shout over the popping balloons to a boy wearing oversize flapping clown feet.

"How do you spell headache?" Daintry said to me over the din. "P-a-n-c-a-k-e."

I laughed and raised my own voice. "Has it always been like this, or was it" — I was equally reluctant to cast aspersions or to say his name, afraid its very syllables would betray me — "your husband's idea?"

"Peter thought it might be a good way to involve the older kids in something worthwhile." Though I continued to watch the chaos, I felt Daintry's eyes on me. "He said you'd given him the idea, actually."

Had I? I couldn't fully remember the content of our conversation about Mark on the columbarium bench. What I remembered was our embrace, our kisses. I hadn't been back since. With January's cold and plantings gone dormant there was no work to do, no reason to visit. And I didn't trust any other reason.

Hal was standing in line for coffee. Wendy was tying the strings of a fresh white apron at Mark's rear. Ceel noticed and made an exaggerated pointing gesture with her hand, laughing. Ellen was on her second round. Doesy and Bill Howard sat in one of the few upholstered chairs in the room, picking at plates.

Doesy had barely acknowledged me when I'd said hello, and I'd chalked it up to our terse exchange earlier in the week. She'd been out of town for the weekend, and though Wendy was supposedly spending the night with a friend, lights and music were on at the Howards' house until late. Mark could tell me exactly how late, in fact, since he'd been forbidden to go over there and had watched from the window.

When Doesy pulled in the driveway, I was picking up cigarette butts. "Have a good trip to Atlanta?"

"Great fun with my old pals. So nice to get away this *dreary* time of year. Did I miss anything?"

I debated, then plunged on. "I think you missed a party at your house."

Doesy shook her head. "That Wendy." She lifted her shoulders with helplessness. "But what can we do? She has to have a key."

I'd gaped at the patent lameness of the excuse, but Doesy was on to other news. "Did Mark tell you about Laura Cathcart giving — oh, what was his name — Dennis, that's it, Dennis Hunter a blow job in the high school parking lot? That's what teenagers consider safe sex nowadays. I didn't even know what a blow job *was* in ninth grade, did you?"

I closed my eyes and rubbed my temples. I didn't know because Mark hadn't told me; didn't know Laura or Dennis; didn't know what a blow job was in ninth grade. I wondered how Doesy would respond if I'd said, *I didn't know anything about sex unless your minister's wife told me.*

Doesy, though, assigned her own interpretation to my expression. "Wendy still talks to me. She still tells me everything." Clearly Doesy pitied me.

Now I watched my neighbor slowly push a sausage link to the lip of her plate. "Doesy doesn't seem her usual, uh —" I began.

"Sunny self?" Daintry finished.

It felt good to gossip harmlessly, natural in a way that so many of our conversations weren't. "Wonder why."

"Lent," Daintry suggested wryly. "What are you giving up this year?"

"I'm giving up giving things up. It's hopeless. Last year I gave up chocolate and Hal begged me to go buy a Snickers after day three. Once in college, Hal gave up alcohol and I nearly died of boredom."

"Was that before or after I saw you in the library?"

I had a flashing, punishing vision of my mother striking her deal with Daintry, but she'd turned her head back to the chaos. "What does" — it was easier now — "Peter give up?"

She blinked slowly. "Instead of giving

something up, Peter takes something *on*. A cause, usually."

I hated that it hurt. He wasn't mine. I couldn't know. I handed a string of purple beads to a towheaded child crawling around my feet. "And you?"

"Sex. Ever heard that one?"

A thousand times. Another punishing picture. China crashed somewhere.

Daintry sighed. "I hate Lent. Re*lent*less."

"Oh, I do, too!" Lent was a kind of darkness, forty days of gloom. The pall stayed with you even after church services, with their absence of alleluias and dirgelike hymns.

"I hate it because it takes Peter away from me so much. So many extra services." Daintry's reasons felt like a rebuke. "Remember getting paid to pull weeds from between the terrace stones and then spending it all instead? Cheating on our mite boxes?"

I watched Peter, hand on Ben's shoulder, then realized Daintry was waiting for me to respond. "And cheating on giving up. Making all these exceptions to not drinking Cokes — it was okay on Sunday, it was okay if it was at someone else's house. There were a thousand ways to . . . cheat. Small sins."

Daintry was watching Doesy Howard gather her things to leave. "Southern women dye their hair too blond," she said, and idly scratched a gabardined calf with her other foot. "The reason Doesy's unsunny is that she's sulking. She got blackballed from the Historical Garden Club." She cut her eyes at me. "La-di-da in Rural Ridge. You probably know that." I knew nothing of the club, had never even heard the name. "Not to mention the fact," Daintry continued, "that Frances Mason is the member who wielded the ax."

Frances excluding Doesy? "But I thought they were such good friends."

"Not good enough, apparently. Maybe someone was faking. And there's always spite."

I watched Doesy, and what I saw didn't look like sulking. It looked like sadness. Maybe Daintry couldn't tell the difference. "Where did you hear that?"

"Church grapevine, a very thick weed. I'm sure you don't have anything like it in the columbarium."

I was saved from this oblique observation by a sixteen-year-old busboy who knocked over the basket of bills and change at the entrance. At the table nearest us, a toddler wept in his mother's lap while the father ineffectually mopped up spilled milk with a shredded paper napkin. Daintry shook her head at the ruckus. "I could never have kids. They're too . . ."

"Loud?" I suggested.

Daintry paused. "Needy. Face it, doesn't it all boil down to mud on the rugs and braces on the teeth and nightmares and piano lessons and wrecking the car and having to bail them out and shore them up?" I was taken aback by her quiet vehemence. She shook her head. "Never."

Peter extracted himself from the general fray to join us. "Should have had mimes," Daintry said as we were showered with a handful of hard candy. "At least they're silent."

"Daintry," Peter said patiently.

She elbowed me. "Look at Maude Burleigh." The church secretary was sitting across from two boys calmly roasting their fork tines in a candle flame. "So far out of her comfort zone she's in another galaxy. Old biddy. Reminds me of Mrs. Mormon."

Mrs. Mormon was our seventh-grade social studies teacher. "Young people," she addressed the class. "Young people, turn to page ninety-four." Despite her gracious facade, though, she'd kept a paddle labeled BOARD OF EDUCATION and didn't hesitate to use it.

"I don't know, though," Daintry mused.

259

"Maude's kind of sexy when she sweats."

I clamped a hand over my mouth to stifle my laughter. Not Peter. Peter clamped his own hand around his wife's upper arm. "Daintry," he said softly, asking her to rein herself in. I knew; I'd heard it on occasion from my own husband, who was mouthing, *Let's go,* across the room.

Daintry looked at Peter's fingers, then directly into his eyes. "Don't do that to me," she said, equally softly.

"Good night," I said, and left them.

"What's better?" Ellen asked. I was teaching her to play gin since Asheville Academy had held its own Mardi Gras celebration that day and she had no homework. Her small fingers were tensed with the effort of holding ten splayed cards. "Should I discard a king I already have two of, or take a second three since it won't count as much against me if I get ginned?"

"Discard it," I said, "and start saving the threes."

Hal unzipped his briefcase. "Keep the king," he advised. "You already have two of them."

Ellen kept the king. "Can I get my ears pierced?"

"When you're older. You're only in fourth grade."

"Wendy Howard got her ears pierced in third grade."

"If Wendy Howard jumped into the fire, would you?"

"Huh?"

My mother's hypothetical question had the same negligible effect on Ellen as it once had on me. Except that if Daintry O'Connor had jumped in the fire, I would have willingly, instantly followed her into the flames. *Go ahead. I dare you.*

"I want to be older. If I was older, I could be in fifth grade and not in the same grade as Jennifer Tomlinson."

I'd heard about Jennifer Tomlinson all year. I'd never met her, but I knew her well. One of those children — always girls — who instinctively have their fingers on the pulse of all things desirable: clothes, music, slang. The ringleader. What Jennifer Tomlinson said, went. "Ignore her. I knock with four."

"Knock! That's not fair." Ellen put down her cards and slumped in the chair. "She's mean to me."

"How, mean?" Though I knew. Knew what girls require of one another and do to one another. I was well versed in the unshakable intimacies and unspeakable cruelties, the hourly hurts and daily revenges, the lunchroom manipulations and recess whispers.

"She hates me because my father is a teacher and my uncle is the head. She leaves me out. She says my peanut-butter crackers are gross. She laughed at the skirt I wore for our skit."

Hal made no comment. Had we ever been mean, Daintry and I? Laughing at Margie Simmons with her chigger-bite legs and eat-up socks. Laughing at Timmy Blanton, who picked his nose. Laughing at Marsha Ellett in the spelling bee, who began "drastic," "T, r, a . . ." *Hurt me,* I thought, *but don't hurt my child.*

I gathered the cards. "Let me tell you something about girls. They're awful." Hal shot me a glance, but I ignored him, trying to explain in language Ellen could comprehend. "Awful to each other. Girls always want other girls to like them best, so they say mean things to make sure other girls don't like you better. Some girls just need to know they're the boss. They want other girls to follow after them. They'll cuss, or shave their legs first, or they have a phone in their room. And here's the worst part: You're just beginning. It'll be like this until your friends — and then only *some* of them — realize that it's not worth competing."

"Hannah," Hal said warningly.

"Just be yourself," I continued on obsti-

262

nately, the easiest advice to dispense, the hardest to follow. "If you're just normal and nice, people realize it eventually and come back to you." How could I convey to my daughter the awful dependencies of childhood, once essential, eventually despised?

But I might as well have been spouting Marxism. "We have to do an interview with someone for a language arts project," she said. "I want to interview Daintry. Can I call her now?"

"No. It's late. Run and get your pajamas on." When she'd left the room I said, "I don't like the sound of that Jennifer Tomlinson business."

Hal shrugged. "You know what teachers say: If you believe half of what you hear about school, we'll believe half of what we hear about home."

It was small comfort. "Why is it that childless people are magnets for children? Seems to me Ellen could find somebody more worthwhile to interview." Was Ellen in the throes of an innocent crush, or was Daintry deliberately wooing her? I wasn't resentful that Ellen was smitten; I was afraid for her.

Hal laughed. "I'm sure your friend Daintry would love to hear herself described as not worthwhile."

Ellen had her face to the wall when I went to give her a kiss. "Hey, pal," I said. "Don't pull a pout on me here. Give me a you fix."

Ellen grudgingly turned over but crossed her arms tightly on her chest, denying me. "Tell me a story."

"I thought you were too *old* for stories."

"I mean out of your mouth."

"Stories out of my mouth" were "When I was a little girl . . ." tales. "When I was a little girl," I began, "I used to build Barbie houses on Saturdays out of cardboard boxes from the grocery store. I glued leftover pieces of rugs and wallpaper in the boxes to make real rooms. And we stacked them up to make three-story houses, made little stairs out of the stiff cardboard that came in my father's shirts. Folding them the way you make fans, you know?"

Ellen nodded.

"And we knitted blankets for Barbie and Ken's bed. And Skipper. The blankets were thicker than the dolls, though, with threads hanging off that we were afraid to cut because they might unravel."

"Who's 'we'?"

We. Of course "we." "My friend and I."

"Daintry?"

I nodded. When had our connection begun to fray and unravel? Who pulled that

264

first thread? *You left me.*

"What else did you do?"

"One Saturday we made brownies."

"In Mommy J's kitchen?"

"No, hers." It was always hers. "And her big brother wanted to eat them before we'd even cut them out of the pan. So we were trying to keep him out — pushing our shoulders against the swinging door, and he kept banging and pushing and we were laughing so hard that she peed right down my leg."

"Gross!" Ellen laughed.

"Right into my sock." I pulled the sheet over her shoulder. "That's enough stories out of my mouth for tonight."

"What's pussy?"

My own smile faded, though I was glad for her courage to ask. "Why?"

"Jennifer Tomlinson told Grace Albright that I was a pussy."

Oh, I hated it. Hated Jennifer Tomlinson and Grace Albright and Ellen's innocence and the inevitable destruction of it. Hated what lay in wait for her. "It's not a nice word."

"But what does it mean?"

"It's a bad, ugly word for girls' private parts. For vagina."

"Who made it up?"

"I don't know," I said, and tickled her soft,

warm armpits. "Probably some bad, ugly boy." She giggled, and I thought of Daintry and myself at Ellen's age, snickering over an assigned report on Phineas T. Barnum, how wicked we thought we were to notice the similarity of the huckster's name to *penis*. So harmlessly wicked and wise, giggling at the word "pupa" in our science texts, so close to *pubic*. And not so harmlessly wicked to each other, competing privately and ruthlessly to achieve the next level in the SRA reading program, on from red to blue to aqua, scarcely knowing what we read as long as we beat the other, could report during recess that we'd gotten to the brown level. And gotten there *first*.

"I wish it would snow," Ellen said.

I leaned to kiss her, glad for the short shelf life of ten-year-old anxiety. "See you in the morning," I said as the phone rang downstairs.

"That was Daintry O'Connor," Hal said. "Mark's at the rectory and needs a ride home."

"That's strange. Wendy was going to bring him home after they finished cleaning up. I'll go."

I'd never been inside the rectory, though I'd thought about it often enough, picturing

Peter there. The two-story clapboard looked appealing in the February darkness, the rectangles of lit windows vaguely reminiscent of something. I walked up the steps and knocked on the door. It opened immediately, to Peter.

"Hannah," he said, and though his eyes were kind and concerned, a look I couldn't interpret crossed his face. "Come in."

I stepped over the threshold into their house, Daintry's home. Perhaps I expected an organ, beloved and disdained, in the foyer. But there was only a killim rug and a table with the usual droppings: keys, letters, gold clip earrings in the shape of knots. I was instantly, acutely uncomfortable. I didn't belong here, and he didn't belong to me. "Peter, I . . ." In the mirror over the table I saw Daintry approaching. "I came to pick up Mark. I'm sorry he barged in on you like this. He could have called us from the parish hall."

"Mark's fine," Daintry said.

Fine? "Is something wrong?" I asked Peter. "Where is he?"

Daintry answered with a soft, mirthless laugh. "Upstairs taking a shower." I heard the *sush*ing noise of falling water somewhere and thought of Daintry's clear shower, that remark made months ago. "He's been in there awhile."

Whatever she was suggesting, I ignored it. "He could have waited until he got home to take a shower. What did they do, have a food fight?"

"No, no," Peter said. "Mark left early, before we were finished. He said he was getting a ride home."

"Yes, with Wendy Howard."

"No, he . . ."

I'd never seen Peter so uncertain. "Where did he go?"

"The cemetery, I think."

"The cemetery? Peter —"

Daintry interrupted. "Mark *needed* a shower. He got sick all over himself because he's drunk."

"He *was* drunk," Peter corrected, as though trying to soften the blow to me.

"Vomiting sobered him up, I expect," Daintry said briskly. "Usually does."

Save me, I thought wildly to Peter as nausea glutted my throat. *Touch me.* But I couldn't so much as glance at him because Daintry's eyes held mine. "He knocked on the back door and Peter was still at the church, so I've been" — she chuckled again — "ministering to him." She fingered the diamond stud in her ear. "He's clean and he's sober. But he's going to feel like shit tomorrow morning."

I hated her.

"Daintry?" Mark's voice. She'd told him to call her Daintry, too, then.

"Mark? It's Mom."

The responding silence was thick, fraught, and though I couldn't see him, I could picture the workings of his brain. The concocted and fumbled defenses, the urge to flee, the dread and longing and the wishing it was days from now. He didn't answer me, directing his question to Daintry instead. But I heard the tremor. "Did you say you had some clothes I could wear?"

I moved toward the stairs, but Daintry's hand closed on my arm, reminding me of who she was and where I was. "Let Peter." He strode past me, my elbow bumping his chest as he mounted the stairs.

"He'll be a minute getting dressed," Daintry said. "Come sit down."

Sweating with shame and fury and discomfort, I followed her into the den. She motioned to the sofa, and I promptly sank deep into its down plushness while Daintry herself took a wing chair, firmer and higher ground. "Did you know Mark had been drinking?"

Oh, that tone. When Mark was two, we found him in the bathroom surrounded by a papery cloud of unrolled toilet tissue and clutching a crumpled tube of Neosporin. Afraid he might have eaten the antibiotic like toothpaste, I'd called poison control and asked what symptoms to watch for. They questioned me closely about every detail of the incident and for several days afterward had called back asking, asking, checking up on me. I was angered by their suspicions, by what seemed an indictment of my parenting. Daintry's question, its superior tone of the concerned social worker who clearly faulted the mother, sparked the same anger now. I wanted to defend Mark even as I wanted to kill him. *You know how teenagers are,* I might say. Or *Yes, we suspected.* Or *No, not my child. I had no idea.* Or *He's been under pressure.* And they all seemed lame, if true. Too similar to Doesy Howard's denials. "We wondered," I murmured. "Hal will be furious."

"Aren't you?"

There it was again, both censure and scolding. *Didn't you know Ellen was supposed to bring two liters of soda for the class party? Didn't you know Mark was running a fever when he came to school today? Didn't you know the birthday party was over at six?* "Of course I am. I can't believe he's done this. And involved you and Peter."

"I hardly call it *involved*," Daintry re-

270

sponded dryly, then changed tack, to non-chalance. "Little Mardi Gras gaiety, that's all. He's a good kid, bless his heart."

I knew the low-blow cut of "bless his heart," disparagement disguised as sympathy. My son wasn't hers to compliment or punish. "Thank God nothing worse happened. Thank God he wasn't in a car."

"God looks after children and drunks. It's a rite of passage. Haven't you ever been drunk in your life?" She laughed. "You know you have. *I* know you have. To this day I can't hear the word 'Woodstock' without thinking of you."

Before our senior high school year, at the end of that mind-numbing summer of belting and buttoning, Daintry got me a date. I was unenthused, but she was insistent. John Waring, whom she was dating casually, had a friend named Sam Troxler. "I've told him all about you," Daintry said on our break as we swung our legs from the loading dock outside the showroom. She knuckled my arm. "You need to get out more. It'll be fun. Don't you want to see *Woodstock*?"

A year after its initial release, *Woodstock* was finally playing in nearby, more cosmopolitan Shelby. I was curious not only about the movie, but about Daintry, what she could possibly be doing with John Waring since her name was linked with Mike Simpson's, in whispers, at least. I agreed to go.

That night she paid me back for my sixteenth birthday. I sat in the backseat of John's car with Sam, excluded from every nuance of the conversation, every private joke and piece of gossip and question about the upcoming year. I didn't know the teachers they discussed, or the couples, or the athletic stats. John and Sam snuck a fifth of rum past the sleepy-eyed ticket seller, and we gulped it down with Coke and popcorn. The film was long, and the return ride to Cullen was another thirty minutes. The rum lasted; I didn't.

By the time John parked near the fourteenth hole of the Cullen golf course, I was smashed, reeling onto the green just yards from a giant oak where Daintry and I once peddled lemonade from a rickety table to golfers on weekends. Where we picked at errant golf balls, certain we were the only people in the world who'd discovered the marvelous sphere of rubber bands beneath the dimpled skin. I was drunk because I was drinking, and I was drinking to escape from the unfamiliar; from what I'd grown beyond or left behind or wasn't grown-up yet enough to confront. All the things Daintry already was.

"She's shitfaced," Sam said, pulling me onto the green. I remember how good the soft itch of the cropped grass felt against my arms in my sleeveless shirt. Remember the good feel of Sam's fingers on my breasts when he unbuttoned that shirt and pulled up my bra around my neck like a scarf. Daintry and John had stayed in the parked car, and now and then I would hear Daintry's low laughter, and once, the horn honked, a comical blare in the night, followed by John's sharp swearing. I don't remember whether there were stars or a moon, but I remember how the earth spun when I closed my eyes.

"Shut your eyes," Sam grumbled more than once. I wanted to, wanted not to see his face, but it spun so, the world and the sky and the golf course and Sam's head at my neck. I remember how the vomit bubbled up from my mouth into his, thick with popcorn bits and burning with rum. Sam had jumped up and back, hollering. I remember his disgust. "She puked on me!"

"Get it in the hole! Par three!" John laughed from the car. Dizzy, stinking, drooling, disgraced, I waited, trying to button my shirt and wipe my mouth with it at the same time. Waited for Daintry to come.

But she didn't. It was Sam who pulled me

up like a rag doll and stumbled me toward the car.

"Watch the upholstery," John directed Sam as he shoved me into the backseat.

"Next time," Sam directed Daintry, "find me somebody who can hold their liquor. Somebody from Cullen."

I was still waiting, in the murk of my misery, for Daintry's rescue. *She* is *from Cullen,* I waited for her to say. *Lay off my friend,* I waited for her to say. Something. Anything. But she merely stared out the dashboard window, silent on the subject of me. She rubbed her face. "How about a closer shave next time, John? My chin's chapped."

Like milk or laundry, I was deposited curbside. My parents were safely away for the evening, visiting a couple who summered in Tryon. Ceel took me in, my bad-girl sister, washed me and consoled me and tucked me into bed. "How was the movie?" Mother asked the next morning.

"Fine," I said. I was fine, too, but for a queasy stomach and a hickey above my nipple no one would ever see.

"And . . . what was his name — Sam — how was he?"

"Fine."

"Did you want to get new tennis shoes before school?"

All I wanted was to be gone, away, confined at Wyndham where I was safe, protected.

"You've hardly seen anything of Daintry," Mother had remarked once during the two weeks remaining before school began. I had, but only from the hall window upstairs, where I watched Daintry bake herself in the backyard those final days of August in her attempt to look like a South Pacific native.

"I have summer reading," I'd told Mother, and held up *Cry, The Beloved Country.* "Daintry has play practice."

"Oh yes, I forgot. Who is she again?"

"Liat."

Now Daintry clasped her hands round her knee, an avuncular, advising posture. "Don't be too hard on Mark. Nobody was hard on you, were they?"

I sat forward on the squashed cushions. "I didn't want to go on that date. You made me."

"Why didn't you want to go?"

"I wasn't interested in Sam Troxler. I didn't even *know* Sam Troxler."

"Was there *anybody* in Cullen you were interested in?" It was challenge, pure and simple. There was something dangerous simmering between us.

"You. I went to be your cover."

Her hands dropped.

Peter came down the stairs followed by Mark, dressed in clothes obviously not his and clutching a grocery bag of his soiled clothing. In his expression and thin, gangly posture — loose and shambling as a marionette — I recognized conflicting emotions of guilt, gratitude, self-pity, fear, defiance. A plea to be loved, forgiven. I knew an equal play of emotions was visible in my own face and didn't want Daintry to catalog them.

"Mark," I said evenly, "let's go home." Whatever scene was to follow, whatever explanation there was to hear, belonged only between the two of us. "Thank you," I pointedly told Peter, and only Peter. *You left me,* I told Daintry silently. *Again.*

Mark was quiet on the drive home, his face turned to the window. Waiting, no doubt, for the boom to lower, the yelling to begin. "Mark," I said. He drew a finger down the shallow channel separating nose from lip where fuzz was sprouting. What breaks your heart most? When they ask for deodorant, for boxers, for a razor. They're gone then. You've lost them. "Tell me what happened."

"She told you what happened."

Not the right approach. "Why were you drinking?" Silence. "You wanted to be drunk." Silence. "Why did you, Mark?"

"They left."

"Left the cleanup?"

He nodded.

"Who?"

"The other people."

"Did you know them?" Another abbreviated nod. "Did they give you the liquor? Is that how you got it?"

"Mom." Specifics and logistics were too embarrassing to relate. I understood. You can do anything, get anything, if you put your mind to it. Seconds ticked by at Rural Ridge's single stoplight. The streets were empty.

"Wendy," he finally said, and began punching the door lock back and forth, back and forth, taking some comfort in the obedient responsive *clunk,* an action he could control. "She said I couldn't come with them. She left me. She told them what to do and they left me. They're my friends," he said. *Muh frenz,* I heard. *"It's muh stuff,"* he'd said that afternoon of packing months ago. Playfully then, wounded now. It wasn't Mardi Gras gaiety. It was exclusion.

"Did you do something that made them — her — act like that?"

"No," he said miserably. "I don't know." I waited for more, but he turned back to the window, his expression a blurred burgundy in the stoplight's glow.

"Mark. You haven't — you're not —"

"You can't understand it," he said finally, and the light turned green.

Oh, but I could. Did, had. For there was another part of the drunk equation.

The production of *South Pacific* marked the first time I'd been back to the Cullen High auditorium since Up with People. Daintry had been in school for two weeks, but Wyndham didn't begin until mid-September. As Liat, Daintry was deeply tanned, her long black hair set off stunningly by bronzed skin and a scarlet sarong. I don't recall who played Lieutenant Cable; by then I knew scarcely a soul at Cullen High, had lost touch. Notwithstanding the rumors about Daintry and Mike Simpson, her performance was lovely. I and everyone in the audience were rapt with her "Happy Talk" grace, the mute misunderstanding and pain she radiated as the bewildered native girl who couldn't comprehend why she was being left.

I'd waited then, too, in the wings. Waited with milling parents and siblings and well-wishers to congratulate the players after the performance. Backstage was noisy and hot and chaotic, the actors animated and excited with success. I glimpsed her black head and tanned shoulders, but she didn't acknowledge me. "See you at the cast party!" they called to one another, these strangers to me, and I left without having spoken to her.

I'd been leaving for two years by then. Coming home for brief respites from school at Thanksgiving and Christmas, hectic, family-filled times when either Daintry or I was often out of town. My March spring vacations didn't coincide with the Cullen schools, and I begged off church on Sundays with the excuse that I had twice daily chapel at Wyndham Hall.

But I knew as I walked up that auditorium aisle away from Daintry that this time I was gone for good. There was nothing left for me in Cullen. Summer was ending, I was returning to Virginia a senior, and the soft night, the parking lot filled with dark moving silhouettes and erratic beams of headlights, were in themselves a kind of elegy.

I sat on the hood of the car, the old station wagon I'd practiced a three-point turn in, using the O'Connor driveway as practice pavement just as Daintry had used our opposing one to practice hers. Sat until the last car had left the lot, scratchin' out, gettin' a wheel. Daintry and I could perfectly imitate the redneck accents of Cullen, twanging away with our ain'ts and cain't hardlys and ever'whichaways. *What you know good?* We never thought twice about it.

I got in the car and drove around. "Driving around," the time-honored small-town means of adolescent socializing, one I'd never taken part in because I'd been away. And tried to picture what Daintry's life had been without me. Hers had gone on as mine had gone on, parallel lines with few intersecting points.

I drove to the Little League field, dark and flat and fenced, the refreshment stand a sagging shack. I drove to the golf course, site of my recent debacle and my date's disgust. Drove to the town pool, bumping over the risen roots of the pines, and parked there. The Ping-Pong table was gone, naked sawhorses the only evidence of where it had once stood. Drove past St. Francis, where through the stained-glass windows whose dates I'd long ago memorized I could make out the dim red lamp burning in the sacristy as it did day and night. Drove past the elementary school with the oiled wood floors that my sixth-grade teacher had made Jimmy Lawson cover with "A preposition is always followed by an object." In between the desks and our legs, he'd struggled to chalk the words.

Drove past Ledbetter's, where we bought Kits and Black Cows and ice-cream sandwiches with our lemonade money, and fart cushions that burst within hours after their purchase. Drove down Main Street past First Methodist and the Rexall, whose fountain with warmed oatmeal pies had been closed and whose shelves were no longer enticingly laden with Yardley and Love's Baby Soft cosmetics. Drove past the library, where I'd checked out so many books that summer before Wyndham Hall, fearful that my unknown classmates would be smarter, ahead, more learned. Unfounded fears. Teenage girls are the same everywhere, though there is always someone smarter, someone who has more. It's how you interpret yourself against the knowers and the havers.

Drove past the showroom, where headless, limbless mannequins stood stiff in the bay windows, wearing the shirtwaist dresses Daintry or I had likely belted and buttoned. Taking it all in, all of Cullen, the geography of my childhood, what I'd been there.

I found her near the factory, where we'd spent so many Saturdays with my father. The sign had always stood there, at a junction on the outskirts of Cullen. It was ugly, a brick-and-timbered eight-foot wall beaming WELCOME TO CULLEN to passing motorists. The thick plastic letters were surrounded by plaques and metal signs of civic organizations, no different from any small town anywhere proud of its citizens and anxious for more members to live among their supposedly contented company.

When I pulled to a stop at the intersection I glanced toward the looming sign as though regarding it for the last time. In the wide conical beam of a spotlight poorly hidden among scrubby shrubs some well-meaning Jaycette member had planted at the base of the WELCOME sign, a figure was silhouetted, straddling the narrow slanted roof sheltering the sign. It was Daintry. Barefoot, red faced, disheveled. Alone.

She didn't notice as I threaded among the knee-high bushes, trampling a border of tired summer salvia. "Daintry," I said, shielding my eyes from the thousand-watt glare.

She lifted her head from the board and peered down. "Well now. Well now, look what the cat drug in."

"What are you doing?"

"Having a swell time," she said thickly, tonelessly. "Almost as swell a time as I had at the cast party. Good stuff, PJ. Purple Jesus. Mixed in a trash can this high," she said, and held her arm out as if to measure. Her body lurched forward. "Whoops," she cackled, grabbing on to the roof again. "Wouldn't want to lose my balance." Her legs dangled, then jerked, and she vomited down the front of the sign. As she gagged and spat I stood transfixed and horrified. "Think I'll just lose my cookies instead," she said, and leaned dangerously forward again, looking. "Did I get them all? Did I?"

"Get what?"

"Lions!" she shouted. "Ruritans! Woodmen of the World!" she brayed, and with each name kicked one of the soldered metal plates. "Civitans, Jaycees, a smorgasbord of belonging! Home, sweet home, here's where I belong, forever and ever, amen." She sighed, hiccuped. "Gross," she said, drawing fingers through her hair. "There're puke chunks in my hair."

"Daintry, come down. You're going to hurt yourself."

"Remember, Hannah?" she crooned. "Remember Woodmen of the World? I won them. Won them over. Yep. Woodmen of the World Citizenship Award. Top banana. Eighth grade." She lifted herself momentarily from the slanted board and dramati-

283

cally put her finger to her cheek. "Or was that the DAR? That was you, no, wasn't it? DAR?"

I thought of my paper, "The Battle of the Coral Sea." "No, Daintry. You won that, too."

"Yeah. Yeah."

"Come down. Please."

"What are you doing here, Hannah? This is a private party."

"I came to see you in the play. You were great. Perfect."

"Perfect. Happy talk." She began a sing-song chant I recognized, one that had nothing to do with Rodgers and Hammerstein. "Behind the 'frigerator, there is a piece of glass, and every time you step on it, it goes right up your ass me no more questions, tell me no more lies, the boys are in the bathroom, pulling down their —"

"How did you get here?"

She frowned, slitted her eyes. "Friends. I got lots and lots of friends. This is my god-damn deadbeat *home*," she said with slurred, sickening bitterness.

"I'm your friend, Daintry. Please come down. I'll help you get cleaned up."

She pulled herself to a sitting position. "Go away, Hannah. Go away." Her voice was strident and accusing. "You . . ." Then, as if she had suddenly been drained of fury, she slumped against the slender roof again, pressed her cheek to the weathered board, and began to cry, bashing her heels against the disk of the Civitan logo, a hollow, mournful clang. "You can't understand it," she said. "Go away."

I stepped forward, grabbed her foot, and stretched my other hand toward her hip. But she'd gone limp again, limbs dangling. Her head lay against the wooden framework, her face turned from me to the dark fields behind the sign. I got back in the car and sat watching her inert body for long moments, debating what to do. Finally I drove away. Just as I always had, I did what she told me to do. I left her.

"How was Daintry?" Mother asked the next morning.

"She was good," I lied. *We've left each other.* "Looked the part perfectly."

"Sunlamp," Mother had said. "Ruins your skin."

I killed the headlights in our driveway. "Mom," Mark said. Contriteness and fear quavered in his voice. "Dad —"

"I'll handle Dad," I said. "But let me tell you, son." I took his hand. "It's not worth it."

Only inches from mine, his eyes — Hal's eyes — were huge in the dark car. He didn't ask, *What? What's not worth it?*

None of it, I would have said. The exclusion or the meanness. Not even the hangover. None of it, I could have told him. But as Daintry was, and I had been, he was still too young to understand.

From Hannah's quote book:
But suppose, as some folks say, the sky should fall?

—Terence

Chapter 13

When Mark was nine, a neighborhood chum shoplifted a pocket flashlight while his mother stood in the checkout lane at Kmart. The mother never found out, but the confessional urge and that old push-pull of thrill and terror compelled Mark to tell me, adding, "I'll *never* do anything like that."

"I know," I replied. What I should have said was, *You'll never know what you'll never do until you've already done it.*

I'd always wondered how people did it. The mothers with the tennis teachers, the fathers with the aerobics instructors, workers with co-workers, students with professors, wives with husbands of friends. The next day phone call after a nighttime party. Over a lunch, at the office, during golf dates. The mechanics and logistics.

An assignation is astonishingly simple to arrange. There are a hundred ways to do it.

Hadn't I myself heard how from my father on dozens of occasions? You can do anything if you put your mind to it. Until the unknowns — the mitigating and propelling factors — are all that remain. Is there any single catapulting component? No. There's never one simple reason.

It's the trivial, the accidental, the correction veiled as comment. The dinner table conversation. "These don't taste like regular baked potatoes," Mark said.

"Did you use baking potatoes?" Hal asked me.

"I think they're russets."

"No wonder they don't taste right," he said. "You didn't use the right kind of potato." *That.* "Why is it the Girl Scout cookies always arrive during Lent?" he groused good-naturedly. Five weeks earlier, on Ash Wednesday, Hal had come home from work still bearing the dark bruise of ashes on his brow from the morning service at St. Martin's. As though he'd been not smudged, but bludgeoned with the fundamental agenda of Lent: repent. For five long weeks he'd eschewed desserts, substituting apples and cheese for sweets. Tonight, as the children and I ate thin mint cookies, a pathetic pile of raisins lay on Hal's straw placemat. The dark pellets seemed to accuse my inability to deny myself. *That.*

"You'll make it," I said. "Less than a week of Lent left. Lent comes from Middle English, *lencten,* meaning longer days."

"How do you know that?" Mark asked.

"I know everything." Not exactly; Peter had told me. *"Teach me something,"* I'd asked him. And he had.

As I was tucking Ellen in, Hal stuck his head in the door and said, "Did Mommy say your prayers?"

I looked him dead in the eye, remembered Peter's hand and Daintry's warning. There were still a few things Daintry and I had in common. "Don't do that to me," I said.

Hal's face was a blank, bland mask of innocence. "Do what?" *That.*

"No, I didn't say her prayers," I said, and brushed by him. "I knew you could do it better."

There are mornings you rise immediately content, with a sense of well-being that gilds the day. Then there are the mornings you wake ambushed by malaise, a funk with no reason. The day progresses, and the front doorknob falls off in your hand and the car's rearview mirror comes unglued. You open a window and notice how rotten and splintery the frames are. So many popcorn kernels have collected in the back of the sofa that if not for the layer of lint balls, they'd rattle. You know how it is. You eat cold leftover pizza for lunch and a milkshake midafternoon and some potato chips to counteract the sweetness and maybe a candy bar while you're running errands, and even though dinner is planned you have to go out for french fries or nachos because once you start throwing your day away it's a lost cause. *That.*

Ceel understood. Only her head was visible from the woolly afghan she was wrapped in on the sofa. "I have a case of mild despair."

"Like how?"

"Like it's afternoon and I haven't made up my bed yet. I can't explain it," she said with an audible sigh. But I knew. "Tell me something good," she said.

"Here's what I learned this week: If your teenager calls past nine o'clock and asks to spend the night out, always say no. It means they're drinking and don't want to come home because you'll know."

"Oh yeah," Ceel said. "I can really use that advice."

The sarcasm was unlike her. Ceel knew about the wretched night at the rectory,

Mark's vomiting on Daintry's doorstep. "I can't shake the feeling that Daintry was enjoying my humiliation. Whenever I'm around her I keep waiting for the other shoe to drop."

"Maybe it's already dropped."

I looked at her, wrapped to her chin, circles beneath her eyes, and tried again. "Worrying about Mark takes up most of my time."

"Is that what's taking your time?" Unsure where my sister's questions were leading, I said nothing. But she only pulled her face from the swaddle of striped wool and cocked her head inquiringly. "How's the columbarium?"

"The bulbs are beginning to come up. Doesy brought me all of her dead forced flowers to replant."

"It won't work."

"I know."

"They've shot their wad. Like me." She reached for a mug of tea, and though I waited for an explanation she said, "I stopped by to get the altar vases last week. Maude Burleigh mentioned that you were in Peter Whicker's office. I didn't interrupt you. The door was closed."

I made my voice steady. "What were you doing with the vases?"

"I do flowers for the altar when no one else volunteers. In Daddy's memory." She paused. "What were you doing with Peter?"

"I don't remember. Discussing plans for the project. Nothing."

"Doing nothing or just haven't done it yet?"

Both. Neither. "What's going on here, Ceel? What's happened?"

She barked a bitter laugh. "Nothing. Absolutely nothing. I thought you'd never notice. SOS. Same old shit. Been there, done that. Quick, give me another cliché." She snapped her fingers, tossed her head. "I'll tell you what's happened. They turned us down. *She* turned us down. We were next in line and she didn't want us."

"Who didn't want you?"

"The mother. She was eighteen. Ancient."

"Why?"

"A very simple reasonless reason. Because she herself was an only child, so she wanted her baby to go to a couple who already had a child. Wait, I have another good one: The rich get richer."

"Oh, Ceel. Ceel, I'm sorry. I know how disappointed you must be."

"Know?" She glared. *"Disappointed?"*

"But there are other mothers. What about

292

another try with the infertility specialists? Surely there's something, some treatment you haven't —"

"Stop right there." She cut me off. "Do you have any *idea* what I've been through? The time, the pain, the years of fucking on schedule?" She tossed her head with disgust. "Do you even know the names of the drugs or the procedures? Spell hysterosalpingerigram, go ahead. Or laparoscopy. Seven hours of Fallopian tube surgery. For something that might, only *might* succeed?" Her voice was gravelly with both rage and anguish. "How would you like to hear some, some *stranger* suggest in presurgery counseling that possibly you've never *reconciled* your infertility?"

Instantly I was beside her, kneeling on the rug. "You're right. I can never know. Forgive me."

"No. But you know enough to tell Peter Whicker all about it, right? Because *that's* what you were doing behind closed doors, right? Isn't it? Weren't you? Telling him *my* problems? What's the trendy word — *sharing* confidences with him?"

"I . . ." Relief and guilt fused. Her accusations were true, untrue. "I have, yes. But not like you think, Ceel. I didn't go to him with that, not purposely, it just . . . came out when we were talking. About Daintry, and her, their, choice not to . . ."

"Tell me more," Ceel said evenly. "Did the two of you arrange a circle prayer for me? Announce it in the Sunday bulletin?"

"Listen, Peter could be a real ally for you and Ben."

"Oh, I see. A go-between with God?"

"Stop, Ceel. You can shriek as loudly as you want, and I'm not going to sit here and talk about some payback God. It's because he's going on the board of the state adoption agency."

"God?"

"Shut up. Peter."

"How do you know?"

"He told me. It isn't public yet because his term doesn't begin until next fall."

Her eyes narrowed. "Why would he tell you?"

"Because . . ." I floundered. "Because we're friends. Peter knows about Jack O'Connor's history, finding homes for babies all those years, thinks it was a good, decent thing to do, a kind of Christian mission no matter what the rest of Cullen thought, and . . . if Peter can influence an adoption decision on your behalf, wouldn't you want him to? He'd do that for you, for me. He knows how close Daintry and I . . . were, and

—" I meant to say it comically, but humor failed me: "I ought to get something out of all those years of . . ." I heard my mother: *You were in thrall to that child.*

"Did you tell him about Geoff?"

"No, I didn't. I swear."

Ceel turned her head. In the clear slashing winter light her profile was sharp. "You still think about him, don't you," I said. "What he did to you?"

She wiped her eyes. "Geoff O'Connor hasn't mattered to me in a long, long time. I know it's no one's fault. It's just convenient to blame someone, myself, God."

I sat on the sofa, pulled the rumpled afghan over her bare cold feet. "You won't give up, will you? Not now. You're too close."

She pulled her feet away from my clasp and drew her knees to her chin. "I'm reconciled, Hannah. You be reconciled, too. She's gone."

"Who?"

"Everyone has a Daintry in their life. Let her go."

"Asheville Academy is wrestling with whether there should be a full-time chaplain or a full-time librarian," Hal said. "There isn't enough money for both."

I looked over my book at the gridded Scrabble board, an unfinished crossword. "I vote for the librarian," I said, and for the third time flipped the tiny hourglass timer Mark had given us for Christmas.

Hal was unfazed. He lingered over his letters for so long that I read a book between moves.

"Faith has to be caught, not taught," he said.

That. I fingered the seven lettered tiles in my tray. "Isn't seven the number mentioned most often in the Bible? Seven plagues, seven tribes, seven something? Someone taught me that."

He fit his word in a corner already cluttered with words: *jig,* and said, "You know what I'm talking about."

We approached the game so differently. I hoarded valuable consonants, the M and B and J, until I could create words with substance: JUMBLE, MERGER, MAYBE; words with *integrity,* I'd once explained to Hal. He'd laughed. He concentrated on the triple- and double-word scores to form intricate combinations of three-letter words yielding forty points: *axe, jet, zoo.*

Sender I put down, points paltry but opening a quadrant, and said, "That's a gift." Prepared for a wait, I returned to my book, one of the volumes I'd brought to Rural Ridge and vowed to read. It was a collection of John Updike stories, tales of overt suburban infidelities amid subtle struggles with morality. "I get the impression everybody but us is jumping into bed with their neighbors."

"They're just bored baddies looking for mischief."

"The women or the men?"

Hal opened the dictionary. "You read too much."

"Wait a minute. You can't look up a word before you put it down."

"What's the big deal?"

"It's against the rules. It's cheating."

"Are you getting your period? Do you have PMS?" *That.*

Zero Hal put down, sealing off the section I'd opened to benefit us both. *"There isn't a spontaneous bone in your body,"* my husband had said. *"Quit following the rules,"* Daintry had said.

The reasons and the justifications tumble and accumulate and gain mass like a fist-size snowball rolled along the ground until it grows too large to move and stops dead. Or hits an immovable wall of sheer desire. Then you get the bound-tos, forgetting how you told him that the bound-tos are closely connected to the re-and-res, regrets and remorses.

I hadn't lied to Ceel, not entirely. Someone had inquired about making a gift to the columbarium, and he wanted to talk to me about it. It had been a business meeting. Or begun that way.

I'd been to his office before, when we'd moved the four urns from the columbarium for safekeeping while I was installing shrubs and plants. I remembered the mission fondly, a lunchtime caper charged with hilarity and delicacy and secrecy as we hid the urns inside a crawl space corner in Peter's office where the paten and chalice had once been kept. Maude and the other staff member had gone out for Chinese. The urns had been returned to the columbarium by now; by now Peter and I had a different secret.

I opened the door. Walls on either side were filled floor to ceiling with shelves of books and the odd, haphazard object, a pottery piece, a sketch of some nameless church. Opposite the door was a window above a cabinet ledge, looking over the church courtyard. The office was a small square, and with his back to me, gazing out the window, Peter seemed too large for the space. Hemmed in by the bookshelves, crowded by the single armchair pushed beneath a standing lamp on which he'd thrown his coat. His energy was checked by the desk between us, but visible in those taut fabric wrinkles across his back. As though the shirt were too small. As though he were straining against it.

"Peter."

He swiveled. The shoulders slackened. "Come here. Around here with me."

"Peter —"

"Please. I want to show you something."

I eased by the narrow space beside the desk, by wastebasket and rolling chair, and stood beside him. He pointed out the window. The day was gray and bone chilling, February to the core. "Acuba, euonymous, sasanqua, berfordia," he said, tapping a pencil on the sill, "and . . . and the tall skinny green bushes that grow fast and hide things."

"Leyland cypress."

"Leyland cypress. You taught me all that."

Taptaptaptaptap.

"Give me that." I managed a laugh and tugged the pencil from his fingers. "What is it?"

"I'm sorry."

"That I took your pencil away? That I taught you?"

"For Daintry, with Mark," he said. His voice was low. "Sometimes I think Daintry has, has worked so hard for what she has and where she is in a male-dominated career that she forgets how to be with women. And I know she doesn't understand what it's like to be a mother. I'm sorry."

I looked down at the vents that topped the cabinet. *Dear God, don't talk about Daintry.* "Forget it, it was weeks ago."

"But I haven't seen you alone in those weeks, to tell you so. Is he all right?"

"Yes."

"Are you?"

Though warm air flowed through, the metal strips were cold. I looked at my hand spread across the horizontal metal slats, amazed that it was still, not quivering. Not from cold, but from a coiled, high-strung tension his tender, genuine question didn't appease. Nervous tension, sexual tension. So distracted by it that I thought I might cry if I didn't touch him. Or bolt. "It's so raw and gloomy," I said desperately. "Will winter never end?"

"I thought you loved winter. I thought you wanted it to snow."

What I wanted, at that moment, was to

have someone taller and larger and stronger tower over me and cup me into his body. To warm me, want me. He was all those things. "I don't know what I want."

He covered my hand with his. I pulled it away, utterly conscious of the metallic *tink* of my wedding band against the slats. I stepped around to the other side of the desk, pulled the chair to it. "Tell me about the gift."

His eyes were pained, but he sat, kneading his forehead, knuckling back the hair. "Someone wants to make a gift, as I said, and I wanted to check with you to make sure you hadn't planned on anything else, some piece of statuary, or a sundial, or . . ."

I shook my head.

"Just the bench."

"Just the bench." Just the bench where we'd kissed, held each other on a similarly bleak afternoon.

"I'll tell them to go ahead, then." Peter ran a finger between collar and flesh, the unconscious gesture I'd so often seen. Suddenly, reaching behind his neck, he unfastened the white band of collar and placed it on the desk blotter. "Maude ordered a size too small. She thinks slow strangulation will get rid of me. Then she can go back to doing things the old way."

The collar lay beside a small metal cross with lettering along the vertical length. "Sportsman's Paradise," it read, and I knew the story behind it, that a prisoner in Louisiana had made it from a dented license plate.

I reached for the circlet, white against green. It was stiff, a cardboard rim sheathed in fine-textured fabric, linen, perhaps. "I've never touched one." I fingered the snaps at the back. "Just ordinary snaps."

"Yes, ordinary. Just like I once told you."

I looked across the desk at him. "Was there anything else you wanted?"

"Is that what you're going to say, Hannah, talk to me like some employer?"

"What did you want me to say?"

I moved to put the collar back, and he reached across the desk and covered my hand with his. "I want you to say you'll see me."

Noises amplified in the sudden profound silence: the tick of sleety rain against the panes, steps in the hall, the chug of the basement furnace, the race of my heart. "I shouldn't have come."

Peter's grip tightened, and the collar curled inside my palm. "Say you will. Please."

Say you will come to my first sermon. Say

you will take the job. Say you will see me, meet me. In the face of being wanted, doubts dissolve. Being wanted is powerful, irresistible motivation. Being wanted is an aphrodisiac that generates its own heat, often having nothing to do with love. And though I learned this fact late in life, I should have known already. His wife had been a good teacher. "Yes," I said for the third time. "When?"

Then the opportunity presents itself: the abracadabra of adultery.

I looked at my watch. Ellen was going home from school to spend Friday night with the admired and mercurial Jennifer Tomlinson. Mark had an away wrestling meet and wouldn't be home until after ten. Ben and Hal had left directly from school for a two-day Independent Schools Conference in Winston-Salem, picking up Ceel on the way. The phone rang. I glanced at my watch again.

"What are you doing?" Ceel said.

"Checking the time." The truth, if the last of it.

"I called to apologize again for that . . . attack of hysteria. Every now and then I need to blow someone out. You just happened to be conveniently on hand. Usually Ben's the unlucky target."

"Better me than Ben. Besides, I asked for it. What are you doing at home? I thought you were leaving."

"Supposedly. I'm waiting to be picked up, but I don't know, I'm feeling fluey. Maybe I'll stay. You can come over, we'll make hot chocolate from scratch." *No,* I said to myself, mentally willing her to go. I couldn't say no to Ceel's invitation, but I'd already said yes to his. "Looks like you're finally going to get your wish."

"What wish?" I answered too swiftly.

"Don't tell me you haven't heard the forecast."

"Oh, that. I don't believe it. It's too close to Easter." Not today. Not now. I looked at my watch again. It's a well-known fact that priests have scattered, unpredictable schedules. Even through the phone I could hear the horn honk.

"Oh well," Ceel said. "There they are. Might as well go."

And after dates and times are fixed, what do people think about as they wind toward liaisons? As they bank back-road curves, pass steep-roofed homes and rusting farm implements and whitewashed tires outlining dirt driveways. Dogs tied to trees, metal gliders on porches, fallow vegetable gardens with defunct pie-plate scarecrows. Are there as many humble whitewashed churches that leap out from grass parking lots on journeys to illicit couplings, or was it only here, on my road, that Matthews Memorial Baptist and Pathways Chapel lay in the same measured mile?

One time, they think, recalling a dorm room avowal among Sissys and Charlottes and Megs. *Just one time he screws somebody else and that's it, it's over.* When we were so certain of our faithfulness and our futures.

And on past ramshackle roadside buildings with hand-lettered signs: GARDEN OF PRAYER APOSTOLIC CHURCH; CHURCH OF THE HOLY SPIRIT. *It would depend,* they might remember amending the avowal, *whether it was just a one-night stand or a long-term affair. It would depend.*

Longevity counts for something, they might remember deciding even later, an avowal's reversal, when children and homes and years were part of the package. *You don't throw everything away because of one mistake.*

THE DEVIL IS NOT AFRAID OF A DUSTY BIBLE, they might read on a roll-away rent sign parked outside some cinder-block structure. *"What are you doing with Peter*

Whicker?" Ceel asked. *"Haven't you ever heard your parents doing it?"* Daintry once bluntly asked me. Not having sex. Not making love. Doing it.

They must look the same everywhere: the stippled walls and pebbled carpet and cellophaned cups, a sense of squalor despite sanitized strips. The blatant bed in the rented room, and there too the bedside Bible. The heater's gushed blow did little to permeate the thick chill. I waited for Peter and thought of Peter, longed for Peter, for his car to appear in the pitted parking lot, imagined his arms finally around me, someone to hold me closely, closely, use his body to loosen the tightness in my mind. A tightness that was both absolute desire and absolute fear.

I turned on the television, whose single snowy channel reported nothing but the weather predictions. I flicked it off and pulled aside the heavy curtain to study the weighted skies. I knew about watching for snow. It required dedicated staring at a dark, nearby backdrop — magnolias, pines, a rooftop. As a child I was superstitiously convinced that if I looked away even once, dropped my guard or lessened the wanting for an instant, the snow wouldn't fall from sheer spite.

As the daylight drains you check for cars, you check for snow, you check your watch. You fret, begin to doubt yourself and him. You wait. For a knock, for a noise, for your lover. For the snow, for the phone, for your heart to stop hammering. *"Just remember A for aorta, V for ventricle, A comes before V in the alphabet, so you can remember the blood from the aorta goes into the V for ventricle and —"*

"Right or left? I'll never remember."

"All you have to do is remember it once, Hannah. You'll never need to know how the heart works again. Ever." She'd been so sure. And still I'd failed the test.

I looked in the mirror. And do any of these lovers who were wanted, who agreed and arranged, do any of them ever realize, ever admit, as they wait with quiet terror and thumping desire — that sometimes it's not attraction, or proximity, or timing? Sometimes it's as simple as the fact that the one they wait for belongs to somebody else. Do they look in the mirror and see this stark, dark truth: retaliation? Was I sleeping with Peter Whicker to punish Daintry O'Connor?

I picked up the phone and dialed not Peter, not the church, but home. I punched in the message code. Surely he'd never be so foolish, but —

"Mom, answer," the thin voice sobbed, clotted with crying. "Mom, pick up, where are you?" *Click.* A whirred silence and another message: "Mom. Dad's already gone. So are Ben and Ceel. Mom? I'm not spending the night with Jennifer anymore. Mommy, I'm at school and I want to come home. She cheated off my paper and got in trouble and we're not — Mommy, please . . ." The trailing despair. "Mommy, she took my underpants from my cubby during gym and showed everybody. They laughed." A choked and pleading finale: "Where *are* you, Mommy? Please."

That swiftly, that simply, it's over. Love and duty and a new fear intervene, collide and conspire to save you from yourself. Or maybe it was God. Perhaps love and duty and fear are all one and the same with Him. I left the key in the motel door.

"I've come for Ellen Marsh. She's waiting for me."

"Yes, there was some mix-up about whom she was supposed to leave with. A change of plans, apparently. But even for faculty children we have to have a note, Mrs. Marsh —"

"I understand."

"Before we —"

"Where's Ellen?"

"She tried to call."

"I know. I've just gotten the message."

"That was some time ago, she was quite upset. I —"

"Which building is she in? The library? Where does the after-school care meet?"

"Everyone's gone now, they —"

"Where is she? Did she go home with another friend?"

"She tried to call Mrs. Carlson, but no one answered there, either. And with your husband away with Mr. Carlson, we didn't have another emergency number."

"Where is my daughter?"

"She said she knew someone who could look after her until you came home. A woman, a friend of yours, she said, Irish name. O'Brien?"

"Daintry?"

"Yes, I believe that's what Ellen called her. The phone number is right here —"

"She went home with Daintry?" Another child, another night. The same savior and captor.

"We couldn't find you, Mrs. Marsh. Ms. O'Connor was home and picked Ellen up." The woman straightened pink phone slips and called after me, "Ellen seemed very glad to see her."

The door's brass knob was frigid. This time I didn't wait for it to open. "Ellen?" The foyer was empty. "Ellen!"

"Mom!" Not a plea for help, but a squeal of pleasure as she bounded barefoot down the stairs, her hair in a dozen cornrow plaits. My knees buckled with relief, and I stooped to meet her, hold her, enfold her.

"Don't touch me, don't touch me!"

"Why, are you okay?"

" 'Course! Look, but don't touch. It's not dry yet." She displayed her fingernails, ten small ovals lacquered with pink stripes and red polka dots. "You can't do this to yourself. Daintry painted them for me."

Descending the carpeted risers, she looked scrubbed and girlish, hair pulled cleanly back from her face with a hairband. A black-headed Alice in Wonderland dressed for lounging in a pale gray cashmere robe. The color of my sweet, dumb, clumsy doves. The cat, still graceful despite the bulk of pregnancy, followed. Ellen left me and climbed the stairs again toward both of them, sitting at Daintry's bare feet to stroke the animal's fur with a carefully flattened palm. I thought of my smilax cardinals. Whenever I'd heard the baby birds' frantic cheeps, I'd whispered, *Don't cry, don't cry. A cat will hear you, find you, eat you.*

"Ellen, what happened?" Though clearly whatever had happened no longer worried her. Daintry had brought her around and made it right and taken my place.

A tight frown pulled Ellen's face. "She cheated."

"Jennifer?"

"She looked at my paper during the *James and the Giant Peach* test. That's cheating. So I told Mrs. Davidson. You're supposed to tell, aren't you? Daintry says so."

"And . . ."

"And Mrs. Davidson called Jennifer's name and told her to stop. She didn't even get punished. And that's okay, I didn't care, but Mom, Mom, she got so mad at me and told everybody not to sit with me at lunch and not to play with me at recess and . . ." She stood, her features crumpled and her voice cracking. "And she went to my cubby and took my —"

"Ssh, Ellen." I stooped again to kiss her, kissed the brimming eyes. "I know, I know."

"Seems Jennifer changed her mind about Ellen coming to spend the night," Daintry interjected.

Ellen nodded, recovering. "And I didn't have any friends all day long." She blew on her nails, satisfied with her version. "But I'd missed the carpool. And then you weren't home for a long time."

Daintry sat on a step, pulled the fabric over her knees. Waiting.

"Where were you? It was getting dark. I was afraid."

"I was in the car. Running errands in case it snows. Then I had to wait, and —"

Daintry casually rested her chin in her palm. "You really should get a car phone, Hannah." Telling me as she always had. "Take your mother's coat," she said to Ellen, rising. "Take her near our fire." *Our*, as though Ellen lived there, belonged there, intimately familiar with her rooms and closets and rituals. I took off my coat with shaking hands that Daintry noticed. "Is it that cold out there?" she asked. "Has it started snowing?"

"Yeah," Ellen said, "snow would make this whole night perfect." She led me into the library, close with an embered fire. "Look, Mom, just the kind of fire you like. No big high flames. We haven't had a fire in *ages*."

There'd been no proper hearth at the O'Connors' house. The chimney had been sealed by old Mrs. Payne. *"You're so lucky,"* Daintry had said as we lazed before the flames, *"I wish we could have a fire."* Backsides to the burning logs, we staged endurance tests, heated denim scorching our

312

thighs with a cold-hot combination of plea-sure and pain, bearing it until the last mo-ment until . . . *"I won,"* Daintry had said. *"I lasted the longest."*

Ellen held out a bowl of popcorn. "Daintry has Jiffy Pop, it's so cool! A big shiny balloon on the stove. Better than ours. Better than microwave." She lowered her voice, looked around. "And she let me have a Coke since it's not a school night."

Daintry poured wine from a bottle on a chest. "Wine? Red wine just seems to go with fires and snow."

"We stopped at the video place to get a movie, too," Ellen said.

"She was very upset at" — Daintry seemed to choose her words carefully — "not being able to get in touch with you."

"Look," Ellen said, holding up the video box. "It's *Ghost*. But we haven't watched it yet because we've had such a good time. Daintry's going to be my im-migrant."

The glass was halfway to my lips. "What?"

"Didn't you know Ellen had a project on immigrants?"

"Yeah, Mom. I told you that."

Daintry smiled indulgently at my daughter. "Seems I'm the closest thing to an actual immigrant Ellen can find. All those old stories of living abroad you used to love."

"And she's going to take my wrapping paper form to her office and everyone who works there will buy some."

I finally found my voice. "Yes," I said. "She always took our Girl Scout cookies to her father's office for his patients to buy."

Daintry's eyes sparkled. "But your mother wouldn't let you send yours to the factory with your father."

In the fireplace a log shifted and collapsed into fiery chunks. "My mother didn't want the employees to feel pressured to buy. She thought it was an unfair advantage."

Daintry laughed. "That's all in the interpretation."

"Can we play Clue now?" Ellen asked. She lifted a battered box and looked at me apologetically. "We were just getting ready to play before you came."

"A closet upstairs is full of old board games," Daintry explained. "Some priest with children, no doubt. I don't know, though, Ellen. Your mother was always terrible at Clue."

"She never wins any games with Daddy, either. What about cards? We could all play cards. I've learned how to knock."

"Only two can play gin, El," Daintry said, winking.

I rose and picked up my coat. "Let's go home, Ellen."

"Daintry invited me to spend the night. She's going to do my hair again. I told her about when you rolled up my hair in those awful Velcro curlers and had to cut them out!"

"Because you —" I stopped. Why was I justifying some past accident to a ten-year-old? Because of Daintry. "No sleep-overs tonight."

"I want to."

"No."

"Why not?"

"Yes, stay." Daintry tilted her glass, staring at me through its ruby glow. "Peter should be here any minute." I hadn't let myself wonder and now forced my fingers to keep buttoning. "He —" she laughed. "I'm not sure where he is, to tell you the truth. The minister's wife is always the last to know. He said something about preparing a couple for a reaffirmation service. I'd never heard of such. But you know Peter, always on to the new thing. The next thing."

Ellen sat stubbornly on the floor, surrounded by video and popcorn and nail polish and Clue. "No," I said.

"Yes," she countered. "Yes yes yes yes yes."

God help me. "Don't you want to be at home when it snows?"

"If," Daintry said. "Probably won't." She shook her head, a sage old owl.

"Tomorrow we can do snow angels, Ellen," I said. "And make snow cream. We'll save some in the freezer for summertime. And you have those new snow paint pens from Christmas." The warring factions in Ellen's head were nearly as visible as the warring factions standing on either side of her.

"Okay . . ." She sighed and began lacing her hiking boots over the thin ankles bound in zigzag leggings.

Daintry set down her glass, followed us to the door, and gazed mildly up into the black sky. "Still no snow. Too bad." She pulled the limp belt of the robe more tightly about her waist and tweaked one of Ellen's tiny braids. "I'll give you a rain check, El."

I turned up my collar and reached for the handrail, afraid of what I might say. Then my daughter did it for me.

"Only Mommy calls me El," she told Daintry solemnly.

I listened as Ellen told Hal everything. He was attentive to the cheating issue, angry about the gym scene, less interested in Ellen's tales of the wondrous Daintry. He was tired, had driven five hours since three that afternoon. "Attendance was low because of the forecast, some speakers had canceled. And it's not even going to snow. A waste all around."

Not a waste, no. Not in my version of the day.

"What's your take on what happened to Ellen?" he asked me after she'd gone to bed.

"Someone was vicious to her."

"Vicious?"

"Boys don't do it. They don't count their slights and advantages, their grades and their girlfriends and their talents. They don't tally and compare. But girls have a god-awful history of it, right there alongside the history of nurturing and sacrifice and soldiering on. A history of doing each other in."

Lacking siblings or sisters, Hal was perplexed. "How?"

"Bloodless battles."

"But not you," he said. "Not grown women."

Oh, that certainty, that rock-solid sureness. "Me too, Hal. I've done it, too." He showed no surprise, and I was grateful. "And Mark's already in bed? I thought he was going out after they got back from the match."

"Well, that's the damnedest thing. He just *chose* to come home. Found himself with a bunch of people drinking and driving. He told me that he had them drop him off here, said something about blaming it on you. You ought to leave him a note next time you're going to be gone like that. Maybe you should get a cell phone if you're going to spend so much time at the columbarium, or with Daintry, or whatever."

"I don't need a phone. It's finished."

He seemed not to have heard me. "You know, I'm not sure I much approve of your friend Daintry. Ellen told me they'd rented *Ghost*. Isn't that rated R?"

And even then there was the instant impulse of defending her, no differently from the way I had with Mother. Protecting her, preserving something. "It's not the movie. You don't like her, do you?"

"There's something . . . unpredictable about her." He pulled back the blanket and climbed into bed. "I guess she just doesn't seem like much of a girl's girl."

I tried to laugh. "Hal. What would you know about girl's girls?"

Like always, he checked the blanket dial. "I know you," he said, and like always, he kissed me good night.

But the day, and the night, what had been

318

and what almost was, churned my consciousness, resisting rest.

My own robe was plain, flannel, blue. For once Hal had forgotten to draw the curtains. I never did close them and never would. In Cullen we even left our doors unlocked. *"Old habits die hard,"* Daintry had said that night at Ceel's. So do old friends.

Not wanting to ever again hear Ellen's recorded plaints for help, I pressed the playback button to erase the tape on the answering machine. There were three new messages, though, the library with a book on hold, a stockbroker cold-calling Harold Marsh. Then Wendy Howard. "Mark? Pick up . . . Mark? I thought you might like to . . ." Giggle. "You know, go out." I quickly punched erase. I didn't want to hear that again, either.

I switched on the outdoor flood, checking more from habit than hope. Then stopped, pulled a chair to the window, and tucked my feet beneath me. It looked like falling ash, so scant that I could count each tiny one before it drifted from the beam's reach. Stars are said to twinkle, but so do snowflakes under a light at night.

There is always something unattainable that shines and glitters and beckons. Should you summon courage enough, grow reckless enough, it may be nothing but trickery at the bottom of the pool, an optical illusion. And even if it's a piece of treasure — a coin or locket, a silver button — and even if you retrieve it, it still belongs to someone else. You can hold it, you can even keep it, but you'd always know it had first been someone else's.

I barely exhaled, afraid my warm breaths might cloud the pane. When you least expect it, it finally comes. Snow at last. In no rush, the flakes floated gracefully, increasing in number. Miraculous.

When Daintry and I watched *The Wonderful World of Disney*, our favorite part was the time-lapse photography of blooming flowers, the tulip and daisy and crocus unfolding incredibly before our eyes. I knew about flowers. I knew about snow. So did Daintry, once. Fat, mothy flakes were prettier, but dangerous. Big flakes meant temperatures were rising, and the snow would surely stop. But these flakes had grown even smaller as I watched, become diamond dust in the light. It would snow all night, something I was finally sure of. The morning landscape would be white, blanketed, cleansed. I drew the curtains, for Hal.

In Mark's room, by the faint lights from the cassette player, the illuminated face of the alarm clock, the lurid lava lamp, I could make out the stolen STOP sign, the posters on the walls of writhing rock stars. Their eyes were blank, staring, *Children of the Damned* eyes. We'd done that, too, Daintry and I, licked erasers and whitened out the pupils to blindness. The more things change, the more they stay the same.

Wendy Howard would come again, and call again, and take him in again with her predatory and catlike slink. *"The Howards are getting one of Daintry's kittens,"* Ellen had said. *"Can we?"* And maybe Mark would or maybe he wouldn't do something he was too young to do with her. There's no legal age or statute of limitations on sexual stupidity, not for a son, not for his mother.

And if not Wendy, it would be some other girl who loved him, and I'd feel again that uneasy combination of dread and gladness for my hurt and Mark's delight. *"It's bound to happen, Hannah,"* Hal had said. *"It happened to us."* I leaned over my sleeping son and carefully removed the headphones from his ears.

Ellen clutched a sand-art pendant even in sleep, a homemade trinket she kept stashed in the velveteen case my pearls had come in, her makeshift jewelry box. I pried it loose from the gaudy fingernails, Daintry's handiwork, and bent to kiss one of the baby plaits. Daintry, again. I kissed the forehead smoothed by carelessness, restored after a day of childhood's anguish.

"Doesn't it all boil down to diapering them and cooking for them and cleaning for them and driving for them and buying for them?" Daintry had said.

But those are temporary troubles. Temporary, like my move to Rural Ridge. Like my friendship with Daintry. She'd said so herself. *"When your children are young,"* my mother once said to me, *"you wear them on your feet. When they're grown, you wear them on your heart."*

"I could never have children," Daintry had remarked. *"They're too needy."*

Just, I thought, and shut my children's doors.

The sheets were chill with vacancy, and as I waited for the warmth to blossom and surround me, I cried, grieving for what I'd nearly done. Cried for Hal, the husband I loved. Cried for Ceel's childlessness, for my children's growing up with all its tender and terrible and unavoidable pain. Cried for my sickened, dying friendship with Daintry O'Connor.

As girls we'd collected Joan Walsh Anglund books, copied the chubby-cheeked, dot-eyed illustrations of moppet children in *Love Is a Special Way of Feeling*, *A Friend Is Someone Who Likes You*. I'd given Daintry another slim Anglund volume for graduation, this one a collection of short poems written for adults. Because we believed we were grown then, at eighteen. Before wrapping it, I'd copied a verse into my quote book. *What matters? Very little. Only . . . the flicker of light within the darkness, the feeling of warmth within the cold, the knowledge of love within the void.*

I hadn't known that when you cry lying down, your ears fill up with water.

The bed grew warm. When Ellen was born, I couldn't hold her for shaking under the epidural's anesthesia aftereffect. I was freezing with teeth-chattering cold, my muscles rigidly contracted. The hospital bed vibrated with my shivering. Nothing helped, not layers of prewarmed blankets, not the nurses' suggestions to relax. My fingers curled and my jaws ached from trembling. Hal had climbed into the elevated bed, amid the sheets and blankets and pads, never mind the bloody gown and my clammy sweat, and held me close, and tight, and whispered that I was wonderful, that it would all be fine.

Tonight as it snowed, my husband was a

dark hump in our warm bed. Tonight there was no restless twitching. Hal was still, and still beside me.

From Hannah's quote book:
"And remember this," he continued, "that if you have been hated, you have also been loved."

— Henry James

Chapter 14

The snow went as quickly as it came, no more than a memory now of the bright glare those few hours before thermometers rose and tree branches dropped their melting weight and white blankets slid tiredly from sloping roofs. Peter had used that mid-South miracle, the swift transformation into an early spring, as text for his Easter Sunday sermon. *"Listen to the words,"* my mother had said as we waited to follow the choir down the aisle at my father's funeral. I'd been teary, afraid I'd collapse with grief in that public procession. *"Listen to the words and you will be all right."* Without looking at him or thinking of him, I listened to Peter's words. Once, though, I glimpsed his eyes travel upward and wondered if it was inspiration he looked for or the organ loft and Daintry.

Hal and Ellen and Mark went to Sunday school. So did Doesy and Bill Howard, so did Frances Mason and Maude Burleigh. So did Ben with Ceel, who tried to persuade me to come, too. We stood outside beside a five-foot cross spilling flowers. At churches everywhere children had brought spring blooms to adorn chicken-wire crosses. "It's Speakout Sunday," Ceel said. "The congregation has an open forum to discuss what they want in a new priest."

"On Easter?"

"Schedule change. Ben's hired the new chaplain for Asheville Academy, and she's going to fill in at St. Martin's luckily, since Peter's leaving earlier than planned. You didn't know?"

I tucked a sprig of redbud more securely into the wire and shook my head. We'd spoken only once since that day, by telephone. Hurriedly, sadly.

"It was a —"

"Reaffirmation service."

He was silent a moment. "Yes, last minute. The couple was afraid the snow would cancel their plane, a second honeymoon. How did you —"

"Daintry."

I envisioned his quick, rueful nod. "Should we ... We could —"

"Peter." There is and always will be that inescapable pull between the comfort of what is

known and the lure of what isn't. "No, it's . . ."

"The children. If they —" But my silence stopped him.

"It's . . ." How could I put this?

"Tell me what you're thinking."

"I was thinking . . ." The afternoon was clear. I'd held a bedraggled forget-me-not; he'd held an abandoned bird's nest. "I was thinking of the time I asked you if being good meant always letting someone in your lane of traffic when they were waiting. And you said, no, being good meant not thinking you were good for letting them in."

"Hannah."

"We can't because . . . because I like the old light bulb."

"I know," he said finally, "I know you do. And English box in the churchyard."

He'd remembered. I'd known he would. I slid down the slick chintz of the bedspread to the floor, knees to chin, cradling the phone. "Remember me telling you at Ceel's, and later in the columbarium, about wanting something new all the while you're fighting for the old? Or trying to tell you."

Wanting to be outside and beyond Cullen, yet wanting the security of returning. The good girl longing for the outlaw boy. And wasn't part of Daintry O'Connor's appeal — her house and her family and Daintry herself — the fact that I *could always leave her, walk across the street to home?*

"The paradox," Peter said. "The old conundrum."

"Is it? Or is it just wanting your cake and eating it, too. It's wrong."

"No," he said. "People grow when they're pulled between poles. Children want to be gone, then want to be home. So do couples, friendships. Even religion. People need to belong to something or someone, then they resent it. Finding a balance is hard. It isn't wrong to look for it."

He couldn't see me, but I smiled. Smiled at that sweet, insistent sincerity. The essential reverence beneath it all.

"Hannah, we —" His voice grew distant. "What is it, Maude?"

"Take care," I whispered, and hung up.

Instead of Sunday school I went to the columbarium, a sodden mess after the snowstorm and winter weeks of absence. The soil, so carefully prepared, had sunk. Puddles dotted the plot, the water staining my shoes. Moss had taken root in one quadrant, seeded perhaps from droppings the afternoon Peter had helped me gather it. A few lonely daffodils were blooming, February golds meant to withstand the cold. But they couldn't withstand the snow, whose weight had cowed them, matting the buttery heads to the dirt.

Mindless of my dress and stockings, I knelt to examine every inch of a plot that had looked desolate and barren from a distance. Still, I found millimetered darts that would become Virginia bluebells, thin burgundy stalks that were the beginnings of peonies. Though frost-heaved, the campanula had lived, enduring the winter, and the ridged leaves of primroses safely hugged the earth. I'd done my autumn raking well; no crackle of leaves announced her approach.

"Hello, Hannah."

I looked at her across the columbarium, a chasm between us. "Daintry."

"You were expecting . . ." She paused as if I might volunteer an answer. "I know, the Easter bunny."

There's a formula for Easter's date, Peter explained to me, established two thousand years ago. That formula hasn't stuck with me, either. Memory is selective, and my memory selected Daintry. "Remember sitting on the doghouse that Easter, eating dyed eggs until we hiccuped?" Brittle pastel bits of eggshells had drifted down our legs like confetti as we straddled the metal S&H Green Stamps sign bent to form a roof.

"I'll tell you what I remember about

Easter," Daintry answered. "The O'Connor kids always had to borrow flowers from your yard for the cross at church, because we didn't have any flowers in our yard."

She strolled around the columbarium's perimeter, more careful with her shoes than I'd been with mine. "I came to see what the great attraction — or inspiration — is. Doesn't look like much."

"No, not yet."

She toed the flimsy foliage of a jonquil. "These the bulbs you bought at the pumpkin place? Looks like the snow ruined them."

My knees were wet. "They'll come back. That's the thing about bulbs."

"I heard your mother planted tulips for your wedding. A hundred tulips. Did they come back?"

They hadn't. "You didn't come," I said. "Every minute of my wedding I kept thinking I'd look up and you'd be there."

Daintry picked up a sweetgum ball, slowly touched each prickle as though she were counting the barbs. "My mother planted daffodils in Nashville when I got married. Daffodils are cheaper than tulips, aren't they." She tossed the pod away, shoved her hands in her coat pockets, and exhaled noisily. "He's good, isn't he, my husband?"

She rested her foot on the stump where I ate lunches all fall, sharing them with her husband. "And fatally charming, as well." Daintry had inspired any number of emotions in me throughout the years. But never this. Never naked fear. "Yes . . ." She sighed noisily. "A good preacher. Jean would hate that word, wouldn't she, your mother? So . . . déclassé: 'preacher.' "

My mother. Who'd manipulated Daintry's dominance by acknowledging my dependence. Something I'd always known, after all.

"Peter's never *bad*. He's just . . . flawed. And what's more attractive than a flawed priest?" She moved closer, towering above me; I smelled her perfume. "He means so well. It's hard not to love someone who means so well. Isn't it."

I willed a neutral expression to my face. Never have I been quick on my feet, never able to fling the cunning, impaling phrase. I lack killer instincts, a capacity for conflict Daintry had learned somewhere.

"Churches are sexy places. Having women throw themselves at you is an occupational hazard." She raised her chin. "You'd be surprised what female parishioners believe falls under the term 'pastoral care.' "

I pressed my fingers into the cold earth. Though perhaps Daintry had rehearsed this revenge, envisioning an elegant rationality in her every utterance. "It usually happens in counseling sessions, not" — she dismissed the area with an airy wave — "cemeteries."

I sought truisms: Rise above it. Kill her with kindness. All the tattered, fraudulent advice.

"Good thing the Episcopal faith is such a forgiving religion." Daintry raised a foot and frowned at the grime that rimmed it. "Fortunately, there are bonds other than sex. Peter and I need each other. Something beyond, you know" — her gaze was steady — "lust."

I stood then, still silent and unprotected and defenseless as the spikes of new foliage at my feet. "Daintry, nothing —"

"Don't tell me nothing happened. I know what happened. You crossed a line, but not *the* line." I gasped, but she took no notice. "Just like I did with Mike Simpson. Poor Mike. I look back now and realize he was just another way I was trying to get out. Away from Cullen." She knocked her knuckles against the bench. "Are we even now?"

"Even?"

"Tit for tat. Clean slate. Even steven."

Within my coat I shrank from the seasonal chill and Daintry's hostility. "Were we competing?"

"Oh, I think we were. Don't be daft. Remember that? The year we decided to talk like books. 'Ever so much,' and 'awfully decent of you.' Ever so much," she said again, softly. "It was ever so much fun."

I remembered. Seventh grade.

"Except there's no such thing as equal," she went on. "Not even in pairs of eyes or thumbs. One heel is more worn, one arm or leg is stronger than the other. There's nothing equal in marriage or in families, either, and there was nothing equal between us. Our mothers understood that. After you left for Wyndham and I moped around, know what my mother said? 'Leave Hannah alone,' she said. 'She's gone to find her own.' 'Her own.' Talk about your tough lessons."

"That's not true. My mother was trying to get me away from you. It didn't work. I loved you too much."

"Oh, I think it worked fine."

It hurt to say it. "But I was always weaker. You knew it and you used it."

"Until you went away. Until you left me."

She craned her neck, pulled a sleek length of hair caught in her coat collar. I watched

her, intimately acquainted with that ha-
bitual action. A hundred times, a thousand,
I'd observed the identical gesture, as this
ally, mentor, savior, and competitor had
freed her hair from a sailor middy blouse, a
T-shirt, a poor-boy jersey. Even a paper
dress with a newsprint cat face.

"Did you like the recessional 'Jerusa-
lem'?" she went on. "I picked it for you, suggested it to Peter. I remember how much
you liked it. A big boarding school favorite,
right? While I stayed home at good old
Cullen High with the rest of the" — she
laughed — "Trojans. An unfortunate mascot
choice. The marching rubbers." She leaned
forward, tweaked a fragile stem. "I know a
few things about gardening. Isn't it time to
put in pansies?"

What could I do but answer? I told the
truth. "Fall's better. So they can harden off
over the winter."

"Harden off, yes. Like people, who get
stronger while no one's noticing. Like you
did. That first Thanksgiving you came
home with a shoeboxful of grosgrain ribbons. Pretty striped things," she said in the
low tone of reverie. "You got a corduroy
backrest for Christmas that year. A 'husband,' you called it. Your new friends called
it."

"I wasn't trying to be different. You began hardening off, too."

"I know it. That's the whole goddamn tragedy of it." She sat on the bench. "We were blindsided, Hannah. Blindsided for the simple reason that we were young. What happened was that we got old enough to realize it was never going to go any further. Any further than sidewalks and bunk beds and matching garter belts and sex ed and roller-skating together on Sunday afternoons. We realized that the world was bigger and the avenues were wider."

"I never thought that, never."

Her expression was pitying. "Of course you didn't. I had everything you wanted up to then, didn't I? Tell me."

A pair of robins scuffled several yards away, fiercely yet soundlessly fighting, and I thought of how they fly into windows, breaking their necks out of jealousy for their own reflection. "Yes," I murmured. Brothers and sisters and house and mother and possessions. Everything.

Daintry's lips were a narrow slash. "Like always, I saw it coming before you did. The scales began to balance and we began to equal. You no longer wanted what I had, and I began wanting what you had. Everything you'd done to me our entire childhood

— the needing, the imitating, the listening — I suddenly found myself doing to you. I needed *you*. I wanted to copy *you*. I wanted to know the things *you* knew. But the stakes were higher. It was more desperate and dangerous then."

"But you deliberately hurt me. I never consciously hurt you."

"No, you're not capable of it." She made it sound like a deficiency. "So, yes," she said. "I started punishing you then." She gripped the bench armrest. "I'll tell you what else I know about gardening. It takes a long time for a plant to die, doesn't it, really die? Even if I stomped on it, the roots would live, wouldn't they?"

"Daintry, what —"

"Don't you see, Hannah," she said in a voice gone from badgering to insistent to querulous, "I *needed* to hate you. It was the only way I could let you go." She painfully mimicked my question posed months earlier. " 'What happened to us, Daintry?' But just like with flowers and with affairs and with dying, it happens by degree. When a plane crashes it's never *only* an engine malfunction, *only* an electrical failure, *only* a broken propeller or inclement weather or pilot error. It has to be all of these. It's never *one thing*. No single, pivotal event." Her voice was raw with sarcasm. "No, and friendships don't die for one reason."

There was nothing in the wreckage of our relationship left to hide or salvage. "Why didn't you tell me what my mother did for you?" I said. "The sorority . . . deal."

"What, and have you gloat?"

"Gloat? Do you know how hearing that hurt me?"

"Hurt *you?* Do you know what it's like to take something and despise yourself for taking it? Hannah, I *wanted* it. I wanted what you had. And I left because I couldn't *afford* to stay in the sorority."

"I didn't know Mother had . . . done that."

"I suspected as much on Christmas Eve. Jean was as nervous as a" — Daintry laughed — "as a whore in church." She examined a fingernail. "I like the way you put it: 'deal.' Believe it or not, I admired your mother. The arrangement had a certain . . . tooth-and-nail quality."

I believed it. "Would you have gone tooth and nail for me without an 'arrangement'?"

Daintry's expression served as answer, contempt naked in the slant of her eyes. She squared her shoulders, stretching as though she were vastly weary. "My God, but you and Peter are alike. I told Peter all about your quotes." My stomach contracted. "Idealists, both of you. That's what you have in common. His idealism gets him in trouble. Does yours?" She swiveled her plain wedding band. "It's why we're leaving Rural Ridge early."

"Because of —"

"Don't imagine you have anything to do with it, mind you." *Mind you,* Kathleen O'Connor's old Irish expression. "I wouldn't want you to enjoy any kind of martyrdom. A blue-haired parishioner doesn't approve of all the changes Peter's made at St. Martin's. So she withheld her usually generous pledge. It's the time-honored way of protesting a ministry. Peter went to her and suggested that she find another parish if she couldn't support this one."

Daintry shook her head. "So biddy blue-hair and Ultrasuede contacted the bishop. The good bishop doesn't mind so much about the changes; change has become the battle cry of the Episcopal Church. Oh yes, I know all about how it pains you — Peter told me that, too. But the bishop minded like hell about Peter's un-Christ-like suggestion. Didn't I tell you it was all about money?

"So we're leaving. Fortunately I can take my career on the road. This time I get to leave you. But there's a benefit to moving

338

you taught me your first Thanksgiving home from Wyndham. With moving, you get to reinvent yourself."

Reeling with a dizzying suspension of time and a pain I couldn't place, I began walking through the woods. Away from the soggy columbarium and into the weak sunlight toward the cemetery. Away from a past I couldn't change and a present I couldn't escape.

Though Daintry followed step for step, I kept going. Through the graveyard, across flat and buckling graves, old acquaintances of mine. I touched an obelisk here, a listing, squared monument there. I knew where I was going.

But as I neared, something looked . . . not right. Something had changed since I'd last visited the rocking horse rider. And reaching it, I discovered what.

The chubby angel's body was headless, severed at the neck. Vandals, perhaps, though I hoped some invisible crack in the concrete had finally succumbed to the elements, unable to withstand the freezing force of the snowstorm, the dramatically plunging temperatures. Despite the age of the grave the break itself was jagged, raw, rough, the pale gray color of new cement. The head, its curls and cheeks and parted lips intact, lay on the ground. The lovely perfection of the marker had been forever altered, its sweet innocence irretrievably ruined. I knelt beside it, my eyes welling as they had two seasons earlier, with Peter.

"Take it. Go ahead and take it," Daintry said. "Can't be fixed." As though we were childhood partners in some harmless conspiracy again, she continued, "Looks like there wouldn't be any living relatives anyway." I picked up the cherub head, surprised by its heft and weight.

"You always were a saver," Daintry said. "You had an ad tacked to your bulletin board, a photograph of a snowy little farmhouse. Remember?"

I did remember the picture, the squares of warm window light winking onto a violet-tinted farmyard iced with snow, the promise of comfort within the cottage. That photograph was what the lit rectory had reminded me of the night I'd come for Mark.

"I wanted to use it on a collage," she said. "When we glued all those headlines from *Seventeen*, pictures of the baby oil hunks to cardboard, and hung them on our walls." Daintry tapped her chin. "What did that damn ad say . . . something . . ."

" 'When you think that nothing can go wrong, that is called security,' " I answered softly.

"That's right. Couldn't remember the line, but I remember it was a stock market ad. Some symmetry there, huh?" She cocked her head. "What I do remember is that you weren't allowed to hang *your* collages on your walls, couldn't mar the paint. So you had to come to my house, where things were always a little slacker. Where rules were broken."

"There's something I want to know."

"Be my guest."

"The afternoon at the pool when you sent me down, twelve feet down, to get the money, or locket, or button. You already knew the silver circle was just a patch of paint. You'd already checked, hadn't you?"

"I don't remember that afternoon."

I had my answer. "I apologize, Daintry. No, it's more than that. I'm sorry."

"Don't be sorry. I know nothing happened between you and Peter. You don't have it in you. You're too pure, goody-goody to the end. But I can hate you with good conscience now."

The words couldn't hurt me, because I was sorry. Because I was never pure. Not even at seven and eight and nine. I looked at Daintry and remembered the private measurements, my running list of self-comforting comparisons. *She has stilts, but I* have a unicycle. Her hair is prettier, but I'm thinner. Her house has an elevator, but my house has a basement. I'd been dishonest with myself. I didn't like competing, yet it was all about competing, a dark swift current running invisibly below our friendship. *She has bunk beds, but I have a pool table. Her cursive is better, but my printing is. She's tall, but I'm cute. She's adopted, and I'm not.* So worthless — jealousy, envy — yet exacting such a high price.

"I'm sorry because I never meant to be . . . callous, or exclude you. I'm sorry I didn't try to change the way things were, sorry I didn't know how. Sorry we're grown. Sorry we can't have it back, still share something."

"There's nothing left for us to share."

I cradled the head. "Yes, there is. Guilt. Guilt that we let it happen." I looked at the sightless eyes. "I moved to Rural Ridge thinking — hoping — to find something uncomplicated. Then you appeared, the . . . embodiment of all that was perfect about my past. Our past. I thought it would all be so simple. And look at us, Daintry, look at us."

The church bell began to peal. Long and loud from up the hill it reached us, Easter's glad chimes. "It was never simple, Hannah," Daintry said. "The only thing

342

that was simple was you."

Then she turned and left me. And though I stood still, I left her, too. We let each other go again, and for the final time.

Hannah's final quote book entry:
...for as the self bends over the past it identifies what it responds to, vibrates with — what it recognizes; the rest is worth little. That is what memory teaches us — the discovery of the essential.
— Catharine Savage Brosman

Chapter 15

In the plots of movies or books or hammock-hatched fantasies, the characters you're meant to hate get their just fate. It's traditional. The beauty queen or the bully or the cheerleader or the football star become alcoholic, addicted, get pregnant. They grow fat, ugly, are divorced, beaten, left in the dust. Havoc is wreaked, revenge is sweet. You know the drill: comeuppance all around.

But of course those are only useful and retaliatory fictions. In real life it's never that simple. My slutty college friend is now an investment banker. In real life the movie or the book or the fantasy ends and people move on to the next book or movie, the next house or job. As I am moving on, packing for a new beginning again. People begin again every day. Daintry and I will not.

Hal has bought a cardboard box manufacturing operation in Hickory. Not so far from the mountains. Already he spends several days each week working there. I commute, too, but at night, taking classes toward a degree in horticulture and design from the community college. My ability has surprised me. Some holdover from Daintry's hold over me? Doesn't matter. On those evenings Ellen prepares her own kid-friendly suppers, and I'm glad. If my absences do nothing but give her self-sufficiency, they'll be worth it.

I went a final time to the columbarium, at sunrise. Rose quietly in the half-dark, pre-dawn chill. Hal stirred under the covers, propped up on an elbow. "Would you like company?" he said. "Would you mind? I've never seen it. You've never invited me."

"Come. Please."

I'd driven and he'd sat beside me, eating toast wrapped in notebook paper because there weren't any paper towels. I'd forgotten to buy them. "I'm sorry," I said. And again, "I'm sorry."

"No big deal," he said. "I'll live."

"He's not exactly an unstable isotope, is he?" Ceel had once laughed of Hal. *What do you love? What attracts you in a man?* Stable isotopes. Adaptability. Two qualities that a year

ago were negatives, not positives. Timing is everything.

Watching the sun creep across the mountains was like watching roof frost melt from white to gray to black slate. Iris-colored clouds cloaked the Blue Ridge, and behind them the sun bloomed slowly from rose to peach to yellow to white. The clouds broke away into high wisps, leaving the backlit mountains bare and whole. "They look like women's breasts, don't they?" I said. "Some conical, some rounded, some perfectly triangular?"

Hal draped his arm over my shoulder as we descended the hill. "I wouldn't know," he said. His fingers played about my braless bosom. "Yours are the only breasts I know." I smiled and threaded his wandering fingers into mine.

The bulbs had come and gone. Shrubs wore their new ruffled growth like furry animal ears, pale against the darker green of older foliage. Hosta scrolls were unfurling their broad, variegated leaves. Elbow-high perennials were still slender and pliable with newness, but on their own, established and secure. I wouldn't see their maturity, the splendor of summer fullness. It's occurred to me that I never really had a summer in Rural Ridge. But among other things, I

346

came for the snow.

Two tongue depressors poked from the dirt. "What are those?" Hal said.

"Reservations."

"As in 'Build it and they will die'?"

I laughed and stooped to lift crinkled foliage of astilbe sheltering the original four marble markers. There, beneath a bleeding heart's dangling row of ruby teardrops, a plaque was embedded in the ground, centered between the simple markers. Its background was grained and deep brown, the plain lettering raised in burnished brass. It wasn't a grave marker, or reservation, but a prayer, and though I knew it already by heart, I read the words through twice.

O Lord, support us all the day long, until the shadows lengthen and the evening comes, and the busy world is hushed, and the fever of life is over, and our work is done. Then in thy mercy grant us a safe lodging, and a holy rest, and peace at the last. Amen.

"Hal, look. From the old prayer book. Wonder where this came from. It's so beautiful. Who . . ."

"It came from me."

I stood and looked at him, suddenly remembered the anonymous gift. Hal had been the giver. In secret, and for me.

"I didn't want you to know," he said. "So you'd be surprised. Haven't even seen it myself. But it looks good, doesn't it? You like it? You approve? It doesn't . . . ruin anything, does it, because it doesn't have to stay."

"Hal." My throat stung with not crying.

"I thought it would fit in a columbarium. Might, well, encompass a lot of things. Your father's death, anyone's death. Forgiveness. What you said about tallying up, how worthless it is. Looking around at the end of the day or the end of your life, and realizing contentment is enough, and love, or grace, and hell, I'm no preacher. I just know." He was embarrassed, his hands huge and empty and gesturing.

"How did you know it was my favorite prayer?"

"Oh, Hannah, give me credit or don't ask me. I've lived with you eighteen years. I just know that, too."

Of course he did. "I'm sorry. But it's absolutely right. You're absolutely right. I love it. And you."

"Come here," he said. "I need a you fix."

I went to his lean height, pressed my forehead against his open collar where tendrils curled, blond that wouldn't so much go gray with age as bleach silver like the undersides

348

of aspen leaves before a storm.

"You already have me," I said, and his arms went round me tight.

I felt a trowel in his jacket pocket. "I thought you'd packed all the tools. What's this?"

"For the arum. To transplant it to Hickory. Where is it?"

With the change of seasons the arum would soon die again. Not die, though, no; it would merely become invisible to anyone but me. I thought of Hal's rock retaining wall, where white candytuft was spilling over prettily. "You're leaving your wall. I'm leaving the arum."

"But you brought it all the way from Cullen. All these years."

I shook my head. "I'm leaving Cullen here, too."

"Yoo-hoo."

Without looking I know who it is. "In the kitchen, Doesy."

"Already echoes in here," she says, and I smile, remembering the day I'd searched every corner of the house for a hair scrunchie Wendy believed she'd left. *It must not be here,* I'd told Doesy, *"I can't find it anywhere."*

"I know," she'd said. *"Your house is so small*

there's just no place for anything to get lost, is there?"

"Everything packed?" she asks.

"Almost." I ball another pair of socks. "Laundry goes on, though. One of the eternal mysteries of life is how a family of four manages to wear thirty-two pair of socks in a single week."

She giggles and displays a flowered gift bag with the Picky-Picky logo of Frances Mason's sucker store. "I brought a going-away present. Open it."

Beneath the ribbons and tissue lies a frame made of twined kudzu vines. Doesy had already put a picture behind the glass, of Mark in the driver's seat of Wendy's car with Wendy beside him. Both were grinning.

"It's really more for Mark than you," Doesy admits. "I thought he might like to have this for his desk next year. They do have desks, don't they?" Mark is going to boarding school in the fall, in New England. It was his decision.

"Yes," I say, suppressing a smile, "they have desks." But no hair dryers.

"Wendy's going to miss him so." Doesy never knew how Wendy treated Mark that bleak night. She leans toward me, asking in a confidential tone, "Tell me the truth,

Hannah. What did he do?"

" 'Do'?"

"That you're sending him away."

I fish through a carton marked KITCHEN STUFF and find the little tin box containing ink and stamper. I'm familiar with that old stigma of boarding school as a punitive measure. "He didn't do anything, Doesy. He wants to leave."

Her eyes widen. "But how can you let him go?"

I ink the pad, considering how to answer this question carrying both stun and accusation. Life is that, letting go. People wrestle themselves insistently away like Ceel, or they drift, or they're severed like a tree limb. Mother couldn't let me go. Her pact with Daintry was part of that tenacious clinging. Daintry and I did them all. We wrenched and wrestled and severed and inched. We let each other go.

"For the whole experience," I finally answer. "Having to be on your own and responsible to yourself. It . . . ," I grope, "it cuts the cord."

Doesy straightens with offense. "I don't want my cord to Wendy cut."

"I know. I understand."

"Come back and see us, now," she says on her way out.

"Yes," I say. No.

I stamp Mark's name on a boxer waistband. And on another and another. Indelible now, this imprint, this evidence of departure. It begins again.

Mark ambles into the kitchen and reflexively opens the refrigerator. "There's nothing to eat."

I wave my hand, asking for the positive.

"But" — he looks at the table — "but you're stamping, so I don't have to do it."

My stomach flips at the new deepness in his voice. "Who's going to wave their hand at you far away from me in the frozen North?"

"Nobody, I hope." He looks forward to this freedom. And though school is three months away, I ache for him already, the pain that awaits him. Leaving friends, defining yourself for new ones, the discomfort of returning home to find life has gone on without you, happy to be there yet ready to leave again when the two weeks or month or weekend is over. "Back to the womb," my father used to say as I packed the last day of every vacation.

Mark has a job in Hickory, too, for the summer, working at a local nursery. "I'm heading for management," he'd told me, and I'd laughed, delighted he'd be toiling among dirt and growing things. "Saving to buy a laptop for school."

"Listen," I say now, and lean toward him. "Next fall don't let anybody give you any shit about your accent."

"Mom!"

"Yes" — I sigh — "now you know. I learned how to cuss at boarding school."

"Not until then?" He laughs.

I take his hand, rub the knuckles where dark man-hair sprouts. Even the sight of them fills my eyes, and Mark does something he hasn't done since I can remember: he kisses me, just at my ear.

Like the day I'd first visited the columbarium with Peter, the St. Martin's sidewalk was empty as Hal and I walked back to the car that sunrise morning. Suddenly I'd wanted to test the theory I'd wondered about aloud to Peter.

The door was unlocked, confirming it. The rubber barrel for powdered milk still sat in the entrance; there were still wicker baskets instead of brass collection plates. Peter's changes survived. Hal picked up a copy of the previous Sunday's sermon by the Asheville Academy chaplain who's filling in. The text was titled "A Call to Forgiveness," and I thought of Mother and our post-Christmas conversation.

"Oh, Mother," I'd said. *"You'd forgive a murderer if he was a good Episcopalian."*

"Murderers can be forgiven," she'd maintained, a good Episcopalian herself. In that hurtful New Year's Eve revelation, she was asking, in her way and in her confession, to be forgiven. And as Peter forgave his mother, I've done the same. Mothers all, we are doing the best we can.

A small article clipped from the diocesan newspaper was tacked to the bulletin board just inside the vestibule. He was reassigned to a village parish in Mount Pleasant, twenty minutes south of Charleston. Daintry, no doubt, commutes to the city proper. I keep this, too, not the clipping, but the knowledge of what I am capable of doing, nearly did.

I looked around the lovely chapel a final time. "I know you say a prayer every morning," I said to Hal. "I feel like an idiot, but will you tell me what you say?"

He didn't laugh. "I just pray, 'Come into my heart today.' " He smiled mischievously at me. "That wasn't so bad, was it?" But this was never about religion. It wasn't about Ellen, or Hal, or mothers and daughters. Nor was it about Peter Whicker. It was about Daintry and me.

Standing there, I hadn't prayed. Phrases and fragments from the Bible ran through my mind instead, the brief bits even children know: *Jesus wept. In those days a decree went out from Caesar Augustus. In the beginning.* And this: *When I was a child, I spoke as a child. But when I became grown, I put away childish things.*

"You always were a saver," Daintry had said to me that Easter Sunday. I leave the desk, my childish things, for last. My savings nearly obliterate the surface of the desk, items I've extracted this morning like archaeological artifacts from the seven drawers, three on each side and one slender, shallow middle drawer. A piece of petrified wood glossily striated with blues and browns that my father brought back from a sales trip to California. Plaster molds of my bucktoothed preorthodontia teeth. The homemade blueprint smudged with erasures and translucent with grease spots from lunches those fall afternoons. Stationery engraved with my newly married initials on which I penned thank-yous and sympathy notes, replies to wedding invitations. *Mr. and Mrs. Harold Cheshire Carlson accept your kind invitation for Saturday the seventeenth* . . . A creamy sheet

held to the light bears faint impressions of my scribbles, replicas of my refusals. Even *Letters to Karen*, still unread, the stiff spine intact.

The smallest items are scraps of paper: lists. A list of funeral hymns. Ellen's Birthday List, the uppercase title precisely centered with requests prioritized by number.

1. *Hang-head doll*
2. *A journal with lines*
3. *A bible*
4. *A silver bracelet with a heart-half charm that says Best Friend*
5. *Other surprises*

The collection is so touching, so telling. A baby doll, a charm bracelet. She's still straddling that delicate balance between childhood and adolescence. There's time yet. I haven't missed her silent leap.

And this, the list of reasons justifying our moving to Rural Ridge and defending our staying in Durham.

FOR
small town
good time to move: Mark starting high school
temporary job

no social requirements
gardening
Ceel and Ben

AGAINST
small town
not a good time to move: Mark starting high
  school
temporary job
no social requirements

Well. Anyone can see the pros are longer than the cons.

I test the deep bottom desk drawer, and it sticks stubbornly, a result of the wood's expansion one humid summer. One night, frantic to reach something stashed in the immovable drawer, Daintry and I had taken a hammer and dementedly pounded on it until it opened. The wood is still marred with gouged dents, crescents of desperation. I've no idea what we wanted so badly, remember only the fierceness of our wanting. I touch the permanent imperfections, fit my fingertips in each small curve.

Thirty feet of a gum wrapper chain is coiled clumsily in the back. The delicate paper rope slips through my fingers as fluidly and limply as the overwashed grosgrain Daintry had envied. The zigzagged links are

357

still colorful, still scented with the sugary aromas of Juicy Fruit and Teaberry and Spearmint. The chain was a collective gift, when Daintry marshaled the entire sixth grade into chewing, collecting, folding, and connecting hundreds of gum wrappers after I broke three ribs in a horseback-riding accident. Daintry wasn't taking riding lessons with me; the O'Connors couldn't afford them.

All here but for that seventh-grade timeline. I had a chance to be the best on the assignment, unlike the booklet on China, when Daintry got top honors. She was allowed to cut pictures from *National Geographic*, while the yellow-bordered magazines collecting at my house had to remain whole and unscavenged for some later need that never arose.

For two decades I kept the timeline stashed behind books on my shelves. Kept it until our yard sale the summer after my father died. Strangers hovered and browsed among the remnants of a life. There were thirty-four Barbie dolls. No one bought the *National Geographic* issues.

Along with an unsold manual typewriter and a fondue set complete with eight diminutive spears, I threw the timeline away. But I can still envision its unwavering progress, straight and true with bold slashes at predictable intervals: birth, childhood, high school, college, marriage, children born, father dead. Friendship isn't so easily and tidily charted. It curves and meanders and deviates.

In this story there's no cataclysmic accident, no gory or revelatory epiphany. In the grand scheme, this isn't a tragic tale. No one dies or divorces, loses a child or a husband. Yet it's a story of unrequited love, betrayal, accidents in which people were wounded. And it's about loss. Loss on a smaller scale is no less painful for the person who is losing something. And like any tragedy, there are lingering questions. Might it have been avoided? Swerved or dodged like highway debris? Were we destined to divide?

"Did you ever think," I'd asked Mother after the sale was over and we folded card tables in the dusk, *"that everyone's life is like a timeline?"* My father's abbreviated life was still so recent. *"That events are already laid out and just waiting for you to walk into them, for the moment to arrive that they happen?"*

"Certainly not," Mother had replied, visibly aghast and swift with assurance. *"That's nothing but predestination. Episcopalians don't believe in predestination. Fate ordained. Certainly not."*

I suppose she's right, again. Our lives intersect with some, collide with others. And sometimes we are saved by the grace of the accidental.

Among the collection of objects is a recent acquisition: a concrete cherub head. Another gift, in its way, from Daintry O'Connor.

Ceel was right, too. Every woman has a Daintry. It matters not the size of the town, or the house, or the circumstances of rich or poor. Delve deeply enough and you'll find her somewhere. Stuck in a drawer, perhaps, though there's no actual evidence. Moreover, this woman will be hard-pressed to define exactly what it was about her particular Daintry. She knows things. She has things. She's gifted, blessed, endowed. She looms large and vital, invincible and untouchable. She's the one who pulls you through and pushes you away. She allows you access, then seals the entry. She feathers the nest, then shoves you from it. Every woman has one, and you love her all the same. Mine lived across the street.

Items litter the desktop. *Things,* only. As we get older we discard objects that no longer have significance. Out goes the threadbare baby blanket or stuffed sheep smelling of spit. The lanyard from summer camp draped over the mirror is tossed a season later without a thought. The unfinished needlepoint belt labored over for a boyfriend. The wedding gift pair of silver candlesticks consigned to tarnish and attic. So that the things we choose to keep are a tangible lament for something lost.

One by one I put each article in a trash bag. The teeth, the wood, the lists. And the little book of quotes. To go.

We discard people as well. But do we discard them because they no longer have significance in our lives or because they're no longer comfortable, remind us of someone we were but no longer want to be? You can't keep a person. There's no adhesive strong enough or flexible enough to hold a psyche, a personality. You can't crate and tape it, label and store it. Because people change.

The angel head stays, a keeper. I might need it one day. It'll make a fine baby present for Ceel.

Ellen pirouettes through the room, the sand-art pendant thumping against her chest. "Are you having a clean-out?" she asks. Ellen loves clean-outs. There's always the possibility she'll come away with treasure. She peers into the bag, sticks her arm inside, and pulls out the chewing gum chain. "Wow. It's as long as the room! Is it yours?"

I hesitate. "No."

"Whose is it?"

"Someone I used to know."

"Are you throwing it away? Can I have it?"

"If you want."

"Cool."

"El, how'd you like to have this desk for your new room in Hickory? We'll paint it, fix it up."

"Purple? Can it be purple?"

"Whatever you like."

"Awesome."

"Do you know any other adjectives besides cool and awesome?"

"You're not going to make me get the dictionary, are you?"

"No, but you have to promise me something." Tit for tat. Even steven. "If I give you the desk, you can't grow up and away from me."

"I don't want to grow up at all," she says. The clunky digital watch on her wrist emits faint electronic beeps, and she kisses it.

"Why'd you do that?"

"It's three thirty-three," she says. "You kiss it for luck when the same numbers are all the way across. I set the alarm so I won't miss it. You don't know about stuff like that," she says with matter-of-fact assurance.

But I do. I knew about picking up our feet over railroad tracks and holding our breath when we passed a cemetery and not stepping on sidewalk cracks and crossing our fingers and touching the car ceiling when we passed beneath a yellow light. I knew that three sneezes equaled a wish and putting your ring around the candle on a birthday cake made certain our wishes came true.

"You know Daintry?" Peter had said to me that August night, the brink of fall, the beginning of the end.

"So you knew Daintry O'Connor growing up?" Hal too had asked.

Forever, I could have said to Peter. *I hardly know her*, I could have answered Hal.

Ellen twirls a tiny dial, resetting the alarm. Daintry had a watch with interchangeable colored rims. "How did you get so wise to be so young?" I ask her.

"What are you talking about?"

I take my daughter's hand, kiss the soft pulsing inside of her watchbanded wrist. "I don't know."

"Hunh," she teases. "I thought you knew everything."

Don't you know anything, Hannah? "I thought I did, too."

"Dad," she calls, bolting away. "Guess what Mom gave me!"

Oh, Daintry, I think, and close the drawer. *I'll miss you so.*

The employees of Thorndike Press hope you have enjoyed this Large Print book. All our Large Print titles are designed for easy reading, and all our books are made to last. Other Thorndike Press Large Print books are available at your library, through selected bookstores, or directly from us.

For information about titles, please call:

(800) 223-1244
(800) 223-6121

To share your comments, please write:

Publisher
Thorndike Press
295 Kennedy Memorial Drive
Waterville, ME 04901